D1066751

HAPPY TRAIL

PARK RANGER SERIES BOOK #1

DAISY PRESCOTT

WWW.SMARTYPANTSROMANCE.COM

COPYRIGHT

CHAPTER ONE

JAY

Mid-October
Great Smoky Mountains National Park
Cades Cove, Tennessee

"Yo, bro." Jenni's chirpy voice greets me when I answer my phone and I am immediately wary.

"Hey." I drawl the word out to stall the inevitability of finding out why she's calling me in the middle of a Tuesday morning. "What's up?"

"Mom call you yet?"

"No, why?" As soon as I ask, I know. "Ah, thanks for the heads-up."

"Jay." Mimicking my drawl, she stretches out my name like she always does when she wants something from me. When we were little and she couldn't really pronounce her J's, my name was one never-ending A. It was adorable and annoying. My older sister is still both.

"No."

"Why not?" she whines.

"I have to work," I grumble.

"Six months is plenty of notice to ask for time off."

"April is when the AT hikers begin coming through the park and it's the start of the busy season with campers and school visits. Plus, all the spring bird migrations will be happening, not to mention, fawning season for the local deer. And the bears will be out of hibernation."

Muffled laughter reaches my ear.

"What's so funny? I'm presenting facts."

She mumbles something I can't understand and more laughter follows.

"Your facts are excuses. The birds and fawns will all be fine if you aren't there. Nature doesn't need you to babysit. The birds and the bees have been perfectly all right for many years without your help. *Obaasan* isn't getting any younger, and the trip from Kyoto to Nashville is too long for her."

Ah, there it is—the guilt. My mother and sister are masters. If guilt were a martial art, they'd both have a black belt.

She continues, unabated and building steam. "It would mean a lot to both Mom and *Obaasan* for us to both be there next year. You know how much Mom loves it when her family is all together, and she can show off her son, the doctor."

My laugh gets caught in my throat. "Always fun to remind them I'm not the right kind of doctor."

"You've saved lives before as a ranger. Kind of the same thing."

We both know it isn't, not in a family of lawyers and corporate titans.

"You're the favorite," I remind her. "Everyone loves and dotes on you. Meanwhile, Uncle Ken pretends to pat the top of my head and I hear the cousins calling me *hāfu* or *gaijin* like I don't know what they mean."

"They're just teasing you."

"Right." I sigh. "Then why don't they call you *hāfu*?"

"How do you know they never do?" Her loud snort reverberates against my ear.

She makes a good point, but it doesn't sway me.

"I'm sure the aunties place bets on my marriage prospects and the fertility of my uterus. I'm thirty-two." She switches her voice to sound like an old woman, or a witch, saying, "Well past my prime. What man will want a shriveled-up, old prune?"

I groan. "Ugh. Can you not put that image in my head, please?"

"Which part? My anatomy or the dried, raisin-like quality of my over-the-hill womb?" She barely contains her giggling.

"The latter. And you're not old."

"Mom was twenty-two when she married Dad, twenty-three when she had me, twenty-five when you were born. Widowed at thirty-five." Her voice trails off the way it always does when she brings up our father, wistful and apologetic.

My brain flips through flashes of the day he died, but I tamp down the memories.

In four years, I'll be the same age. No wife or kids, no family of my own. I have a neat stack of diplomas and a closet full of uniforms to show for my life. Maudlin isn't an emotion I enjoy, so I switch the subject back to visiting our grandmother in Japan.

Clearing my throat, I say, "I'll think about it."

"Ask for the time off," Jenni implores. "It will be fun. We can escape the disapproving glances together, take the fast train to Tokyo for a night of *okonomiyaki* and karaoke. Who can say no to either of those?"

She knows my weakness for good street food. *Why does putting something on a stick make it taste better?* Same goes for fair food. My stomach rumbles at the thought of a corn dog. I skipped breakfast and am now regretting it.

"I'll think about it," I repeat, not making promises I don't plan on keeping.

"Fine. I'll tell Mom you're ninety percent sure you'll make it. She'll be thrilled. Gotta go. Bye."

"Jenni!"

She doesn't hear me because she's already ended the call.

Shaking my phone in frustration, I curse under my breath.

"What about time off in April?" Gaia asks from behind me. "Sorry —it's hard to not listen to your conversation in this tiny office."

"Nothing." I spin my chair to face her, my knees barely avoiding bumping hers in the tight space between our desks. "My sister is bugging me about a family reunion."

"Are you close with your family?"

"Not outside of my mom and sister. Mom's family lives far away, and we don't see them much. I barely know them." I never talk about personal stuff at work. Not sure if it's a matter of being private or avoiding the awkward questions and comments.

"Yeah, I get that. At least you have your sister. My parents each have four siblings. Big families are like living inside a circus run by the monkeys."

The image makes me chuckle.

"Sure, laugh, but I have three cousins named Bobby. Not Robert or Bob. Bobby. They all go by Bobby. Grown men, too, which should tell you everything you need to know about my family." She rolls her hazel eyes toward the ceiling. "Speaking of annoying idiots, Griffin is telling people it's skunk season again."

"Someone needs to take away his press privileges," I suggest.

"He's forbidden from speaking to journalists or writing releases, but found a way around the ban by calling into Cletus Winston's podcast."

"Thought Cletus banned him after he showed up at the studio uninvited back when Dr. Runous was out of town."

Gaia rubs her temples as if she might be able to erase The Great Skunk Makeup fiasco from memory.

"Send him into the backcountry to check on the Appalachian Trail hikers. Keep him out of cell phone range." I tug on my beard to fight my laughter.

The dark, coarse hair is in need of a trim and I could use a haircut soon. No one is complaining, though probably because there's no one in my life who cares if my whiskers are too long or my hair brushes my collar. Rangers have a dress code when it comes to our uniforms, but as long as we're not scaring the kids, personal grooming is left up to us.

"Trying to get out of your turn?" She gives me a knowing arch of her eyebrow.

"Nah. I love escaping the confines of this cage."

I'm not cut out to spend my life working in an office, lab, or classroom. Anything with four walls, a floor, and a ceiling is a box. No, thanks. I'm much happier with the sky overhead and dirt beneath my boots.

"Guess we'll find out at the staff meeting. You ready?" Gaia stands and picks up a clipboard.

We all call her Guy out of laziness and because she's the only female ranger amongst our motley crew. It's become a lame inside joke. She's the most senior staff member, right after our boss Ed.

We join the others in the staff lounge and go over the week's schedule.

"We're getting reports of a sizable storm heading this way from the Gulf. Could bring some nasty rain and wind. The last of the hikers should be coming through soon and we'll need to set up patrols of the trail to make sure everyone is safe and healthy." Ranger Ed pushes his glasses up his nose. In his late fifties, he still has the air of the high school biology teacher he was for twenty years before joining the Park Service.

I refill my thermos of coffee. "Thank goodness. Feels like this year's been cursed with accidents and weird idiosyncrasies. Will be nice when the snow comes and we don't have to worry about the ATs until spring."

Guy nods. "Still have the day hikers and leaf peepers to worry about, at least for another month or so. Of course, if the snow shows up early, people will lose interest in finding themselves in nature."

After a busy summer and September, we're tired. The college kids who work with us during their break have left, and so we're down to full-time staff only. Burned out, all five of us are ready for the quiet of the coming winter and a much-deserved break.

"Who wants to take the first patrol?" Griffin asks from his spot on the hideous plaid that has been in headquarters longer than any of us. Totally possible the sofa is original to the building.

"I will. I could use some time in the mountains." I sip the semi-burnt coffee before adding half-and-half from the carton in the fridge. It's godawful, but it's still better than the concoction involving molasses and vinegar Cletus Winston used to drink when he visited his brother Jethro.

Since Ranger Winston's retired, we rarely see either brother unless they're visiting Dr. Runous, who's married to their sister. Green Valley's a small town, and there are enough Winstons around the area to make it practically impossible to not know at least one or two of them. Despite what the local gossips say, they're good people.

Ed's still talking and I realize he's focused on me. Having no idea what he's said, I sip my coffee and nod as I pretend to know what I'm agreeing with.

He gives me a pointed look. "Plan for an overnight trip, but bring enough supplies for a couple of days in case the storm hits early. Head north toward Clingmans Dome."

"Roger that. I'll pack up tonight and start tomorrow." Looking forward to the time outdoors, I begin a mental list of supplies I'll need to restock before heading out.

"Don't forget a bear can." Griffin reminds me. "Cooler weather means they'll be more active. Whatever you do, don't pack honey. Or a picnic basket."

Then he laughs at his lame joke. At least one person finds him funny.

"I don't get it," Guy says.

Griffin's grin falters. "Are you kidding? Yogi Bear? Come on. It's only the greatest cartoon about rangers ever. Jay? Ed? Help me out here."

Ignoring Griffin, I nod at Ed. "Gotcha. I'll grab a canister from here in the morning."

* * *

Next day, I'm packed and ready. The bear can and my bivy tent take up most of the space in my bag, but I don't need a change of clothes for the quick trip. Bedroll strapped to the bottom of my day pack, food and water, warm socks and a fleece, and I'm set to go.

After checking in with the team, I verify my radio is charged and working before heading into the woods.

For the first few hours of the hike, I'm alone on the trail. No signs of bear tracks. Birds chirp in the colorful canopy of leaves and wind whistles through the mountains under a blue sky.

This is why I love being a ranger in the Great Smoky Mountains: peace, quiet, and an endless vista of nothing but trees and mountains. No houses, businesses, or even a church steeple. This feels like America before the settlers and colonies. I can lose myself in the idea that I've traveled back in time to a land without McDonald's and Walmart. There's no such thing as a strip mall, let alone strip-mining to mar the perfect landscape.

I climb up through the dense woods to an elevation that affords me a view of the surrounding valleys. Pausing to drink from my water bottle, I hear the sound of human voices approaching from around a bend in the trail.

The Appalachian Trail hikers have a certain look to them at this point in their journey. Unlike the fresh and eager spring starters, the southbound summer hikers have almost two thousand miles behind them. They're in the home stretch by the time they hit Tennessee and can practically taste the victory awaiting them just over a hundred miles from here in Georgia at the official end of the trail.

Two thin, wiry, young guys with long, scraggly beards and shaggy, dark hair come into view. Large packs and gear strapped to their backs, they both use hiking poles to navigate the uneven surface of the trail.

"Morning." I greet them with a friendly smile.

"Ah, a sight for sore thighs." One of them chuckles at his joke. "A ranger by any other name wouldn't smell so sweet."

Did I mention these hikers get a little odd after months of walking?

"How are you gentlemen doing? Need any assistance?" Scanning for any visible signs of injuries, I note neither appears to have a limp or obvious bandages, nor are they too thin or visibly disoriented. No sign of illness either.

Before saying more, both take long drinks from the straws of their camel-style water bags.

"We're doing good." The younger of the two gives me a thumbs-up.

"Where'd you start?" I ask.

"Katahdin in May," he replies, subtly shifting his shoulders to adjust his pack.

I catch the flash of the red thru-hikers tag.

"Whoa. You're hardcore." Hiking in either direction isn't easy, but beginning in the snow-covered mountains of Maine in spring is considered the more challenging route.

"First time hiking the AT?" I ask, using the abbreviation favored by most hikers.

The one with a red bandana holding his hair back answers. "Yep. We graduated from Bowdoin College and headed out the next week."

"You've made good time," I tell them, the compliment sincere. Given it takes most hikers five months or more to complete the trail, this is impressive.

"Once we decided to do the AT, we trained with hikes in the White Mountains for a year," his friend explains, removing his baseball cap to swipe his brow with the back of his hand.

The morning started off cool, but the sun is stronger at this altitude and heats up the day, despite the tree cover.

We chat for a minute or two more before they get restless, eager to continue with their trek.

As we part, I ask, "Pass any other hikers today?"

"We stayed at a hut north of Clingmans Dome night before last with three others. You'll probably encounter them at some point. Two older men and a woman," Baseball Cap replies.

"Everyone healthy?" The more information I can get from these two, the better prepared I'll be if there's an issue up ahead.

I'm hopeful the three hikers behind these two will be down from the highest elevation before the storm hits. It's rare, but snow isn't out of the question below five thousand feet. The Park Service would all feel better if the AT folks spent a night or two off the trail if the storm's going to be as bad as predicted.

"For the most part. One of them has a cough, but doesn't seem serious," Bandana tells me.

"Good to know. Thanks." I twist the cap back on my bottle and tuck it in the side pocket of my pack. "Ranger station is about eight miles ahead. If you need anything, stop in and we can assist you. You're welcome to weather the storm in the valley with us."

After a quick goodbye, we head in opposite directions.

I don't encounter any more hikers for another couple of hours. Turns out, the guy with the cough is a man in his fifties with buzzed, silver hair and the thin physique of someone who's been on the trail for months.

He's happy to chat for a few minutes and I get the sense he's a real talker. He hacks a few times and I'm concerned he's on the verge of bronchitis or pneumonia, especially given how common respiratory infections are among hikers once the weather cools.

"You might want to check in at the station for your cough. We're not far from Green Valley and you can see a doc in town," I suggest. "Storm's coming in and you don't want to get caught in the bad weather."

He thanks me and promises he'll think about seeing the doctor. "By the way, there's a young woman hiking solo. She said she was taking an extra day back at Clingmans Dome. Be sure you find her. She's not traveling with a cell phone and won't get the weather warning unless she hears it from another hiker or ranger."

Great. Nothing like being at the highest altitude of the whole damn trail when there's a major storm blowing up the east coast and we're the bull's-eye.

For the record, I'm not being a sexist asshole about a woman hiking the AT solo. Plenty of women complete the trail every year, but I've met enough of the male hikers to know it isn't easy to be a woman on the AT.

What annoys me is the lack of cell phone in case of emergency, especially this late in the season when other thru-hikers are few and far between. Unless she runs into day visitors, she's not going to meet up with anyone heading in the opposite direction.

Rescuing a damsel in distress is something best left to fairy tales.

I'm a national park ranger, not some Prince Charming, who swoops in on his noble steed to save the princess and falls in love at first sight.

CHAPTER TWO

OLIVE

*L*ove makes us do crazy things.

For his thirtieth birthday, my boyfriend Tye decided to hike the Appalachian Trail. For the record, that's over two thousand miles. Two hundred miles would be a lot. Honestly, twenty would've been inconceivable for me prior to this year.

He promised it would be an "epic adventure."

I said yes.

Mostly because I'd watched part of *Wild* on a flight once.

In hindsight, I should've read the book.

I don't come from outdoorsy stock. The Perrys aren't hiking people. We don't even march in parades, should we be required to attend. We're the people waving from floats or the back seat of a classic convertible, and in my grandfather's case, behind bulletproof glass in an armored limo.

My mother sometimes walks on a treadmill while watching The Today Show or strolls down Madison Avenue to shop and have lunch with friends. Dad is known to occasionally decline a cart on the golf course. That's about it.

Hiking wasn't exactly on brand for Tye either.

We'd met at a young patrons night at the Guggenheim. Surrounded by contemporary art and the babbling *blah blah blah* conversations of New York's elite, our eyes locked. Sutton Wallingford III, known to everyone as Tye, was recently single and the hottest bachelor in the city. Barely back on the market after breaking off my engagement, I was available and interested. His family was thrilled about their son's connection with the Perrys. My parents remained tepidly optimistic that this relationship would stick. In other words, we were perfect for each other. At least on paper.

At a cocktail party for the latest YouTuber's book launch, someone asked how we were training for hiking the Appalachian Trail. I joked I'd been walking for almost thirty years and was more than adept at putting one foot in front of the other, especially in four-inch heels.

After the laughter subsided, two people simultaneously asked, "No, seriously, how are you training?"

And then the enormity of hiking every single day for months hit me.

This wouldn't be a walk in Central Park.

Tye found my panic "adorable" and only reluctantly agreed to attend wilderness preparedness classes and spend Saturday afternoons tromping up the hills of Fort Tyron park on the northern tip of Manhattan, wearing backpacks stuffed with canned goods to simulate carrying all of our belongings on our person.

"This gives new meaning to the term pack rat," I complained, flushed and out of breath while sitting on a curb next to a suspicious stain from either an animal or a human. Hard to tell without getting closer and I was already close enough.

"Darling," he reassured me, "we're not ordinary hikers. I've hired a travel concierge to plan our route and make all the reservations and accommodations."

"We need reservations to sleep on the ground?" I asked, naïve to the world of camping.

I mourn for that girl, the one who'd only ever gone to the bathroom in toilets. Sweet, innocent Olive no more. I've seen and done things I never imagined possible for myself.

Months later, I could still hear Tye's laughter at my questions. "No, at hotels, and if necessary, the occasional bed and breakfast along the way."

"Feels like cheating." I don't know why I protested the idea of a mattress instead of sleeping on sticks and rocks.

He scoffed. "Says who? We're not beholden to some sort of rule-book. Most thru-hikers stay at hostels whenever they can. If you want to share a room filled with bunk beds and strangers, I can call Mina and amend our itinerary."

Unlike the majority of hikers, we wouldn't be starting in Georgia in April. Turned out, Tye had a strong aversion to the South, based solely on watching the movie *Deliverance* when he was nine during a sleep-over with his older cousins. He also hated all banjo and fiddle music. Made me wonder if his cousins were also musical sadists.

"There isn't an actual prize for completing all two thousand miles, you know," he chided. "If we start in Pennsylvania right after Memorial Day, we'll still hit Maine by the end of the summer. Labor Day in Kennebunkport will be glorious. I can already taste the lobster rolls." He sighed a dreamy sigh, mentally enjoying the monstrous combination of shellfish and mayonnaise.

Give me butter or give me nothing was my motto when it came to cooked shellfish.

"You don't get a trophy or medal for summiting Everest either, but I'm pretty sure it doesn't count if you start halfway up the mountain," I replied, surly and already tired at the thought of hiking for weeks on end.

"Bragging rights and the endless, fascinating stories we'll get to tell at dinner parties for the rest of our lives will be worth more than any trophy on a mantle," he countered, revealing his true motivation for the hike.

I loathed dinner parties with his boring and even more pretentious friends. They'd all seen *Riot Club* and instead of taking it as a cautionary tale, modeled their lives after the morally doomed and pompously horrible characters.

Rules were always more suggestion than set in stone when it came to Tye.

In hindsight, I should've had my eyes checked for color blindness. I kept missing all the red flags.

* * *

June
Delaware Water Gap, border between Pennsylvania and New Jersey
Day Zero
Mile Zero

Starting on the Pennsylvania side of the Delaware Water Gap, we're setting off with our shiny, spanking-new, top-of-the-line gear, bright-eyed and bushy-tailed like two spoiled children going to their exclusive summer camp in Maine. Which, essentially, we are. If kids chose to walk almost nine hundred miles to get there.

Dating a social media influencer has a few perks.

Once Tye informed his legion of followers he was thinking about hiking the "AT," sponsorship deals flowed in like a fast-moving spring river full of snowmelt. All of our high-end equipment was gifted with the understanding that he'll post about it on his accounts.

Easy peasy. Done and done. The man lives his life for likes.

Our adventure has been clearly ordained by the universe—or at least by several multi-national companies and good-deed, environmentally conscious B corps.

Our very long walk is the hiking version of glamping. Gliking? Glaking? Glamking? Insert cool, new hashtag here. Whatever the social media catchphrase, we're doing it.

#livingourbestlives

* * *

Day Two
New Jersey

Mile 10

Oh, New Jersey. You're a lot prettier than I ever knew.

Ten miles took us all day. All. Day.

Why am I doing this?

At this rate, we'll barely make Kennebunkport by Labor Day.

My feet hurt. My toes hurt. My back hurts. My knees hurt. A spot right below my hip hurts. My boobs hurt from my pack's straps digging into my shoulders and across my chest.

I've never been happier for a hot shower, mediocre pizza, and a real bed.

Tye is so exhausted, he hasn't even complained about the low thread count on the sheets.

Our mutual love of the finer things is what brought us together. No one ever expected us to carry our belongings on our backs and hike for months.

Yet here we are.

Ten miles down and almost nine hundred to go.

* * *

Day Nine
Mile 106

Who am I?

Apparently, a woman who's walked one hundred and six miles.

I'd give myself a high five if I could easily move my arms without pain.

Over the past week, there's been a lot of bickering, more crying than I ever anticipated, and several times I've sat down on the ground and declared myself insane for ever agreeing to go on this hike.

All in all, I'd say it's going about as well as can be expected.

Today, we took a zero day (hey, look at me using the trail lingo!)

and picked up a new pair of fancy walking poles for me. I broke one of mine yesterday on the boulders I was heaving myself up and over. Imagine a salmon jumping and flopping itself upstream, only less graceful.

After breakfast in bed, we spent the afternoon at the spa. I decided to skip the mud treatment since I've basically been covered in it every day this week. Sadly, my skin isn't softer and most definitely isn't glowing—unless sweat counts as highlighter.

At this rate, we might make it to Maine for Thanksgiving.

* * *

Day Fifteen
Mile 154

Three summers ago, I visited Paris and walked thirteen miles around the city in wedge sandals and then went out to dinner in heels.

Those same miles on the trail in practical shoes are exponentially harder.

Today there was no going out to dinner. I crawled into bed and ate French fries Tye hand-fed me like I was a baby bird, dropping them into my open mouth from above.

Everything hurts.

I hate my past self and everyone who knows me for not recognizing an episode of temporary insanity when I said I'd do this. Any reasonable person should've had me committed. I could be resting comfortably in a padded cell, enjoying a cup of pudding right now.

Shockingly, I don't hate Tye for being the reason for my current situation. Mostly because he also ordered not one but two brownie sundaes with extra hot fudge sauce for dessert.

* * *

Day Seventeen

Connecticut
Mile 190

Met some guys on the trail who are hiking from Georgia to Maine in one hundred days. According to my calculations, they're walking close to a marathon a day.

Puts things in perspective for me.

Tye and I are sloths in comparison to their pace. Smelly, cranky, slow sloths who make questionable life decisions.

When they saw our light packs, they asked if we were day hikers. I took the question as a mild insult. Did they miss the myriad of bruises, scrapes, and mosquito bites covering my exposed skin? The slightly crazed "what the hell am I doing" look on my face? Come on. I'm obviously walking the walk.

While sharing some jerky by a waterfall, Speed Racer (obviously not his given name) enlightened us about life on the trail.

Turns out they have a name for people like us. Tye and I are slack-packers.

Our people are the ones who don't carry their lives on their backs in heavy packs and get picked up at the end of the day to sleep in a hotel or even at home if they're close enough. Like hiking is their day job.

I'm a little disappointed by the title. Glamking has a nicer ring to it.

The knowledge that we're not alone in taking the easy way is both comforting and a confirmation of my sense of imposter syndrome.

* * *

Day Twenty
Massachusetts
Mile 205

We crossed the two-hundred-mile mark today and still have feet.

I'm down to one hiking pole.

Chatted with more northbound AT hikers during the day.

Apparently, most people use a trail name. Some choose their own, but most people earn a nickname from other AT folks. Hence the name Speed Racer for the guy on his way to completing the hundred-day hike.

No one told me I'd get an alias. I've always wanted a nickname.

Squeaky, so named because he had a pair of noisy boots when he started, assumed Tye and Olive were our trail noms de guerre.

When asked why, he said Tye looked like he'd be more comfortable in a suit and I was small and round but obviously salty.

I took it as a compliment.

Now I want to earn a real trail name.

It's good to have goals that don't involve the number of miles hiked and not peeing on my boots.

* * *

June

Berkshire Mountains, Massachusetts

Day 23

Mile 260

I stopped keeping a daily journal because every entry for the past week would be the same.

We walked.

My body ached.

Things bit me.

The pope might not poop in the woods, but Olive Perry has.

I still regret my decision to do this while dreaming of institutional pudding.

Long-distance hiking can get a little tedious and more than a little painful.

Not for Tye, though. His days have gone mostly like this:

Look at a tree. Snap a picture. Post it to the 'Gram. #deeproots

Look at a cool boulder. Snap a pic. Post it. #thisrocks.

Look at deer poop. Snap. Post. #everybodypoops

Look at a view. #howisthisreal

Keep walking. #miles

Everything is a photo op or a chance for a quick, ten-second story to share the experience with his loyal minions.

Two bowls of bland oatmeal is an #ad for the cooking gear. Doesn't matter that we eat room service at hotels most mornings.

Snack time is a pic of a different protein bar or trail mix. #healthysnax

He even has his assistant upload staged photos for future non-photo-ready moments.

I thought the worst part of walking for hours upon hours would be the blisters and unwanted chafing in delicate areas.

Nope.

Unbeknownst to me, I've signed up to be a model, camera operator, human tripod, and equipment schlepper.

Sure, I've been featured on Tye's accounts many times before this. Early on, I thought that it was sweet he proudly showed me off as his girlfriend. His Instagram is an online highlight reel of our happy life together.

Tye's face is what his followers want to see in their feed. Makes them feel like they're on this adventure with us while scrolling on their phones from the comfort of their own bathrooms.

I miss modern plumbing.

CHAPTER THREE

OLIVE

Day 25
Berkshire Mountains, Massachusetts
Mile 282

*W*hen Tye suggested we sleep in a tent last night, I should've known something was amiss.

I agreed because the Berkshires have always been some of my favorite mountains. Picaresque white church steeples dot rolling green hills and valleys sprinkled with forests and farms. I love visiting in the fall when the foliage is at its peak and pumpkin spice laces the air, a fact Tye knows because he went leaf peeping with me last year.

In hindsight, he probably thought such a tidbit made his grand gesture more romantic. It promoted the lie that his actions were in any way about me.

He woke me before sunrise, hustling me out of the tent. Only a third conscious, with sleep in my eyes and flakes of drool on my chin, I shuffled after him, up a hill to a craggy outcrop of rock.

Below us, undulating green waves of trees stretched to the horizon. Pale pinks and hazy lavender lit the eastern sky. Mount Greylock poked her head above the other hills to our north.

After he handed me his phone and told me to go live on Instagram, I figured he was going to show off some sun salutations like he'd done a dozen times on the trip already. #yogaislife #onlyonetoday

Glancing around, I realized the view probably wasn't the only reason Tye chose this spot. Leave it to him to find a location with a strong signal.

I was grateful not to be on camera. The mosquitoes had held their last supper on my forehead two days earlier. Clusters of swollen bumps near my hairline felt like horns about to sprout from my skull.

The trail was not kind to my vanity. Luckily, I hadn't packed a mirror and had learned to resist using my phone to check on the latest downfall in my appearance. I avoided my reflection in our nightly hotel bathroom mirrors with dubious lighting.

This morning, Tye didn't assume his usual mountain pose.

While I held his iPhone and hit live on the app as commanded, Tye flashed me his most dazzling grin as he got down on one knee.

Honestly, at first, I thought he was mixing up his routine with a crescent lunge.

Until he pulled out a red box.

The kind from Cartier.

My hand shook. I casually noticed the number of people watching had hit ten thousand and was quickly growing. White text flowed up the screen with each new comment. Hearts popped across the image like colorful bubbles when Tye began speaking.

Rushing blood roared in my ears. I must've been in shock because I couldn't process his words. Eyes trained on the red box like it was a venomous snake, I actually jumped when he extended his arm toward me.

Out of range of a possible deadly attack, I blinked at the sparkling stone centered in the white silk of the box. Threatening images of the open jaws of a viper came to mind, causing me to recoil.

"Olive?" His voice cut through the din of my rapid heartbeat and a new unsteady, asthmatic wheezing in my lungs. My body was in full fight-or-flight response and it took everything I had not to run away or punch something. Given Tye was the only thing close enough to make contact with, it's a miracle I didn't hit him.

"O love," he said gently, calling by his favorite pet name. "You haven't said anything."

"Sorry." I shook my head, trying to make sense of the moment. "Can you repeat what you said?"

He laughed and shifted his eyes from mine to the phone I was still holding. "Isn't she the cutest? Can you understand why I want her to be my wife? She's absolute perfection."

Something clicked in that moment—or snapped might be the better word. He'd used those exact words the night we met...when he didn't know me. Over the last year, he had also used the same words to describe a hideous painting he bought at a Chelsea gallery, a yacht in Sag Harbor, and a bowl of cacio e pepe at Luce.

"Are you proposing?" I whispered as quietly as possible, knowing all seventy-five thousand—wait, eighty thousand people watching this on live stream could hear me.

"Was it the five-carat, flawless, radiant cut diamond in a platinum setting that gave it away?" He lifted the ring closer to the camera.

Two sensations occurred simultaneously.

My stomach bottomed out near my knees at the same time bile rose in my throat. I thought I might pass out or vomit. It was possible I might do both.

"Is this a paid sponsorship?" My throat constricted around the words. *What was he thinking?*

A brief flash of confusion clouded Tye's eyes and his perfect smile (#thankslaserwhitening #drkrausisthebestdentist) faltered for a second before he recovered. "Olive, darling, you haven't said yes."

Had he actually asked me to marry him and I'd missed it?

In my silence, he stood and closed the distance between us. His touch on my wrist made me realize I'd dropped my hand. The camera was now recording my bug-bite-covered-legs, filthy socks, mud-caked boots, and the granite boulder beneath them.

This was not how I'd imagined Tye—or anyone—proposing. I was a dirty, smelly mess. There was nothing romantic about this moment. In fact, I could've listed five other more romantic proposals than this one, ones I'd personally experienced.

"I think she's in shock." Gently slipping the phone from my fingers, he laughed into the camera, speaking to the tens of thousands of random people witnessing our big moment. "Guess we blew her mind."

We?

He held up the camera, practically in my face. "O, everyone is waiting for your answer. Don't leave us hanging."

With my mouth hanging open and brows scrunched together, I processed the moment. This had to be a joke, a weird, not-funny prank with me as the punchline. Knowing my reputation as the girl who always says yes, Tye had to be punking me.

"Are you serious?" My voice broke with laughter, which quickly escalated into full-blown cackling. I was certain I sounded as crazy as I looked, a former socialite turned deranged mountain woman. I could imagine the gossip mongers circling like hyenas. Inside my head, I heard my mother's disapproving sigh.

"She has the best laugh, doesn't she?" Tye asked. His kiss came out of nowhere.

Now? He's kissing me now?

Finally recovering myself enough to act, I slapped the phone out of my face, harder than I intended. It went flying, landing with a sickening crunch of glass meeting stone a few feet away, dangerously close to the edge of the cliff.

"Why would you propose to me live on social media?" I stared at the phone and then him.

"You were supposed to say yes!" he shouted. "Who asks so many stupid questions when the man they love gets down on his knee with a ridiculously expensive ring in his hand?"

"You surprised me!" My voice rose to match his. Internally, I asked why the cost of the diamond mattered if the love was true.

"That was the point." Grumbling, he shoved the box into my hand

and walked over to his phone. Holding up the shattered, black screen, he cursed. "Just great. It's fucked. Just like this relationship."

Reeling and still trying to understand the events of the past ten minutes, I stood quietly, slack-jawed and bewildered.

Maybe I was still asleep in the tent and this was a weird dream, a nightmare. We'd eaten weird, packet food the previous for dinner. Probably some preservative caused me to hallucinate this scene. Must be it. My wild imagination was infamous in my family.

"Shit." He pulled on his messy-yet-still-stylish blond hair. "Shit-fuckshitfuck. Fuck."

I slipped into people-pleasing mode to quell his frustration. "We can get you a new phone. I'll call Mina as soon as we have service. She's the best assistant you've ever had. We're not far from Williamstown and they probably have an Apple store. She'll have a new phone ready to go by our meet-up this afternoon."

He shook his phone at me. "You don't get it. My. Phone. Is. Broken."

I stared at him. "Obviously. That's why we'll have Mina buy you a new one."

Ignoring my attempted problem-solving, he continued, "Which means I can't delete the train wreck of a live video."

"Oh shit," I whispered. My stomach clenched and I was certain my heart stopped. "I forgot we were live."

"You were the one filming, Olive—how could you forget? How many people watched me be humiliated?" He fumed as he shoved his phone into his back pocket.

"I wasn't really paying attention. Maybe a hundred thousand?" When he didn't respond, I continued, "Was that a rhetorical question?"

"Give me your phone so I can log in to my account." Palm up, he flexed and curled his fingers, demanding.

My phone hadn't been charged since New Jersey, two states ago. Cringing, I admitted, "It's still dead."

Casting his eyes to the beautiful sunrise lit sky, he sighed deeply. Without answering, he snapped the box closed and then tossed it at me.

Instinctively, I ducked. I'd always hated balls and other objects hurtling toward my head.

Much to my family's disappointment, I was a complete failure at tennis and badminton. Even more embarrassing, I giggled every time someone said shuttlecock.

The box landed behind me, bounced once, skittered off the boulder, and disappeared.

His scoffed, the sound cold and brittle. "Great. I literally just threw away fifty k."

"It can't have gone far." I tiptoed close to the edge and spotted a dot of red. "There it is, only a few feet down."

Without a word, he lowered himself to collect the box. Once he scrambled back to the top, he shoved it into my hand.

I wanted to tell him I hadn't said yes and he should keep the ring, but he didn't give me the chance. Silently, I watched as he stomped off in the direction of our tent. I allowed him a head start, figuring he would need the extra space to calm down, maybe lick his wounds. I knew I did.

I scratched one of the bites in the middle of my forehead before realizing what I was doing. Damn itch was driving me crazy.

Curious, I peeked at the ring again. It was lovely. No one had ever given me a radiant cut diamond before. Tye, or whoever picked out the ring for him, had good taste.

Shame I couldn't keep it. I never did—bad luck. No amount of smudging or crystals could erase the bad vibes of a rejected proposal. Although, technically, I hadn't said no. Or yes. Nor would I. I didn't want to marry a man who proposed to me as part of a social media stunt.

It was a pretty ring, though. Damn.

By the time I returned to the tent, Tye and his backpack were gone.

Grumbling to myself about his stupid stunt and childish pouting, I gathered the rest of my things, collapsed the tent, and cleared our campsite.

Naïvely, I reminded myself he often walked ahead of me. Hiking at different paces, we'd meet up for lunch or at the designated stop for the day.

Sure, I ruined his proposal, broke his phone, and we fought, but he wasn't the kind of guy to abandon me in the literal middle of nowhere. Chivalry ran strong in his blood.

I wasn't devastated because I was in shock.

If he loved me like he said he did, there was no way he would dump me in the woods like an old tire or discarded mattress.

* * *

Day 26

Berkshire Mountains, Massachusetts
Mile 285

There was no sign of Tye at midday. Carrying the tent and the rest of the extra gear slowed my pace, but I felt legit when I encountered other thru-hikers. They would chat with me as we walked or give a friendly greeting as they passed.

For the first time, I felt like I was a real hiker. Not a phony.

When darkness fell, I set up the tent by myself, and after giving myself a high five and then having a dance party of one, I ate a smooshed protein bar for dinner. Besides my chewing, the only sounds were a distant owl and the treetops swaying and creaking in the wind. I didn't allow myself to cry or be afraid.

Definitely still in shock, maybe moving into the denial stage.

The next morning, I asked any southbound hikers if they'd seen him. An older man in his sixties remembered Tye, said he'd spotted a guy matching his description tossing his pack into the backseat of a black SUV with tinted windows, the kind celebrities and assholes ride around in. His words, not mine.

Sounded like my boyfriend.

Ex-boyfriend?

I was pretty sure I'd been dumped.

Welcome to the angry stage.

Another one bites the dust.

A horrible mistake.

An unfortunate incident.

My mother's descriptions of my last three failed relationships. I wondered what she'd call this one. Misguided? Doomed from the beginning? A matter of miscommunication? My own fault?

No, she'd used those descriptions already.

A blip. A bad year.

I could hear my mother's voice in my head. A mere blip. Nothing to settle in and worry about. No one will remember it once the social season is in full swing again in the fall.

When I arrived in Williamstown, I found a coffee shop where I charged my phone. No messages from Tye. I tried calling him. Went straight to voicemail with a full inbox.

Next, I called my best friend, Campbell. Designating herself as my emergency contact, she'd made me promise to check in with her as often as possible. Our daily texting and the occasional FaceTime annoyed Tye, but I didn't care. I'd known Campbell since we were in preschool, long before he or any other boy was on my radar.

She didn't answer either. I sent a quick text with a selfie as proof of life.

Curious, I peeked at my other texts. Even if Tye hadn't managed to take it down, the app wouldn't show the video after twenty-four hours. Apparently, that had still been long enough for it to have gone viral.

From the previews, I could tell way too many people knew about the proposal. I opened my email, skimming the names and subject lines, which gave more evidence that his little stunt had been seen by more than a few random strangers. My stomach sank when I saw Buzzfeed and PopSugar asking for interviews.

If a tree falls in the woods and no one is around to hear it, does it make a sound?

If a scandal happens but you're not online to follow it, does it exist?

If I didn't read the texts and emails, if I avoided all social media, I could pretend none of it mattered.

I couldn't face my family's disapproval yet again.

Turning off my phone, I shoved it and my charging cord deep into the bowels of my pack and set off to find real food.

Over a bowl of pad Thai, I realized I could stop hiking. A phone call or a long Uber ride back to the city could end this whole farce. No more sore feet and aching legs. No more bug bites. No more trying to figure out if the strange sounds in the woods were a warning of imminent death by animal, snake, or insect.

And yet, as I sat there, among summer students from local colleges, tourists, and regulars, I felt like an outsider. None of them gave me a high five or asked me about my time on the trail.

In fact, most of my fellow patrons avoided eye contact with me. A table of young moms scooted their table farther away from me. Couldn't blame them. It'd been a few days since I'd showered or washed my face with more than water. I probably scared their babies.

As I silently enjoyed my late lunch, I eavesdropped on conversations between the waitstaff and watched people stare at their phones instead of engaging with the humans at the same table.

I hadn't missed this life. Sitting there, I knew I wouldn't be going back to the city any time soon.

Waving over a waitress a few years younger than me, I asked where the nearest outdoor store was.

"Are you a thru-hiker?" she asked, glancing at the pack on the chair opposite me. "Wait, are you hiking it solo?"

Instead of telling her my woeful tale, I simply nodded. "Heading north to Katahdin."

"Wow. So cool. You're way more brave than I am." Awe filled her voice. "I could never do it."

I understood. "I never thought I could either. Turns out, if we think we can't, we're right."

Reaching for my wallet, I pulled out my credit card to pay.

She waved me off. "It's on the house. The owner hiked the whole thing back in the nineties and hikers eat for free. The outdoor store is three blocks down on Main. Take your first right. You can't miss the orange awnings."

I thanked her and left a twenty on the table.

Fake it till you make it, I told myself.

I could do this.

CHAPTER FOUR

JAY

Mid-October
Great Smoky Mountains National Park
North Carolina

*S*everal hours later, I cross the border into North Carolina and there's still no sign of the solo female. The half-dozen thru-hikers I encounter promise to ride out the storm in the campground or in town. Low miles or a zero day are better than being dead.

I radio over to the visitor's center at Clingmans Dome to see if she showed up there. Maybe my mystery woman heard about the storm and decided to catch a ride back to Gatlinburg to wait it out in a place with a roof and heat.

No one has seen the mysterious Snowbird, not since she was at the hut a few nights ago. Given I don't have much of a physical description other than brown hair and average height, there isn't much more they can do. They haven't had any long-distance hikers check in today. The famous tower outlook is a short detour from the AT, but this time of year, people aren't taking the scenic side trips. They're so close to the finish line in Georgia, they can practically smell it.

As I gain altitude, the wind picks up, howling through the red spruce and Fraser firs. As I climb higher, the colorful leaves of the deciduous trees give way to the deep evergreens. Riding out a storm on one of the balds would be a bad decision and one I hope I don't have to make. Staying above the tree line with nothing to provide shelter or a windbreak is asking for trouble.

Kind of like hiking solo without a cell phone.

I don't know anything about Snowbird, and I'm already not a fan.

* * *

Giving up on the trail north to Clingmans Dome, I turn south. It's likely Snowbird has found her way off the mountain and into town. Possibly she even detoured into North Carolina after splitting ways with the college guys and the cougher. In the case that his cough was viral, she could be nursing herself back to health at a hostel.

Never into the pack mentality, for me, the entire point of hiking in the back-country is the solitude. Hell, my end goal for most days is to be left alone. Teams, squads, and groups have never been my thing. Growing up, I preferred solo competitions like karate to team sports, mostly to avoid the locker room conversations that drifted toward sexist and racist statements under the guise of humor.

In high school, I kept my mouth shut and avoided calling attention to myself—that is until sophomore year when Kevin Mane said he wanted Jenni to give him a massage with a happy ending. When I punched him in the face and broke his nose, he said he didn't know I liked eating Chinese.

I got suspended for fighting. Fifteen years later, I'm still ashamed. Not for the fighting or for resorting to physical violence; if anyone deserved to get punched for something, it was Kevin Mane. No, the guilt is all mine. I should've explicitly said that no one should talk about my sister or mother like that. Or any woman, for that matter. I never admitted Jenni was my sister or corrected him to say we're Japanese. Didn't matter. To him and a lot of other people, Asians are all the same.

Not saying the stereotypes about mountain folk are true, but around here, if you're not white, you stand out. Easier to play off of people's assumptions than go into too much personal history about my parents. I'm not hiding my true identity. More like not advertising it. And, yes, in my mind, there is a difference.

My walkie-talkie crackles with a familiar voice. "350. This is 324."

"Hi, Guy." I don't bother repeating our call numbers.

"Hi, Daniels. I have a weather update for you. Over," Gaia says, keeping it professional. All park rangers share the same channel on our land mobile radios, so others could be listening to our conversation.

"You know you don't have to say over or roger, right?" I tease her.

"You ruin all my fun." Amusement warms her voice. "Storm's intensifying and shifting course. Did you clear the trails? Over."

I decide to play along. "Roger that. All but one hiker seems to be accounted for. Clingmans didn't have eyes on her either, but she may have headed down into North Carolina."

The radio remains silent for a beat.

"You still there?" I ask.

"You didn't say over."

"And I'm not going to."

"Better make your way back to the station if you can. The meteorologists are saying we're getting gale-force winds, hail, thunder, rain, probably ice, and a few inches of snow." She switches to her serious tone. "In other words, it's going to be bad up at elevation and you might get stuck."

"I've hiked every trail in this park at some point in my life. I don't get lost," I grumble, continuing my march through the familiar woods.

"Won't be a trail to follow if it's buried under half a foot of snow."

"You said a couple of inches," I grumble.

"That's the general consensus, but the outliers have mentioned more."

"Has the guy from the Weather Channel shown up with a camera crew yet?"

"Jim Cantore?" she asks with a chuckle.

"That's the one. Always a bad sign if he's in the area."

"No, not in Cades Cove, but he's all over the news about the storm."

"Shit. Really bad, huh?" Smirking, I scan the steep incline ahead of me.

"Ed wants you to return as soon as possible."

"I agree." The idea of a solo hiker, especially a woman, stirs a feeling of guilt in my belly. "I just wish I had confirmation on the last person."

"I thought you believed she left the trail already?" Guy sounds confused. "Don't risk your life. It isn't worth it. Despite you being a misanthrope, people would actually be sad you're gone, at least a few. Maybe even a half-dozen of us."

"Thanks for making me feel loved, but I need to do my best to make sure everyone is safe." The idea of someone dying because I wanted to sleep in my own bed doesn't sit well with me, not at all and we both know it.

She sighs. "Fine. Radio me in an hour. Take care out there."

"I will." I pause by a tree marked with the white blaze of the AT. "Over."

"Shut up." Her laughter echoes in the stillness of the woods.

Guy is my favorite colleague. We get each other, though not in a romantic way, and not even in the friends with possibilities way. She's smart, kindhearted, and doesn't suffer bullshit. Kindness is underrated these days.

Oh, and she hates people who litter almost as much as I do. Those people are the worst, especially on the trails and in the backcountry. No one is out there following behind the selfish idiots with a garbage bag and a dustpan.

Don't get me started about Mount Everest. My stomach churns with rage at the thought of the thirty plus tons of trash left behind on the mountain. It's like thirty cars packed full of shit. Literally.

Now in a foul mood, I decide to get off the main AT and try one of the smaller trails. There's a chance Snowbird took a detour or got lost. I hope she's at least stuck to the marked paths and hasn't wandered into the thick woods. Too easy to get disoriented, especially on a cloudy day without the sun to guide direction.

The wind swipes the tops of the trees, blows through the under-brush, and scatters leaves. There's a chill to the air. Storm's not supposed to hit until later tonight, but already the temperature is dropping.

I'm running out of time.

CHAPTER FIVE

OLIVE

July
Vermont and New Hampshire
Miles 300 to at least a million according to my legs

*T*ye never came back. #poof #gone.

What happened to the guy who professed his love to me? What happened to #goals and #thatATlife?

Apparently, being rejected on the Appalachian Trail wasn't in his life plan.

According to my calculations, he'd hiked about three hundred miles with me. A mile for almost every day we were together.

Stuck between anger and acceptance on the grief scale, I still wasn't sad.

No Tye meant I was completely on my own. No more car service waiting at designated locations for rides to hotels. No more meals delivered to our GPS coordinates by drone or one of Tye's unpaid interns.

I really missed the yummy food.

What did that say about my feelings for Tye?

I'd thought I loved him and he loved me. Looking back, maybe the only real things about our relationship were the photo ops.

Hiking gave me a lot of time to mull over our history. The relationship I believed was a fairy tale was nothing more than smoke and mirrors. Superficial. Good vibes only. No substance.

For all he knew or cared, I could've been eaten by bears. Or broken my leg and slowly succumbed to the elements in a crevasse, vocal cords shredded from screaming for help. Or tragically bled out in a ditch a few yards from discovery.

I wondered if he'd feel guilty when reading about my death in the Times. I hoped my father would write my obituary. Despite being an engineer, he had a lovely way with words. Mom would probably mention all six of my engagements and zero weddings. *Quel shame.*

For the rest of the first week hiking solo, I occupied myself with imagining my funeral and who would attend. Would all of my ex-fiancés bond over the bland but elegant canapés? Would my father insist on an open bar and generous pours of whiskey, more for his own sake than as a tribute to me? Would Campbell weep over my casket?

I imagined family and friends huddled together, politely and quietly sobbing in the rows toward the front of the little church on Fifth Avenue. My grandmother's funeral was there, and in keeping with Perry family tradition, I knew they'd choose the same location for mine. I always loved the gothic stone building tucked among the skyscrapers.

Sure, I could've stopped hiking at any time. Could've quit and phoned someone to take me back to the city or out to the beach house to heal both my real and mental wounds.

Instead, fueled by sadness, a healthy reserve of spite, and a side of shame, I kept walking. As long as I was on the AT, I could avoid the rest of my life and whatever fallout had been created by Tye's proposal.

Evading any and all direct contact, I only turned on my phone to text Campbell proof-of-life selfies before quickly shutting it off. I didn't even call my parents or sisters. Back in Massachusetts, I'd sent them a group text letting them know my plans to keep hiking. Probably best for me to keep out of sight. There was nothing my family hated more than a scandal.

At an outpost somewhere in Vermont, I discovered a box full of supplies from Mina waiting for me along with the other hikers' packages. Another box showed up in New Hampshire. Made me wonder if she'd scheduled them before Tye bailed, but there wasn't a box for him when I asked.

Grateful for the new trail shoes, fresh underwear, socks that couldn't stand up by themselves, and food, I sent her thank you texts to let her know the packages had been received. I avoided saying more because any dialogue might have led to asking other questions about things I was better off not knowing.

I don't think I would've survived The Hundred Mile wilderness without my fairy godmother.

* * *

August
   Maine
   Day 72
   Mile 895

Yesterday, I summited Mount Katahdin.

After hundreds of miles up and down the White Mountains, over rocks and along ridges, I finally reached Maine.

Scrambling over and crawling through boulders for the mile of Mahoosuc Notch was no joke. Staring up at a granite wall, lashed with metal rungs to aid in the vertical ascent almost had me quitting. This wasn't hiking anymore. I'd become a rock climber. My hands and knees still bear the evidence of the madness.

I even made a few friends along the way, my own trail family, AKA my tramily. As they celebrated completing all 2,190 miles on the mountain's peak, I snapped their pics and smothered my feelings of being a fraud with smiles.

Instead of wanting a trophy or a ribbon for the nine hundred miles I had hiked, I only had one thought.

Finishing what I'd started to prove to myself I could.

I began plotting finishing the trail by hiking south from the Delaware Gap. I figured if I could be in Georgia by early November, I'd complete the remaining 1300 miles before winter weather hit.

My schedule allowed me a week off before beginning phase two, and I needed to decide what to do with myself. Go home? Camp at the beach in Maine with the tramily for a week? Book myself into a spa for seven days of non-stop pampering?

Given the chance to sleep in a real bed instead of my tent in the campground, I couldn't resist booking a room in an economy hotel a block from the water in York Beach, Maine. Lumpy mattress and hard pillows aside, it was heaven.

My new friends were oblivious to my real identity and I liked being anonymous, blending in for once. If any of them had knowledge of Tye's proposal, they didn't tell me.

Showered and wearing leggings fresh from the dryer, I called home.

My mother answered right as I was trying to think of what to say to her voicemail.

"Olive? Where on God's green earth have you been? No one has seen or heard from you in months. If you're going to disappear, at least have the decency to check in with your mother. You could've been kidnapped and sold into sex slavery. Your grandfather was about to rally the troops for a search-and-rescue operation." Her words came out in a rush.

Before she could spin out of control, I interrupted her. "He can't actually do that anymore, and even if he could, it would be a gross misuse of military resources and taxpayer dollars."

"Are you finished? It was a figure of speech. If your sarcasm is intact, I can assume the rest of you is in one piece as well." Her voice was exasperated but hidden in the nooks and crannies of her tone, I heard relief.

"I'm fine. No, I'm better. I'm doing really well. I summited

Katahdin this week. Not only did I walk from Pennsylvania all the way through New England, I've climbed mountains—plural. I've forded streams and scrambled over boulders. I can build a campfire and filter my own water. I also learned to cook. If you close your eyes and ignore the texture, it's not terrible." I rambled, excited to share the little details of the last seventy-plus days of my life.

Her sigh was audible and her disappointment palpable. "Oh, Olive. This all sounds just awful. You poor thing."

And just like that, my pride deflated like a Macy's parade balloon the day after Thanksgiving.

"Weren't you worried?" I hadn't checked in with her since I left a voicemail a month ago for her birthday. I'd received exactly zero texts from either parental unit since.

"Of course, we were fraught with anxiety over this latest demonstration of your need to rebel. I thought you would've outgrown this phase years ago. I should've fought harder to send you to boarding school in Connecticut. Your father was always too soft on you girls."

Leaning against the flimsy wooden headboard, I cast my eyes at the ceiling, willing my voice to remain sarcasm free. "I could've been dead or lying in a remote hospital with amnesia from taking a tumble off of a cliff."

The memory of Tye's ring box sailing through the air flashed through my mind.

She doesn't take the bait. "Your father's been tracking your credit card purchases, so we knew you were alive. Campbell has also been kind enough to pass along updates."

I chose to ignore the serrated edge of guilt she jabbed into my chest. "Oh, good. Nothing like having my privacy invaded for your peace of mind."

"He cosigned the card for you in high school. No one is prying," she said dryly. "When can we expect you home? You know I'm not in the city until after Labor Day. We're spending this week at the house in Westport but will take the ferry over to Long Island on Thursday to beat the weekend Hamptons traffic. Why we can't take the helicopter, I don't know. What's the point of having access to these things if we're not going to use them?"

Knowing she couldn't see me, I closed my eyes and let my head fall back until it was supported by the cradle of my shoulders. Felt good to stretch my neck.

"I'm not coming home," I declared in a soft voice. Clearing my throat, I sat up. "I've decided to hike the rest of the trail."

Silence greeted me.

Checking my screen, I confirmed she hadn't hung up on me.

"I'll be back for Thanksgiving. Probably," I reassured her.

She sighed. "I don't know what to do with you. What does your new fiancé say about all of this? You haven't mentioned Tye once."

"My new what?" The screech of my voice made me recoil. Either I'd gone crazy or she had.

"We saw the pictures. The ring is lovely," she said, drily.

"Hold on—what are you talking about? I'm not engaged!" The gnawing unease I'd pushed to the back of my mind after Tye's disappearance chewed its way through my ability to ignore it.

"Tye shared a picture of the ring on your hand on his account. We watched his proposal to you. I must say, Olive, it wasn't your finest moment. You looked rough." She clicked her tongue in displeasure. "Always be camera ready. How often have I said those words to you?"

"My entire life," I muttered, reverting to being a petulant child. "Tye ambushed me. Do I need to bother saying we'd been hiking for almost three hundred miles when he sprung his stunt on me?"

"He seemed genuine. You were the one acting like a lunatic. I'm glad you two made up. We've been following his pictures of your trip since you never share anything with your family."

Her words sounded like English and made sense individually but, when strung together, were gibberish.

"We broke up the same morning. He left me. In the woods. I haven't seen him since." I stated the facts as I knew them to be true.

"Hmm, this isn't adding up." She sighs. "Sounds like the two of you should have a conversation and get your story straight. The press picked up the story. Another failed engagement is bad optics for you.

You'll never be taken seriously if you keep dumping fiancés, Olive. Is this how you want to be remembered?"

Legacy. She didn't say the word, but we both knew what she meant. The Perrys were all about the family legacy.

"Does Grandfather know about this?" I grimaced at the thought.

"You know he doesn't bother with social gossip, but he's aware you're engaged. Again." She didn't need to add the reminder at the end, but my mother could never resist gilding a lily.

My sigh of disappointment echoed hers. "I'm not engaged. As soon as we hang up, I'll call Tye and clear this up."

"If you need the lawyers, let me know. We keep them on retainer for exactly these moments."

Nice to be reminded my fickle heart and inability to say no were responsible for the annual salary of more than one attorney.

"Please let us know when you have this settled either way," she said.

"What does that mean?"

"If you change your mind about Tye, it would be nice to hear it from you rather than Page Six." Ice clinked against glass. Mom enjoyed her wine spritzers the way some women chugged La Croix.

"Trust me—Tye and I are through. I want nothing to do with him. Once he takes down the photos and whatever else he posted, the story will fade away." Exasperated, I knew I needed to end this call before it became a nautilus spiral, winding in ever-tightening circles of frustration until my head exploded.

"We'll see. Darling, Miranda is here for our tennis match. Call soon. Love you." She disconnected the call before I could respond. Typical.

Instead of calling Tye, I tapped Campbell's name. She picked up on the third ring.

"Hello, stranger." She yawned. "Sorry. Late night."

"I'm engaged?!" I shouted. "Why does my mother think I'm still with Tye and we're happily engaged? What the hell is going on?"

"Shh, not so loud. This is what happens when you disconnect from the Matrix."

43

"That reference is almost as old as we are." I rested my head against the headboard.

"Keanu is having a renaissance so it's relevant again."

"Can we talk about your Keanu Reeves obsession another time? I feel like my life has split into two realities. On one timeline, I'm engaged to Tye. That's not real. I never said yes. He dumped me in the middle of nowhere."

"Open up his Instagram. I'll wait," she instructed me.

I followed her orders and scrolled down until I spotted the ring photo. "Given I never took the ring out of the box, I have zero memory of such a picture being snapped. I'm not sure that's even my hand! What the ever-loving hell?"

"Are you sure? Looks like your fingers."

"We've been friends for decades and you can't identify my hands?" My voice echoed back at me from the phone.

"I was distracted by the diamond. It's a pretty stone."

"I'll send it to you. Tye left it with me. Hold on ... if I have the ring, when did he take those pics?" I studied the hand again. "No, it's mine, but I swear I never put the ring on my finger. Wait, do you think he took a photo while I was asleep? Before he proposed? He wouldn't, would he? Super creepy. What if I said no?"

"You always say yes. He probably knew the odds were in his favor." Her voice grew muffled and faded.

"Campbell? What are you doing?"

"I'm here. You woke me up. I was just getting out of bed."

"What should I do? If everyone thinks I'm engaged, it's going to be a legit pain in my ass to set the record straight." I moan at the thought of having to deal with a publicist to handle this mess. Again.

"Simple. Talk to Tye."

"Ugh. Do not want." I groan and thump my head against the headboard.

"Or don't. Deal with it when you come home. Are you done with your long walk yet?"

Oh, right—my big accomplishment.

"I finished the northbound section several days ago."

"Congratulations!" Her enthusiasm was genuine. "When will you be back in the city? There's a big house party in Montauk next weekend. You should come out. It'll be mellow fun, but we can celebrate then."

"I can't make it. I've decided to hike the rest of the trail."

"But you already climbed the mountain," she says, confused.

"There are almost thirteen-hundred miles left I haven't walked. I want to complete all of them. After I finish, I guess I'll come home."

"And when will that be?" She sounded confused and a little put out by my new plans.

"Thanksgiving. Probably." I'd likely be able to finish well before then, but I wanted to give myself a cushion.

"Have you lost your mind?" she squealed. "Do I need to come get you and bring you home?"

"No and no. If anything, I'm feeling more myself. I need to finish this. For me."

She didn't say anything for a long moment.

"You can't run away from your life, Olive. Hiding out in the woods won't make the Tye mess go away. I think you need to face reality by coming home. This isn't normal behavior."

Her judgment and dismissal only solidified my intention.

"I'll see you in November." My finger hovered over the screen to end the call.

"Olive?" Her voice stopped me. "We can't hang up mad. Rule number one of this friendship. Be careful. Send me proof-of-life selfies as often as you can. If I see Tye, I'll kick his ass for you."

"Thanks, Campbell. Love you."

I chickened out about calling Tye. Instead, I sent him a three-letter text with a screenshot of his feed.

WTF

Not waiting for a reply, I turned off my phone and buried it in the bottom of my pack.

If your life is a mess but you're in the woods, does it matter?

CHAPTER SIX

OLIVE

October
Somewhere in Virginia
Day: Thursday?
Mile one thousand and something
States walked through: 11

*H*iking is putting one foot in front of the other.
One foot.
In front of the other.
Repeat forever.
One step becomes ten and then a thousand.
Eventually, these steps turn into miles.
Miles turn into days.
Days turn into states.
States turn into months.
Months become life hiking the Appalachian Trail.
I officially passed the halfway point in Harper's Ferry, West Virginia.
When I first began solo hiking, I listened to podcasts and music. Turns out, true crime and serial killer stories aren't the best things to

think about as a woman alone in the woods in the middle of nowhere. After hearing about a hiker who was almost trampled by a charging bear because he was wearing headphones, bye-bye earbuds.

In case anyone is wondering, *Please Forward my Mail to the Middle of Nowhere* is the working title of my imaginary biography.

Alone with myself and my imagination, I decided it would be better to be aware and focused on my surroundings, which consists mainly of trees, rocks, dirt, and plants. Throw in random reptiles, toxic looking amphibians and strange noises, and that's pretty much my daily existence.

Other than a few lizards, the snakes I'm trying to block from memory, more salamanders than I've previously seen in my entire life, and the two possible bears, there hasn't been nearly as much wildlife as I imagined there'd be. Except birds. So many birds.

Back in the city, I used to imagine the unbroken quiet of the woods. Ha!

Most days it's a cacophony of bird conversations over the chatter of insects and frogs.

Cicadas are the loud, drunk girls of the woods. No point in trying to shush them. They'll only scream louder.

The constant buzzing, chirping, and squawking reminds me of women fighting over bargains at the Barney's Warehouse sale, only with less screeching.

Back in Pennsylvania, I grabbed a dog-eared copy of *Peterson Field Guide to Eastern Birds* in one of the hiker boxes outside a shelter. It was avian information or a copy of the Bible.

I can't believe the good stuff people leave behind on the trail. Along with the gators for my ankles and the buff I'm wearing over my head, I have two new-to-me pairs of socks and an inflatable sleeping pad. Someone left a mini, cast iron skillet. Shockingly, no one else wanted the heavy, unnecessary cooking implement.

The bird book is the thing I didn't know I needed and can't live without, like a magical wireless bra that lifts without creating a sausage roll boob.

Identifying birds and marking the ones I've spotted has become a small obsession. On a scale of not caring to the Jonas Brothers super fangirl I became when I was eight, I'm definitely closer to the latter. I'm at the point where I can recognize bird calls before I get a visual confirmation.

Heading south means following the migration of several species as well as the local varieties. Given my lack of entertainment, I've also memorized all fifty state birds and can name them in alphabetical order. Because I'm cool like that.

Watch out fancy dinner parties, I'm going to blow your socks off with ornithological facts.

Given my new obsession, my trail name has evolved now that I'm a southbound thru-hiker, AKA a SoBo. They call me Snowbird. Works for me.

To all the haters who think I'll never get married and am going to die alone as a cat lady, I say ha! I'll be the crazy bird woman with binoculars and a camouflage poncho, silently hiding out in reeds or woods. As a stealth ninja, a friend of the beaked and feathered.

After my quarter-life crisis and a weird but thankfully brief music festival phase, I swear I'm not freaking out about the big 3-0. Age is just a number, right? My inner calm partly comes from the fact that the broken timetable in my head isn't working anymore.

For the record, my poncho is orange and also from a hiker box. It's hunting season and I'd really like to not be mistaken for a deer. Plus, neon is on trend again this year.

Current me laughs at former fashionista me. Old me shudders at the idea of wearing the same pair of socks for days at a time. No one tell her about the current underwear situation. I'm down to three pairs: the ones I'm wearing and, if I'm lucky, two clean. Most days things are more dire.

My mother and sister would disown me if they ever found out. Or if they knew on non-raining days, I've been known to hang my unmentionables on my pack and let them air-dry out in the open where God, bears, and strangers can see them. Unfortunately, I lost pair number four somewhere in West Virginia.

There's probably a hiker box with pink-and-white striped panties in it. Wouldn't be the first time underwear ended up in one.

I should probably restock and buy some fresh socks next time I swing through a major town. My shoes are also pretty much shot at this point. Not held together-with-duct-tape ruined, but close. Five hundred miles causes a lot of wear and tear. My hiking pole has a twenty-degree bend to it.

If I can make it to Damascus, Virginia I can do some shopping and resupply.

* * *

October
    Somewhere in Tennessee or North Carolina
    Day: 147?
    Mile one thousand nine hundred something
    States walked through: 13

I've lost track of the days. Not only what day of the week it is, but how many days I've been on the trail. Gotta be close to five months since Tye and I headed north from the Delaware Water Gap, which means I've spent four months pretty much solo hiking.

Alone but not solitary.

This is good. This is fine.

Okay, it's a little weird.

I spend a lot of time having conversations with myself in my head.

The SoBo hikers are an interesting bunch. Some of them started at Katahdin and faced the most challenging parts of the AT first. Those people are hardcore nuts.

Then there are the flip-floppers like me. Those are more my people. For the most part, everyone is nice enough, but I'm over every, single, last dude bro who feels the need to mansplain my hike to me. Over. It.

I get it you know stuff. Is there some sort of chemical stored in testicles, that compels men to explain things to women? Obvious things like why leaves are green or the sky is blue or how to manage a period while hiking in the woods.

Dude, you don't even have a vagina.

The worst ones are the guys who come off nice, but turn out to be stealth cuddlers. I've woken up one too many times on a shared sleep platform in a shelter as the little spoon with morning wood pressed against my back through two layers of sleeping bag. No, thank you.

Not today, and the rest of the week isn't looking too good for you either, Satan.

Hooking up on the AT is a big thing, especially at the larger shelters and hiker hostels off the trail. Even if scraggly beards and general lack of personal grooming were turn-ons, I've officially sworn off any potential romances. Even thinking about relationships gives me the dry heaves.

Presented with the choice, I stick to hanging out with families and other women. Sisterhood of the traveling sports bras unite.

Somehow, I got off pace with the lovely family hiking with their two teenage boys and found myself in a shelter with a pair of dude bros and an older guy a few nights ago.

Actually, those bros weren't so terrible, just young. Right out of college and still puppies who haven't filled out yet. The man was nice enough, except he was sick, and every time he coughed, I swore I could see the germs floating through the air in my direction. I've managed to avoid getting sick so far and I'd like to keep it that way. Thank you and good day.

After they gave me a heads-up about some weather heading toward the Smokies, we parted ways. They took the trail toward Cades Cove while I detoured to Clingmans Dome to see the lookout tower.

CHAPTER SEVEN

JAY

October
Great Smoky Mountains National Park
Tennessee

*R*esigned about the mysterious hiker, I decide to return to the station. Clouds darken the sky and rain scents the wind. If I'm lucky, I'll only have to hike a few hours in the dark and the rain tonight before sleeping in my own bed. I say a silent prayer for the safety of anyone still in the mountains during the storm. It's all I can do at this point.

Following the white blazes, I head south along the AT for a few miles, knowing I need to take a spur trail to wind my way home.

Given the coming harsh conditions, I don't expect to see too many birds, but I keep my ears open for their songs. As the resident ornithologist and one of the park's wildlife ecologists, I'm tasked with tracking the ever-changing bird populations in this quadrant of the Smokies.

Southbound migratory birds have mostly left the area for their winter homes in the Caribbean. Not a bad way to spend a few months, but the flight would be exhausting and I'm not sure my arms could handle it.

The joke is lame, even in the ornithology world. I chuckle anyway.

"I'll be here all week, folks." I tip my hat to my imaginary audience.

"I'm peeing!" a female voice shouts from the woods to my left and up ahead a dozen yards. "Privacy please!"

My feet halt while the rest of me freezes in place. Everything stills except my eyes, which scan the trees for the source of the voice. Behind a good-sized Fraser fir, I spot a sliver of neon orange the color of a safety vest. A roll of hunter orange fabric sits atop a large blue backpack. From this angle, all I can see of her is a bit of a pink down jacket sleeve. I don't want to see more when she asked for privacy.

Waiting for her to finish or declare the all clear, I chew my bottom lip and toy with the strap of my own pack. I think about radioing back to the station. Might be premature given I don't know this woman's identity. It's unlikely she's a day hiker.

Time stretches into silent awkwardness as I remain still, debating if I should continue loitering nearby or walk farther away to give her more privacy. Growing up sharing a bathroom with an older sister was a blessing and a curse. Some bladders are shy.

Blowing out a long exhalation, I'm about to head back up the trail when she speaks again.

"Are you still there?"

Her question is more an accusation than an inquiry. I should've retreated up the path. Great, now I'm a creeper, possibly a peeping Tom. At the very least, I'm a lurker. None of those are good.

Taking a few steps in reverse, I wait to answer her until I've put more space between us. Quietly, staying on my toes, I attempt to remain silent until I can no longer see any of her at all.

"Sorry to interrupt," I shout an apology.

Her reply doesn't come right away, and she doesn't stand.

I check my watch. We're burning daylight and precious time.

Finally, her blue pack shifts into view and rises as the hiker stands, disappearing for a moment before she steps around the tree.

"Are you Snowbird?" I ask, observing her as she picks her way over rocks and branches.

Definitely a long-distance hiker.

Two messy, brown braids curve over her shoulders from under a black beanie. She's fit but not gaunt in her black leggings and jacket. After scanning her body, I slide my gaze up to her face.

Other than the sharp stare and frown, she's objectively beautiful. Not like the Mona Lisa, which we're told is beautiful. Her features are classic but slightly off balance. Her blue eyes are a little too large and her scowl exaggerates her already wide mouth. In contrast, her nose is delicate. Somehow all the elements combine into undeniable beauty.

"Why do you ask, Ranger?" Annoyed, she rubs sanitizer over her hands. "Am I in trouble?"

Her pointed chin juts up, making her neck appear long.

"We're expecting bad weather for the next couple of days beginning tonight, and it's my job to make sure everyone is safely off the trails."

"Very kind of you." She tucks the small bottle into a fanny pack at her waist. "I don't need to be rescued. I heard we're getting some rain, maybe a little wind, nothing I haven't already experienced. I'll find a shelter if it gets to be too much."

Did she just dismiss me? I'm still out here because of her.

"You're too far from any enclosed shelters. Better to head toward Cades Cove and wait it out in the campground, or in town. Given you're the last unaccounted-for hiker in this area, you might be out of luck getting a spot. I'm sure someone can give you a ride to Green Valley." I remove my water bottle from its pocket and take a long draught.

"Is that in North Carolina or Tennessee?" She pauses several yards from where I stand.

"Does it matter?" I ask.

"No, not really. At this point, it's all the same I guess." With a sigh, she shifts her pack and joins me on the trail. "As long as I'm not under arrest."

"Why would you be? Have you done something illegal?" I cast her a serious look. "Poaching? Hunting out of season? Stealing plants?"

Her chin retracts. "Plant thieves?"

"You'd be surprised."

"How bizarre." She shakes her head. "People are weird."

"Understatement." I lift my gaze to the clouds brushing the tree-tops. "We should probably get going."

"We?" She widens her stance and crosses her arms. "Are you escorting me off the trail?"

It takes a certain personality to overcome the mental challenges of long-distance hiking. Stubborn. Tenacious. Idealistic.

This woman definitely ticks the first two boxes.

"Pretty much, yes, miss." I dip the brim of my hat. "Officially, the trail is closed. All hikers need to be off these mountains until we can safely reopen it."

Her wide mouth curls back into a frown. "How long will it be closed? I'm almost finished with this damn walk. I can handle the weather."

"Can't say. Up to Mother Nature and what she wants to do."

She grumbles something about a fickle bitch before tipping her head and shoulders back to yell at the sky. The heavy pack drags her into a backbend and she stumbles to right herself.

Instinctively, I bound forward to catch her before she falls over and gets hurt. Stubborn and reluctant is one thing. Injured would be a bigger mess than I want to deal with out here.

Steadying her with my hands wrapped around her waist, I hold on until I'm certain she has her balance again. "Whoa. Careful." My voice low and my words slow, I sound like I'm talking to a spooked horse. "Easy."

"Excuse me?" She jerks and wide eyes meet mine. Swirled with gray amidst the blue, they remind me of storm clouds.

She flicks her gaze down, and I do the same. My hands remain on her body.

No longer resting on her waist, my fingers grip the curves of her hips, my thumbs dangerously close to the apex of her thighs.

"I'm so sorry." This time it's my turn to stumble back. My body propels itself away like I've touched a high-voltage wire.

Only she doesn't try to stop my fall. I land on my ass, hard.

She doesn't even try to hide her laughter.

"For the record, I had no intention of groping you." From my spot splayed out on the ground leaning back on my hands, I meet her blue eyes with a slow smile.

"Sorry. I shouldn't be laughing at you. If you get injured, who will carry me to safety should I be overcome by rain, sleet, or snow? I might get the vapors and faint. Who will save me if you've been knocked unconscious?" Speaking in an atrocious Southern accent, she presses her hands together over her heart and flutters her lashes.

My hat has landed a foot or so away from the rest of me. Standing, I gather it and place it back on my head before I wipe the dirt and mud from my uniform. My fingers flex at the memory of touching her.

"Was your accent supposed to be Scarlett O'Hara?"

If she identifies with such an entitled character, we might be in bigger trouble than I originally thought.

"Actually, it was Blanche from *Golden Girls* with a dash of Miss Julia Sugarbaker from *Designing Women*." Her pointed chin lifts in defense.

"Okay, sure. Well ..." I stretch out the word. "Shall we?"

Sweeping my arm to the left, I gesture at the trail.

"I never answered your question." She steps around me and leads the way down the narrow dirt path.

Happy to finally be moving, I follow behind her. "Which one?"

She twists her neck to locate me. "I *am* the Snowbird you're looking for."

"Did you just deliberately misquote Star Wars?" I add one point in the positive column for her.

"Maybe." She winks and faces forward.

We walk for a few minutes in silence. Listening to the creaks and sighs of the bows bending from the wind, I release the tension in my neck and shoulders, relieved to have located the solo SoBo. I might not be a fan of people, but conducting a missing person search after a weather event is probably my least favorite part of this job. Finding a body out here sticks with a person for life, no matter if it's the first time or the fifth.

"Now you're supposed to tell me your name. That's how introductions usually go," she says, barely glancing over her shoulder.

"You can call me Ranger Daniels." I point at the name embroidered on my uniform jacket.

"Is Ranger your first name? How convenient for you." I swear she picks up her pace.

"Actually, my mother wanted me to become a doctor." I resist the urge to help her navigate a rocky section.

She stops and faces me, waiting.

I answer her silent question. "It's Jay."

"Short for James?"

"Nope. Just Jay. Since I told you mine, what's your real name?" I cock my head.

She studies me, not hiding how she's sweeping her eyes down my body to my boots and back up. Whatever she finds causes her to shake her head.

"Since we're technically still on the trail, Snowbird will do, Just Jay." With a satisfied smirk, she walks away.

This is going to be a long hike.

CHAPTER EIGHT

OLIVE

Great Smoky Mountains, Tennessee
Day: 148
Mile one thousand nine hundred something

*T*here I am, squatting behind a tree, having a private moment when this man-hunk shows up wearing a Smokey Bear hat and looking all grizzly in a good way with a thick beard and the prettiest green eyes surrounded by the longest, darkest lashes. Totally unfair. I've paid hundreds of dollars for lash extensions and the gods bestow their bounty on Ranger Smoking Hot. He's probably one of those guys who doesn't care about his appearance. Not even deliberately trying to destroy women with his hotness, just doing it naturally.

Both his light brown hair and darker beard could use a trim. I wonder if he's even heard of manscaping or if all his body hair is wild and free.

I cover my mind's eyes before they can start picturing him naked.

How many months have I been out in the wilderness? How many dude bros and thru-hikers have I encountered? I haven't imagined any of them naked. With some I didn't have to use my imagination, not when skinny-dipping in streams and lakes happens on the regular.

59

Honestly, the male body is okay but doesn't throw me into a hormone-fueled horny haze. A six-pack is nice to look at but can't satisfy an itch. By satisfy an itch, I mean give me orgasms.

One thing about being outnumbered by men out here is the knowledge that dick is plentiful and easily available. Sounds nice, but the reality is disappointing. Supply and demand. When there isn't a scarcity, there's no reason to get riled up and flustered. I wish I'd had this realization back in college.

Ranger Jay in his spiffy gray and olive uniform exudes authority. I didn't mean to be snappy with him from the start, but the rebel in me doesn't respond well to figures of authority.

I've had enough men telling me what to do, the last thing I want to do is follow orders.

His suggestion to detour down to the valley does not mesh with my agenda. Time's running out to spot the Black-throated Blue Warbler, one of the few species left on my list.

When I heard footsteps on the trail, I yelled out the first thing that came to mind to explain why I was off in the woods and needed privacy.

Probably should be embarrassed, but whatever shame or scraps of dignity I'm supposed to have around bodily fluids has long disappeared.

However, in the moment, I wasn't using nature's restroom.

I thought I'd finally caught the notes of the elusive warbler's call and wandered toward the sound. I know they like to hang out in the underbrush at higher altitudes.

I hoped he would keep walking. He didn't.

There are guidelines about hiking in the national parks. Leave no trace and pack-it-in, pack-it-out are two of the biggest. The number one rule is to stay on the trail. Wandering into the woods, chasing birds is exactly how people get lost.

Instead of continuing on his way, he waited for me. Weird. Most hikers would give a wide berth and keep on keeping on. Catching a glimpse of his hat, I knew I'd been busted. It's not like I was stealth camping or doing anything he listed, but I still feel guilty.

Now he's escorting me to safety.

My knight in a green uniform.

There's no point in arguing with him or trying to ditch him. I attempted the former and know the latter would be pointless. I may have more long-distance endurance, but Ranger Jay seems like he'd be a fast runner. Long legs, lean muscles. Broad shoulders. Strong hands.

Must. Stop. Cataloging. His. Hotness.

This is why I'm walking in front of him.

Eyes on the path, Olive. Pretend he's a friendly bear concerned about forest fires, not causing a fire in your pants, one he could put out with his big hose … the one I caught a suggestion of when he fell.

In spite of the chill in the air, I fan my heated cheeks.

A heavy drop of rain splats on my head, leading the charge of its brethren in a sudden downpour. Low beats of thunder echo around the valleys below us. We're below the balds and in the trees, but still at high altitude. The trail is never the best place to ride out a thunderstorm, especially near a place called Thunderhead Mountain. No, not the ride at Disneyland. Ranger Jay is right—we need to get off this mountain.

"We need to put on rain gear so we don't get soaked." His voice is closer, a few steps behind me. "Once we're wet, we're wet. I'd prefer not to get hypothermia."

I stop walking and shimmy my pack off my back. My poncho is strapped on the outside of my bag for quick access. I'm adjusting the hood over my head while he's still unfolding his.

"Need some help?" I offer in a sweet voice, with a slight Southern lilt to it. I can't help it. He has a drawl I automatically want to mimic. The slow pace of his words is molasses and I'm a housefly with a sugar addiction.

"I'm fine. Thank you." Once encased in his clear body condom, he rolls his wrist, indicating that I should continue walking.

I give him a salute and set off again.

We walk in silence for a while, maybe half a mile or more. The thunder encroaches but lightning never strikes closer than three or four miles away if my one-one-thousand counts are accurate. The rain pelting my poncho makes hearing anything else difficult.

Thankfully, the storm passes and we get a break from walking through the equivalent of an outdoor shower. A light mist follows, enough to keep wearing our ponchos but not terrible.

Swift-moving, low-hanging clouds characteristic of the Smokies scrape the peaks across a valley from where we're currently navigating a narrow ridge. Moisture thick in the air, I can barely make out details of the trees less than a quarter of a mile away.

Slowing my pace, I allow Ranger Jay to catch up with me. "When did you say the worst of this weather is hitting?"

"Last report said tonight." He wraps the long fingers of one hand around the radio near his neck. "Shit, I was supposed to check-in an hour ago. Give me a moment."

He presses a button on the side and speaks into the black mouthpiece. "350 to 324."

"Aren't you supposed to say over?" I ask when he pauses. "So the person on the other end knows when you're finished?"

"Not you, too." He rolls his eyes.

"Daniels?" A female voice crackles over the speaker. "Is that you?"

He lifts an eyebrow. "No over?"

The woman on the other end laughs. "You're obviously still fine. Any luck with Snowbird?"

They've been talking about me? I squint at the radio.

"Found her. We're en route back." He ignores me by turning his back. "Everyone else accounted for?"

"As far as we know. Lightning took out a tower to our north. Tornado warnings to the south. Surprised you were able to get through. Best to keep the lines clear unless it's a true emergency. You going to be okay?"

"As long as we just have a little rain, we'll be fine."

I reach over and knock my knuckles on a tree. Evidently, Ranger Jay isn't superstitious enough to believe in jinxes.

He glances at me and then up. I get a definite impression he doesn't like me.

Which is fine.

The last thing I need is to have a mountain man flirt with me. Don't need him being all charming and sweet with his slow, honey-coated voice.

The very last thing.

I knock twice again on the nearest trunk and remind myself I've sworn off men.

Not forever. Just for the duration of this hike.

Let's be realistic—yes, a lot has changed about me over the last five months, but I'm still the same woman who said yes to six proposals. I still have eyes and a heart and other working parts.

This ban isn't forever.

CHAPTER NINE

JAY

Once the lightning fades and the thunder is no longer audible, I think we're out of the metaphorical woods for a while. This is good news because this section of the trail has a lot of rocks and a quickly moving creek we need to cross.

During our descent, Snowbird keeps up a quick pace. Her steps are sure as she navigates uneven surfaces and inclines, and I can tell she's used to clocking a lot of miles most days. Curious about the why of her hike, I make a mental list of questions to ask her as I try to keep up with her.

Another round of heavy rain pelts us, turning the ground beneath our feet to mud, slippery and sticky. There's no sunset as the sky grows noticeably darker, along with the onset of another temperature drop.

"Can you smell snow?" She inhales deeply. "I swear I've always been able to tell when the first snow of the season is coming."

"I'm not sure that's a thing." I sniff the air.

"Don't be such a grumpalumpagus."

"Disagreeing with you doesn't automatically equate with me being grumpy," I complain. "Snow doesn't have a scent."

Her mouth twists in annoyance. Noticeably inhaling, she says, "I think it does. Frost is in the air."

She's right. Our breath comes out in puffs, lingering between us and floating above our heads before dissipating. Not a good sign.

Tilting my head, I stare into the tree cover. A single perfect flake drifts down from above, followed by another and another.

"Shit," I mutter.

"Ooh," she murmurs. "It's snowing."

If I'm not mistaken, there's a slight hint of gloating to her tone.

"Let's hope it stops soon." I glower at the flakes swirling fast and furious in the wind, willing them to stop. "Typically, we don't see any frozen precipitation until November. Mid-October is highly unusual."

"It's going to be beautiful." She spins in a slow circle, head back and arms spread wide.

If she tries to eat the snow, I'll be forced to share with her about microplastics. No one enjoys hearing about how our planet is so over-whelmed with human garbage now, there's literally plastic falling from the sky.

Instead, I remind her about our mutual enemy: hypothermia.

"We're already wet from the showers. Even with the ponchos, our forearms, hands, lower legs, and feet are exposed. They're at risk for frostbite, and reduced body temperature can lead to hypothermia."

She stills, her face serious when she gazes at me. "How far are we from a shelter?"

I check our position on GPS. "Nothing close. There's an open lean-to a few miles ahead, but it won't protect us much."

"If it's our only option, we should head there for the night." In the dusky light, I can barely make out the worry lines of her forehead.

"What happened to hiking through all kinds of weather?" I rub my hands together and blow on my fingers. I only brought thin gloves and they're mediocre at best, but better than nothing. I drop my pack and pull them on.

"You brought up frostbite and hypothermia. If the professional is concerned, who am I to be arrogant enough to think I'll be fine?" She mirrors my movements and grabs a pair of thick gloves from the bag at her waist.

"I'm more worried about being out here at night and losing the trail in a few inches of snow. We get whiteout conditions, it'll be impossible to spot the white blazes that mark the way. Even with the GPS, getting disoriented and lost is highly probable."

She takes in our surroundings. "Should we set up camp here?"

"Ideally, no. I only have my bivy bag. It's basically a sleeping bag with a storm flap." Because I refused to believe I'd be stuck out here in the snow.

"My tent is for a single person of average size. AKA, me. I'm not saying you're a giant, but I don't think we'd both fit. Sorry."

There's no way I'd ask to share her tent unless freezing to death was inevitable and even then …

Extracting the laminated trail map from my inner jacket pocket, I have an idea. "Give me a second. I think I know a better option."

Snow coats the plastic and I struggle to see the fine lines in the dim light.

"Hold on, let me grab my headlamp." She pulls one out of her waist bag. "Here."

"Thanks." Grateful, I take it from her and hold it above the map.

"What are you looking for?" Leaning into my space, she peers over my hands.

"I grew up hiking these mountains. Let's just say I didn't always keep to the marked trails when I explored."

"Why, Ranger Jay, are you saying you didn't follow park rules?" she teases.

"Young and dumb." I shrug off her words. Pointing to a spot not far from our current location, I swirl the light in a circle. "We're going here."

"What's there?" Warm puffs of air rise with her words.

"An old moonshiner's cabin."

Her mouth opens and closes a few times, not that I'm staring at her lips … not enough to notice her front top teeth are slightly longer than the rest or note that her bottom lip is slightly chapped. I definitely don't stare long enough to realize she has faint freckles across her nose and cheeks that aren't visible from farther away.

She begins speaking, her voice high and thready.

"Has horror movie written all over it. No way. Nope. We can squeeze inside my tent. You might have to sleep on your side curled into a ball like a potato bug, but we can make it work. Or find a cave. Even one occupied by a bear would be a better option than the murder cabin. I'm not a virgin and therefore definitely not surviving a night in the death house." Her head turns from side to side as she speaks. "Not happening."

If she stomped her foot for emphasis, it wouldn't surprise me.

"Okay, you can sleep outside. I won't force you to spend the night in a building with a roof, four walls, a door, a floor, and a fireplace." I shoulder my pack.

"What?" She jabs me in the chest. "You'd let me sleep outside all alone while you're enjoying a warm fire? Aren't you sworn to serve and protect?"

I remove her finger from my solar plexus. "You're thinking of the police, not park rangers. If I'm not mistaken, you just told me all the reasons why you are absolutely not setting foot inside a perfectly good cabin."

She rambles about fireplaces and ski lodges, at least I think that's what she says. She's mumbling mostly to herself.

Snow begins collecting on the fallen leaves near our feet. A gust of wind hits my back, shoving me forward a step.

"Can we at least get moving again?" I ask, adjusting my poncho, which has partially inflated with the breeze. "You can make up your mind when you see your options. All I know is we're not camping here."

Given she doesn't have any other choice but to follow, I take off down the still-visible trail. It's less than two hours to the cabin.

I hope it's still standing.

* * *

Death by a simple padlock.

Well, technically we're at risk of dying from hypothermia if I can't get us out of this storm. Wet gear and dropping temperatures are a deadly combo.

Using my shoulder, I lean into the door, testing the strength of its hinges. They're old and rusted, but they hold strong.

From the outside, the cabin appears to be long abandoned. Thick moss and pine needles smother the roof, and dead leaves crowd the porch. Grime coats the cracked panes of glass in the small windows flanking the door under the low porch ceiling.

Next to me, Snowbird shuffles off her pack before setting it down on the ground next to a small boulder. Snow slides off the top where it's accumulated. Thick flakes land on her black beanie and slowly melt into the fabric.

"Maybe there's a hidden key." She bounces on her heels and blows on her hands.

"People engaging in illegal activities don't generally use a hide-a-key," I grumble.

"Understandable, but it's possible. Why even lock a cabin in the middle of the mountains nowhere near anybody else?"

"See my above statement about illegal activities." I jostle the old lock to double-check it's engaged.

"It won't do any harm if I look for a key." She steps closer to me.

Reflexively, I freeze and hold my breath as she invades my personal space and stands on her tiptoes.

What is wrong with me? She's not going to try to kiss me. That would be ridiculous.

She pauses, gazing at me with her eyebrows drawn together before reaching her hand above my head. "Sometimes people hide keys above the doorjamb."

"People?" I croak out like I'm thirteen and at my first dance.

"Okay, me. I'm notorious for losing my keys or locking myself out of my apartment. I don't have a doormat or a potted plant, so I've been known to slip a key on the ledge."

Empty-handed, she steps away, wiping her dirty fingers on her wet leggings. "No luck."

"I'll kick the door open." I gesture for her to move back. "If it doesn't splinter into a hundred pieces, we'll only have to worry about a broken padlock."

"Not reassuring, Ranger Daniels." Her tone is teasing. I think.

I correct her for the tenth time. "You can call me Jay."

"So you've said." She runs her fingers over the top of the window next to the door.

"Even with a broken door, we'll still be out of the elements and protected from the worst of the storm." Recalling my years of karate lessons from childhood, I assume the proper position for a side kick.

"What's this?" Snowbird's voice halts my movement. Grinning, she extends a metal, key-shaped object toward me. "Why, I believe it looks like a padlock key."

"What are the odds?" Muttering mostly to myself, I drop my foot and straighten. Disappointed I didn't get the chance to kick the door open like a badass, I slip the key from her hand and then insert it into the lock.

The door swings open, revealing a room empty of furniture. The only objects on the filthy floor are a wooden crate, a plastic gallon jug of questionable amber liquid, a fire-poker, and what appears to be the petrified carcass of a mouse near the threshold.

She peers around my shoulder into the one-room cabin. "At least we don't have to worry about sharing a single bed."

I chuckle, the sound awkward. "Thank God for small mercies."

CHAPTER TEN

OLIVE

"Total murder cabin." I back away from the door and lean against the crooked post holding up the rickety roof.

"Porch might be wide enough to set up your tent. I'd be careful of rotting boards." The ranger's smile is patronizing.

With my weight on my left foot, I gently stomp on the wood below my right. It creaks and groans. "Hmm, spongy."

He's gone when I look up. "Ranger Daniels?"

"Inside," he calls from within the dwelling whose structural integrity I am seriously questioning. Light from his flashlight sweeps the room. "I was right—there is a fireplace."

"Any evidence of blood splatter or dismemberment?" I hesitate to enter. Near my boot is a mummified rodent. Using my hiking pole, I push it across the narrow porch. The late Mr. Mouse skitters off the side and disappears from view.

"Surprisingly, no," Jay says from close behind me.

I yelp in surprise. "Don't jump out at me."

"I didn't." He doesn't apologize. "Come inside so I can close the door. You're letting snow and more cold air in, which defeats the entire idea of weathering the storm *inside*."

Picking up my backpack, I step across the threshold. The room doesn't feel any warmer than the porch, but at least snow isn't pelting me in the face. Glancing around the room, I notice a drop leaf table with three legs in the corner behind the door, but zero firewood.

"Do you have wood?" I ask, without thinking.

Jesus take the wheel of my brain-to-mouth bus.

"For the fireplace," I add.

He stands stock-still and does nothing to ease my verbal flailing.

"You know … for heat. I'll stop talking now," I mumble.

He gives me a funny look. "I'm hoping there's some stacked up against the side of the cabin. I'll go check it out. If not, we can burn the table and crate."

The cabin dips into darkness when he leaves since he takes his flashlight with him. I fumble with my headlamp and pray there isn't someone waiting to jump out at me from the shadows.

Tye would absolutely hate this place. It's pretty much his worst nightmare and would definitely take the number one spot if there was a soundtrack comprised entirely of banjo music.

Funny, I haven't thought about him in weeks. Maybe even longer. I've been on a boycott of social media and sworn Campbell to silence, which means I have no idea what he's doing with his life or if he deleted any evidence of our non-existent engagement. I've enjoyed not knowing.

Not my cattle, not my bullshit as my grandfather would say.

I miss him and his wisdom. Next time I'm somewhere with service, I need to call him. He always tells me exactly what I need to hear, though it took me a long time to understand his brand of tough love.

Keeping my gloves on, I gently lift the jug of questionable liquid and set it outside on the porch. Could be moonshine. Could be urine. Either way, it has to go.

If there were a broom in the place, I could sweep up the dirt and leaves. Across the room is a narrow door by a small counter with a sink comprising the 'kitchen.'

There is zero possibility of me opening said door without Jay in the room.

Satisfied I'm not going to die in the next five minutes, I go about removing my poncho. Should Jay get a fire going, I'll be able to dry out my clothes and shoes. Until then, I'm keeping all my layers in place.

Minutes tick by and he doesn't return. Through the grime on the window, I spot the glow of his light. Slightly reassured, I flip the wooden crate and take a seat to wait.

Something heavy thumps into the other side of the closed door. I hold my breath for a second until Jay appears, arms laden with logs.

"Can you take these? I'll grab another load and we should be set for the night," he says from the doorway.

The firewood is heavy and wet, but better than nothing. I'm grateful for whatever Jay can find.

This time he returns quickly, carrying even more wood, which he adds to the pile I created by the old stone fireplace. Over time smoke has blackened the rocks directly above the hearth. I wonder how many years this cabin has stood here and how long it's gone unused.

"Need any help?" I ask.

"Sure. Sort out the smaller branches and any loose bark. We'll use it for kindling. I have a package of fire-starter pods in my pack. I'll grab those and my matches, and we should be good to go."

There's something so confidently capable about him that I find appealing. Must be a caveman/cavewoman response in my ancient lizard brain. If you provide fire, I'll be your mate.

His strong hands and nimble fingers make quick work of stacking the kindling and bark into a neat pyramid. I'm guessing he must be a complete Ranger Romeo, flirting his way through the park, wooing every woman in the campground. How could he not be?

Now I'm flipping through all the other rangers I've met along the way. None of them come close to his good looks, even with the scraggly beard. Must be something in the water around here. I wonder if all the men in the Smokies are as handsome.

A spark of orange catches my attention. Ranger Jay tips forward, gently blowing on the baby flame, breathing life into his creation.

From my perch on the crate, I watch with relief as combustion takes over, spreading along the edges of the dry material.

"I shall henceforth dub you Prometheus, Ranger of Fire." I tap both of his shoulders from behind with a long stick.

Sitting back on his haunches, he laughs. "What an enormous responsibility. Not sure I can live up to being a Titan."

My gaze lingers on his wide shoulders. "I somehow think you're up to the challenge."

Whatever that means.

Standing, I walk over to my pack and pull out my bear bag of food. "Hungry?"

"I could eat." He crosses the room to where I'm setting supplies on the three-legged table. "Have anything tasty in there?"

"Who says I'm sharing?" I attempt to clutch the top closed, despite the fact that I just asked if he was hungry. Mother Nature isn't the only fickle bitch.

"I've provided shelter and fire—you should contribute something. Is this a Pop-Tart wrapper I spy?" Excited, he points to a silver package poking out of the top of my bag.

"Could be." I don't know why I like teasing him. I just do.

He directs his words to my hands. "Please tell me you have Brown Sugar Cinnamon. Or Strawberry. Or at the very least, Frosted Blueberry? I'd be happy with the unfrosted variety too, but know I'll be silently judging you."

I'm taken aback by his list and shift the pack farther away from him. "How did you know?"

"Seriously? Which one?" He pretends to make a grab for my goodies.

And by goodies, I mean my stash of Pop-Tarts.

"All of them?" I don't know what I'm asking when my voice rises at the end of the sentence.

"Really? You have to share. At least split a package of your least favorite flavor. One tart is all I'm asking." He begs, hands clasped together and face shaped into an expression so innocent and hopeful I can imagine him as a little kid.

Widening the top of my bag, I extract all the two-packs. "I tossed the boxes so they're kind of a mystery. Pick one."

"This feels like a Vegas card trick." Slowly, he slides one of the packets out of my hand. "No take-backs. I keep whatever I picked, right?"

"Deal," I agree.

Dammit, he's adorable. I bet he can be a sweetheart if and when he forgets to be grumpy.

Peeling back the wrapper, he breaks off a piece and exclaims, "Strawberry! I win!"

His enthusiasm makes me laugh. "My favorite are the brown sugar ones."

Half a Pop-Tart disappears before he swallows and asks, "Then why buy the other flavors?"

"The Piggly Wiggly only had one box of them in stock so I bought my runner-ups. To quote the Rolling Stones, if you can't have the tart you love, love the tart you're with. Or something."

"Pretty confident those aren't the lyrics." He finishes off the first pastry and tucks the remaining one into his jacket pocket. When he catches me staring, he explains, "For later. I like to pace myself."

"Let me guess, you were the kid who still had leftover Halloween candy at Thanksgiving."

"Made it to Christmas one especially bountiful year." His smug smile puts me in my place. "And you?"

"One Halloween, I ate so much and was in such pain, my mother took me to the ER because she was convinced my appendix was going to burst." I giggle at the memory.

He chuckles and I feel his eyes studying me.

"What?"

"Nothing."

"You want to say something, say it. I won't take offense."

"Somehow I don't believe that's always the case." He holds my gaze.

I fight the urge to glance away. Feels like he can see straight into my soul. Most people don't hold eye contact, but then there's Ranger Jay.

Being exposed makes me defensive, so I deflect. "We don't know each other and will never see each other again. No reason to hold back."

I swear he flinches.

"Fine. It's true we just met, but you seem like the type of person who doesn't believe in delayed gratification." He glances over my shoulder and then directly at me.

I hold eye contact. Eventually, we're going to end up in a staring contest. "Why do I think you're the opposite?"

"Because I am. I believe in hard work and setting goals. Nothing in life has come easy for me. I suspect that's not true for you."

His words are an arrow straight to the truth of me. "I have goals, like the two-thousand-plus miles I'll walk this year. Pretty major accomplishment by any measure."

Feeling vulnerable, I look down and stuff half a Pop-Tart into my mouth.

"You're absolutely right. Never mind." He strolls back to the fire and stabs it with the poker before adding a bigger log. The damp wood cracks and pops as flames infiltrate it. Thick tendrils of smoke creep up and over the stones.

"Shit," he mutters. "Forgot to open the flue."

The smoke billows into the room as the flames intensify. Jay inserts the poker up into the chimney, cursing under his breath as he struggles to get the latch to release.

Afraid we might asphyxiate, I open the front door at the same moment the flue opens, creating a strong downdraft. Our fledgling fire struggles to keep burning, flickering and sputtering.

"Shut the door!" Jay shouts.

Apologizing, I follow orders and slam it shut.

He casts me a sheepish look. "Sorry, I shouldn't have yelled at you. It's fine."

The orange glow in the fireplace restores itself and warmth spreads into the room.

"Think it's safe to take off my shoes and dry them by the fire?" I study the dirty floor.

"Worried someone might steal them?"

"No, was thinking about tetanus and all the other bacteria probably living in here." My mind flickers back to the poor mouse. "How easy is it to contract the bubonic plague? Do you have to be bitten by an infected flea? Or is contact with a body enough?"

Ranger Jay tips his head back and laughs. Real, shoulder-shaking, belly-jiggling laughter escapes him. It's ridiculous and unrestrained. Utterly contagious.

Although I suspect he's laughing at me, not with me, I join him.

Catching his breath, he finds enough of his voice to ask, "How have you survived for months in the wilderness on your own? Does your mind think up every worst-case scenario? How are you not crazy?"

"Who said I'm not?" I cock my head. "Most people who know me agree I lost my mind when I decided to continue this trek on my own."

He nods once. "There's a story there."

"Isn't there always?" I ignore his unspoken invitation to share more. Suddenly, I don't know what to do with my hands. If I cross my arms, I'll look defensive. First, I rest them on my hips—too Wonder Woman power pose. I drop one hand to my thigh, and now I'm an awkward teapot handle. Finally, I tuck them into my jacket pockets. "We should get out of our wet clothes."

His mouth pops open and his eyes grow wide. "Uh ... I'm not sure that's a good idea."

I replay what I said. "Oh! I don't mean get naked *together*."

Embarrassed, I cover my face with my hands.

He mutters something under his breath and then raises his voice. "You meant because our clothes are wet and we'll warm up quicker with the added bonus that they'll dry faster on their own. I'm an idiot. Sorry, I'm inappropriate."

"No need to apologize. I'm the one who suggested we get naked. I have other clothes." I lift my small cube from my bag to prove my point.

"Lucky you." He rubs the back of his neck.

"You didn't pack anything?" I eye his much smaller backpack.

"Nope. Wasn't planning on having a sleepover." He frowns at his feet. "But feel free to change. I can turn my back or stand in the corner over there." Pointing to the opposite side of the small room, he follows his own suggestion. "Just let me know when the coast is clear."

"Okay," I confirm, already fantasizing about dry, warm clothes.

Over the last few months, I've become a pro at a super quick outfit change and don't hesitate to lose my damp layers, starting with my soaked shoes and frozen socks.

Wet leggings are difficult to peel off, but I shimmy them down and step out of them. Barefoot and pantsless, I shiver in the cool air when I unzip my down jacket. Despite the poncho, my clothes are damp down three layers to my skin.

Reaching for my one other pair of long pants, I knock over my pack and groan when it lands on my left big toe, which has been sore for weeks.

"You okay?" Jay asks from his corner.

My eyes cut to where he's standing and make contact with his worried stare.

"No peeking!" I pull my jacket closed, which does nothing to hide my underwear.

"Oh, shit. Sorry." He faces the wall. "It sounded like you were in pain and I turned without thinking. I swear I didn't see anything," he mumbles through his hands.

I glance down. "Nothing to worry about. I typically wear less when I go swimming."

"Everything okay? Are you injured?" His voice holds genuine concern.

"Totally fine." Keeping an eye on him, I pull up my clean pants, drop my jacket, and peel off the long tee and camisole. My sports bra feels dry to the touch, so I don't bother taking it off. None of my clothes could be described as clean, but they're dry.

I sigh audibly when I'm fully dressed. "Dry socks are one of life's greatest blessings."

"Is it safe to turn around?" he asks.

Ranger Jay has seen all he's going to be seeing of me.

"You're good." I laugh when he peeks through his fingers. "I don't mind if you want to lose your wet clothes, as long as you're not going commando."

"Uh …" he hesitates.

"It wouldn't be the first casual penis sighting on the AT." I'm attempting to reassure him, but as soon as I say it, I know I've made things more awkward. "I'll show myself to the corner now."

Spinning around, I mentally bang my head against an imaginary desk. I'm not fit company for regular people anymore.

"Snowbird?" His voice sounds unsure. "It's okay. I'll keep my pants on."

"So you *are* one of those commando guys?" My voice lifts to a tween-like squeak.

"Didn't say either way. I just don't want to make an awkward situation more uncomfortable for either of us." He's clearly trying to be professional while I keep bringing up inappropriate topics. Like what's in his pants.

After removing his olive-green jacket, he unbuttons the gray short-sleeved shirt with his badge and patches. Beneath is a plain gray t-shirt. There's a dark line mid-thigh on his pants marking where the fabric is soaked.

I'm not a prude by any measure, but I don't want to cross the boundary of public servant and taxpayer with him.

Geez, sounds like some weird kind of roleplaying.

CHAPTER ELEVEN

OLIVE

"*I*f we lay our clothes on the floor near the fire, they'll dry quicker." I gather my things and carry them over to the hearth, all the while I try not to check out Ranger Jay's broad shoulders and the way the cotton stretches around his biceps. So basically, I'm only staring at my own feet.

He sits on the crate to unlace his boots and strip off his socks. I've seen a lot of gnarly feet and toes over the past five months—missing toenails, thick calluses, bunions, and other pedicure nightmares—so I feel qualified to say Jay has nice feet. No hobbit hair.

Olive, get a hold of yourself.

He reveals his forearms and feet and I'm decoupaging a mental scrapbook about them. A poem waits to be written about his thick belt. Perhaps a short haiku about his boots or a limerick about his hat.

His movement breaks me out of my trance. Neatly lining up his jacket, shirt, boots, and socks in a row, his arm brushes mine when he reaches to flatten out a sock.

The hairs on my arm lift in a salute to acknowledge the contact. If he notices, he doesn't let on. Maybe I'm imagining the pull between us.

"Let's make some real food and eat. We might get lucky and have water."

"You might need to adjust your definition of the word real. All I have is packets and processed food stuff." I know I should eat healthy while hiking. My body is a temple and should be honored with nutritionally dense, organic meats and vegetables. Right. That was me before I had to carry my food supply on my back while heaving myself up mountains. Cheese puffs are both lightweight and delicious.

"Anything is better than nothing," he reassures me.

After standing, he steps over to the counter and then turns the faucet handle. Nothing happens for a few seconds. "Guess we'll have to collect snow and melt it."

A foreboding, deep rumble and then a gurgle draws our attention to the sink. Black, then rusty brown water sputters and splashes into the basin.

"Mmm, mountain fresh," I declare. "Snow it is."

"Let it run to flush out the pipes. Out here it's got to be well water. We can filter it." As he speaks, the water lightens from chocolate to weak coffee before finally transitioning to clear.

"Look at us all fancy with our running water." I slap his shoulder in shared triumph.

"What's for dinner?" He grins down at me. The top of my head barely meets his shoulder.

"You like chicken pot pie?" I grin.

"You have an entire pot pie in your pack? Unrefrigerated?" His nose wrinkles.

"No, of course not. I've come up with the second-best option. Actually, lower your expectations and forget what real chicken pot pie tastes like. Pretend you're an alien from a distant planet and this is your first experience with human food." I pull the packets out and line them up on the counter.

"You're really selling this dish. I can't wait to taste it."

Ranger Jay does sarcasm? We might become friends after all.

"What are you contributing? You must have some supplies with you. Wouldn't be very rangerly to not have snacks."

His eyebrow arches. "I came prepared."

"Where's your picnic basket?" I prod.

"That joke doesn't land anymore. How old are you?" He chuckles and again, I'm pretty sure he's laughing at me.

"My grandfather and I used to watch old cartoons together —*Looney Tunes, Rocky and Bullwinkle, Scooby Doo*, and all the original Disney classics. It was our thing when I was little. I'd get up early and find him then he'd make us each a bowl of cereal and we'd hide out watching shows until everyone else woke up." I love this memory of my grandfather. It's one of the most normal family memories I have. "Do you have any moments like that from your childhood?"

"No, not really. I didn't really know either grandfather. My mom's family lives far away and my dad wasn't close with his parents." His words come out in a rush. "My dad and I watched WWE wrestling sometimes and Godzilla movie marathons on Saturday afternoons."

Going about the process of cooking with limited supplies, I begin by filtering water, and then set up my small pot and single burner mini camp stove, AKA the pocket rocket. Not to be confused with the other pocket rocket also available for sale on Amazon.

"Anything I can do to help?" Jay stokes the fire, adding another log until it classifies as roaring.

"Got it covered." I bring the water to a boil and let it simmer for several minutes to ensure it's safe to consume.

"Guess I'll explore." He slowly turns in a circle to check out the room. "Did you open the closet?"

"No way." I laugh at myself. "I already dubbed this place the murder cabin. If there's a hidden killer or dead body, it's definitely behind that door."

"Might be something useful." He makes a beeline to the closet.

I freeze and hold my breath, ready for something horrible to be revealed when he tugs on the handle.

Nothing happens right away.

"Feels like it's warped." He pulls harder.

"Or God is trying to protect us from what's on the other side."

Laughing, he puts his back into it, and the hell gate swings open.

Secretly I'm hoping it's a hidden bathroom or at least a toilet so I don't have to go outside to take care of business in the snow.

Sadly, it's only a closet. With a broom and an old metal bucket.

"Disappointed?" he asks, bending down to lift the bucket.

"I was hoping for moonshine. I feel misled by this being called a moonshiner's cabin. False advertising. Where's the hooch?" Adding a dramatic sigh, I stir my bubbling dinner concoction.

"Those stills are worth something. If they had to abandon this location, the equipment would be the one thing they'd take with them. Good news, though—we can use this to heat up water in the fire."

"A broom and a bucket?" I ask, disappointed.

"From the mess on the floor, looks like the former residence of our not-so-recently departed furry friend. Wait, there's something up on the shelf." He extends his arm and pulls down a stack of magazines.

"Please tell me you're not holding porn." I cringe, both at the possibility of Appalachian moonshiner pornography and the words my brain insists on vocalizing.

"You have sex on the brain." He's not amused.

Normally, he'd be wrong, but given the things coming out of my mouth this afternoon, he's right. "Too much time spent with the dude bros. I'm no longer fit for society."

"Looks like some old issues of *Outdoor Life* along with *Field and Stream*." He holds up the evidence so I can read the titles.

"Nature porn is a thing, the fantasy of communing with the land," I mumble, lamely defending my assumption.

"Right." After tossing the stack back on its shelf, he rinses his hands in the sink.

"I have soap if you want to clean up." I jerk my head in the direction of my stuff. "In the little green pouch."

"What else you got in there, Mary Poppins? Coat rack? Sugar? Top hat? Semi-feral house cat? Parrot?" He opens the top and peers inside.

"Have you even seen *Mary Poppins*? There's no house cat in her bag." Exasperated, I reach over and hand him the pouch.

"Isn't there a parrot?" His forehead crinkles adorably.

"On her umbrella handle. It talks, though, if that makes you feel better." I pat his arm.

Still looking confused, Jay frowns. "Huh. I thought I remembered the movie better. My mom and sister loved it and watched it on repeat."

"Memory is funny." This conversation has me feeling nostalgic, too. "Food's almost ready. I only have one spork and the mug/pot, so we'll have to take turns."

CHAPTER TWELVE

JAY

*T*he only place to sit other than the floor is the old crate. Being a gentleman, I plop down on the floorboards close to the fireplace.

Our fire has warmed up the room enough that it's almost comfortable in here. My pants are still damp, mostly from the knee down so I angle my legs toward the heat in the hope they'll dry out quicker.

Snowbird's suggestion that I remove my pants took me off guard, and my hesitation to hang out in my boxers surprised me. I'm not shy about my body, and boxers don't reveal anything a swimsuit doesn't.

Living in the park staff cabins means close quarters with my colleagues. Think college dorm meets summer camp. On our days off in the warmer months, we'll go swimming or hike up to a waterfall and spend the afternoon chilling out together. Still, I don't think any of my female coworkers have seen me in my skivvies.

Snowbird falls under the category of park visitor and in my mind she's on the same level as Guy or any of the summer interns or volunteers. In other words, she's off-limits.

There's no rule set in stone about fraternizing with visitors. The line in the sand is my own. I never want "hooking up with a ranger" to be part and parcel of a trip to the Great Smokies. Or any national park. Rangers aren't here for entertainment and personal, um, enjoyment.

Others would disagree with me. Griffin definitely would. Life is an all-you-can-eat buffet for him. He's going to enjoy every moment, every experience. If anyone is an odd duck, it's him.

Snowbird pulls the crate closer and sits, her feet resting on the floor near my knees. Blowing on the beige goop in the mug-pot, she takes a small bite and then hands it to me.

"How is it?" I sniff the pudding-like consistency. "Smells like chicken and vegetables. Sort of."

She waves a hand in front of her mouth before speaking. "It's delicious."

I'm not so sure. "I don't want to steal your food. I have some protein bars and some jerky in my bear can. That'll suit me just fine."

"I swear it tastes better than it looks. Try it. If you hate it, more for me." She refuses when I attempt to give it back. "Don't you know it's insulting to the chef if you're not even willing to try something?"

I use the spoon to poke at something green. Might be a pea. "Chefs might think it's insulting to compare this to food."

She's been teasing and flirting with me all day. Pretty sure she doesn't think I've noticed. As the younger brother, I grew up being teased and quickly learned to dish it out as good as I got. This is a language I speak fluently.

Cautiously, I lift the spoon to my lips and take the tiniest lick with my tongue. The first thing I notice is salt, followed by chicken and an umami flavor, reminding me of buttery crust.

Braving more, I slide the spoon into my mouth. The texture is mush, but she's right—it vaguely resembles pot pie … if my eyes were closed and I have no memory of a real pot pie.

"Not bad, huh? Huh?" Her grin is infectious.

"Far from the worst I've ever eaten." I scoop up another bite. It's probably my saliva glands responding to the salt, but suddenly I'm starving. It's been a long day of hiking and I can't remember if I stopped to eat lunch.

"Well, don't hog it all." She gestures for me to hand it over.

After another mouthful, I pass it back to her. "Not bad. How'd you come up with it?"

"This may shock you, but I've never been much into cooking until feeding myself in the wilderness became a necessity."

Given all of her top-of-the-line, expensive gear, this news doesn't come as a surprise. Typically, the fancier the equipment, the less seasoned the hiker.

"One day I hiked over twenty miles, thinking I'd find some trail magic by the end of the day—a hot meal, cold drinks, and good company before crawling into my tent and falling asleep." She holds out the mug. "Well, a storm rolled in and the sky turned into a faucet. Complete deluge. Too wet for ducks. Kind of like this afternoon. Forced to set up camp before I floated away, I threw in every soup packet I had and only added a little water because I was running low. Mushroom plus chicken plus creamy vegetable. Voila! I'm a genius!"

"Like I said, I've had worse—much worse. One time I got served chicken feet when I ordered chicken soup." I give her a turn with the spoon, pausing to gulp down water from my bottle.

"In Appalachia?" she asks.

"No, Japan." It bothers me to know she travels with the classic stereotypes about these mountains being filled with hillbillies and small-town yokels. We do have our fair share of odd folks around here, but I'd like to believe we're not all so different from state to state if you get to know people on a personal level.

"What were you doing in Japan? Were you in Tokyo? I've only been once but loved the energy. And the food. The sushi—can we have a moment of silence for the sushi, please?"

I can't blame her for launching into her own memories of the country. We as humans want to be heard and acknowledged. Most of us want an opportunity to be seen and share our stories.

"The sushi is incredible there. Nothing comes close around here."

Her eyes lift to mine. "Have you ever been to New York? We have pretty decent sushi. The food isn't all pizza and street meat."

With a mouthful of food, I shake my head.

"Really? Never?" She sounds shocked.

"Cities aren't really my thing. Too crowded. Too many people." Saving the last couple of bites for her, I rest the pan on her knee. "Finish it. If you're still hungry, I have two cookies for dessert."

"Real, honest, baked-in-an-oven cookies? Or packaged ones from the store?" With a hopeful look on her face, she scrapes the spoon on the bottom as she eats the last of the soup.

"Homemade, but not by me," I clarify. Don't want her getting the idea that I'm some sort of domestic god who bakes in my spare time. If I want something sweet, I'll drive into town and grab a slice of pie or a donut at Daisy's Nut House, or I'll swing by Donner bakery next to the lodge closer to the park.

"You've been holding out on me, Ranger Jay." Her gaze pierces mine and I'm frozen, a deer in headlights.

Even in the dim light from the fire, she's beautiful. Dirty and honestly more than a little smelly, she still has trouble written all over her pretty face.

Outside, the wind howls, causing the flames to shimmy and retreat with the draft. Neither of us has checked the state of things outside since we arrived. I assume it's still snowing while remaining optimistic temps will warm enough to switch back over to rain before morning.

"So you live in New York City?" Under the guise of cleaning up from our meal, I stand to put some distance between her and my body's reaction. Must have been sitting too close to the fire and got overheated.

"Don't try to distract me from your stash of baked goods. What kind of cookies are we talking about? Please don't say oatmeal raisin."

"They're oatmeal raisin, which happens to be my favorite kind." I'm full of lies. I'll happily eat any cookie, because I'm not a monster, but raisins are a cruel trick on kids perpetuated by moms who want to slip more fruit into their diets. My number one favorite is double chocolate chip in brownie batter.

"I was afraid you'd say that." She sighs, resigned.

Snowbird excels at pouting, information I file away for future reference. I bet she's rarely told no and almost always gets her way. What I've observed plus the limited amount of information she's shared about herself adds up to a spoiled city girl. That said, the fact that she's solo hiking the AT doesn't fit neatly into this equation.

I'm thinking I can leverage the promise of non-raisin-tainted cookies to learn more about her.

"Hold your thought." She bounces up. "I need to take care of some business. Outside. Um, you didn't happen to locate a recently remodeled bath house while you were gathering the firewood, did you? Something with all the fancy modern conveniences like a flushable toilet?"

I snicker at her fantasy. Beats our reality. "Nothing remotely similar. Might be an old outhouse in the woods, but I didn't spot anything close to the cabin"

"If this were a rom-com movie, this would be a lot less awkward." Shoving her feet into her boots, she pulls her down jacket on. From inside her bag, she extracts a packet of wipes, hand sanitizer, and her headlamp.

Part of me feels like I should escort her outside. With the wind gusting hard enough to come down the chimney and affect our fire, I'm worried about the conditions out there.

"Want me to do some reconnaissance?" I offer, reaching for my boots.

She waves me off. "I'll be fine. Not my first time. Bears and I have a lot in common."

As she opens the door, a blast of air flings it out of her hand and slams the wood against the wall. Snow blows through the doorway, swirling across the threshold before melting on the planks of the floor.

Snowbird appears shaken yet remains upright. I'm by her side in a few seconds.

"You okay?" I touch her shoulder.

"Wow. It's bad out there." More snow scatters across our feet. The light from her headlamp illuminates the blizzard beyond the porch.

Still barefoot, I step outside, regretting my decision when my feet come in contact with the icy surface. "Forecast said snow, but I didn't expect whiteout conditions."

Thick inches of snow coat the ground and tree branches, giving a soft glow to the woods.

"I promise not to wander far. You don't have to stand out here freezing while waiting for me." She navigates around me and down the porch steps. "I'll only be a minute."

"Stay where you can see the cabin," I warn her. Disobeying her suggestions that I retreat inside, I only step across the threshold to avoid getting snow on my toes. "Damn, it's cold."

My breath exhales into frozen clouds around my head. Caught up in our random conversations and distracted by eating, I've forgotten to check in with anyone. It isn't too late.

Locating my radio next to my pack, I attempt to reach the station.

"This is 350." The channel I typically use is quiet.

"350 for 324. Over." No one responds to my call.

Guy did say the tower got struck by lightning, and it's possible they're having power outages from the wind or are out responding to actual emergencies. Reminding myself to check back later, I resume my sentry post near the front door.

Through the static of white snow against the inky black of the woods, I catch a glimpse of a headlamp bobbing through the snow. Relief courses through me.

At the sound of her boots clomping on the porch, I swing the door open to let her back inside.

"What an experience." She stomps her boots to clear them of snow and shakes off her jacket. "Do not recommend unless you're a fan of cryogenic tanks and ice bars."

"Not familiar with either of those things." I lay her jacket out next to mine.

"You're not missing anything. People paying to be cold when you can stand out there and get the same results—nuts." She rubs her hands together. "Brr. If I were a man, I'd pee in the sink."

I choke on my own spit. "You say whatever comes into your head, don't you? No filter."

She blinks up at me, amusement curving her wide mouth. "You

should've met me six months ago. My filter had a filter. I was triple-filtered and rarely said what was on my mind."

"What changed?" I lift my eyebrows, letting my mouth shift into a smirk.

"The better question is what didn't." Her fingers toy with the wet tips of her hair. "Five months of walking. Figuring out how to survive on my own. Being away from my friends and family. Doing something completely out of character to prove to myself I can. Somewhere back in Maine, I discovered I was all out of fucks. Must have lost my last one climbing the White Mountains." With a laugh, she makes a dramatic bow.

It's been a long time since a woman has intrigued me and it's possible she might be completely crazy, but I'm curious to know more about her.

"Why did you decide to thru-hike? You said there's a story."

"Isn't there always?" She gives the same answer as before. "No one wakes up one morning and says, 'Self, let's start a 2,200-mile walk today.'"

"That's not really an answer. What's your why?"

"Why did you become a park ranger?" She deflects.

"I'll tell you—after you answer my question. I'm willing to bribe you with cookies to find out more." I locate my food stash and reveal my bait.

"I forgot all about the cookies. Those don't look like oatmeal raisin." She reaches for the bag and I lift it over my head.

"They're double chocolate. Brownie base with milk chocolate chips." To tempt her, I wave them in front of her face. "And they're delicious."

She sighs, resigned. "Fine. What do you want to know?"

"Everything. Let's start there."

CHAPTER THIRTEEN

OLIVE

I really don't want to get into the details of how I ended up in a cabin in the middle of nowhere Tennessee—nowhere North Carolina? I'm honestly still not sure what state I'm in. Maybe it doesn't matter. To quote Alice, I knew who I was when I woke up this morning, but now I'm not sure.

Yet I find myself opening up to Ranger Jay.

Could be his training or personality that makes him a good listener, the kind who remains quietly engaged, doesn't interrupt, and asks the right questions.

Could be because he's willing to share his cookies.

Pop-Tarts are fine for a quick snack on the trail, but they sure as hell aren't freshly baked cookies. A lot about me has changed since May, but obviously, I'm still easily swayed by sugary bribes.

Is chocolate worth spilling my secrets to a stranger? Past me says no. Current me points out I have nothing to lose. She also reminds me he's an exceedingly handsome man. Not sure why his looks should matter in my decision-making process, but I agree.

Jay's too good-looking to be hiding out in the backcountry. His high cheekbones and almond-shaped green eyes are wasted on wild boar and bears. I doubt there's a skunk alive who could appreciate the

Cupid's bow shape of his mouth or the mole behind his left ear, right below his hairline. Not even wild ponies would understand the perfection of his messy waves. He probably doesn't realize or care he's handsome enough to be a model, and not catalog. We're talking Tom Ford or Gucci building a campaign around the angles of his face.

This type of thinking leads me down a dangerous path, one involving fantasies of the naked variety.

Nothing is going to happen with this nice ranger. As much as it feels like we're the last two people alive, we're not. Tomorrow the snow will melt and we'll go our separate ways.

Present me, the one who lost her filter and her fucks back in New England pipes up to remind me this is a perfect set up for a one-night stand. No strings, just wild sex with a handsome, sexy stranger.

Old me, the one who still has a shred of dignity and decorum, chimes in to remind me I haven't showered in … I try to count the days … a very long time *and* we're in a murder cabin, one which may or may not have been exposed to the bubonic plague.

With a shudder, I decide to spill the tea about myself.

"Where should I begin?" I ask him, sitting cross-legged with my back against the crate.

"Like you said, no one wakes up one morning and decides to walk for five months. Start there." He reclines on top of his sleep pad and bag, using his bent arms as a pillow.

"The quick and dirty is my boyfriend decided to do it and asked me to come along." Knowing how lame the reason sounds, I attempt to shrug it off. "So I did."

"Just dropped everything, quit your job, and took off?" He lifts his head to meet my eyes. "What did you do to train?"

"I set up training hikes and walks around the city with backpacks full of canned goods," I reluctantly admit, not feeling the pride I once did for coming up with the idea.

He scratches his ear, and I swear he hides a smile behind his arm. "How'd that work out for you?"

"Those first couple of days sucked. Hard. Clearly, I had no idea what I was getting myself into. Nothing prepared me for the reality of hiking." I grimace. "And we weren't even camping most nights."

"Slackpacking?" There's no judgment in his voice, which I appreciate.

"The slackiest." I leave out the details lest he think I'm a spoiled princess. "At least at the beginning in New Jersey."

He squints a bit. "You didn't start in Maine and hike southbound?"

I shake my head. "Believe it or not, before May, I wasn't very outdoorsy. If we'd started out climbing mountains in snow and ice, fording half-frozen rivers, and slogging through knee-deep mud, I would've quit the first week, probably the first day if not the first hour."

He laughs at my exaggeration. "Tell me more."

"You know all of it. I'm the girl who's hiked for almost five months because she followed a guy."

He lifts himself up to rest on his elbows. "Where is he now?"

"We broke up, so I have no idea." Shifting my attention to the fire, I deliberately avoid his attentive gaze.

"I'm sorry. It happens a lot. Thru-hiking is one of the most challenging things someone can do, physically, mentally, and emotionally. Takes a toll on the best relationships. Come spring when the NoBo hikers come through, the rangers have a pool about how many breakups we'll witness or hear about on the trail. We've nicknamed April 'Heartbreak Month.'"

My brows scrunch together. "You gossip about the hikers?"

"Pfft. Not *all* of you." His lips curl into a lazy smile. "Only the ones who cause drama and make their personal issues our business. We're here to keep the peace and protect. Doesn't only extend to wildlife. Most of the time we're dealing with human problems, and those include interpersonal relations."

He sounds like he's quoting a human resources pamphlet.

Sitting up straight, he bends his knees. "I suspect there's more to your story than you followed a guy into the woods, he dumped you, and you never went home."

"That's it in a nutshell." I sneak a glance at him.

Jay raises an eyebrow. "Go on."

He remains silent, waiting for me to continue.

"Talking about exes is bad form." Watching the flames, I lift the poker to jab at one of the burning logs.

"I asked. I wouldn't have if I weren't interested," he says, soft, and encouraging, his voice makes me want to confess every secret.

"Never talk about your exes on a date." I clamp my mouth shut hoping he didn't hear me. *Oh filter, where art thou?*

Sneaking a peek at him over my shoulder, I catch him wide-eyed with confused surprise but not the horrified disgust I anticipated.

Instead of moving my sleeping bag to the porch to hide, I decide to go all in on clarifying my faux pas. With more words. This might not be my best decision.

"Not that this is a date. I don't think it is—a date. Of course not, because this clearly isn't romantic. You know what I mean." I press my lips together to stop the flow of embarrassing verbiage.

"No, being trapped in an abandoned moonshiner's cabin definitely is not a first date, at least not one I ever want to go on. No offense." He looks sheepish for a second or two. "So feel free to talk about this ex who convinced you to hike the AT."

Trapped.

The word stings.

I duck my chin and wrinkle my nose. "Are you sure?"

"I can guarantee this tale is more interesting than anything I have to share. There's nothing else to do but talk while we're stuck here."

Nothing? I want to ask.

Boundaries, Olive, boundaries.

"Okay. You'll need a little background information."

"It's always a good idea to begin a story at the beginning," he encourages.

"Right. So Tye is a popular social media influencer ..."

"A what?" His confused expression tells me he has zero idea what I'm talking about.

"An Instagram star with over three million followers. In case you didn't know, that's a big deal."

"Okay." He chuckles. "This is his job? Posting pictures?"

I nod. "And videos. There's more to it behind the scenes. He works with brands, sharing their products with his followers. There are multiple revenue streams for influencers: affiliate commissions, sponsorships, paid promotions. He makes good money. Very good." I stop myself from saying more. There's no way a park ranger makes six figures.

Jay bobs his chin. "Interesting."

"Don't worry, my parents don't understand it either, or approve, which of course made him more appealing in the beginning. I'm such a cliché." I roll my eyes at my lameness.

"My sister went through a bad boy phase in high school. The more broken and toxic, the more she liked them." He resumes his reclined position. "I don't get the appeal, but you're apparently not alone."

No, you probably don't because you're a nice guy. I manage to keep this thought to myself.

"Besides the rebellion aspect, I liked that he made his own money sharing his life and adventures with other people. No desk job or corporate ladder meant freedom, which always appealed to me. Doing your own thing isn't common in my world."

Nor is being open with strangers about my life and failures, but here we are.

"I get that. Family expectations can be a heavy burden," he says, his eyes closed.

I like how he's trying to empathize with me, even if he has no idea what an understatement his words are.

"Is the ex why you have the most expensive gear on the market?" he asks.

"Is it? I have no idea what any of it costs. He was in charge of getting all the equipment. All I know is it was gifted to us."

Staring up at the ceiling, he laughs. "Yeah. Ridiculously overpriced if you ask me, but top quality. When I saw your pack, I pegged you for a spoiled rich girl."

"Maybe I am." I'm testing the water with him. When people find out about my family, they typically react one of three ways. They kiss my ass, hoping to leverage knowing me for their own gain. They hate me, thinking they already know me because of something they've read or heard about me or my family. Or, they act like decent humans who don't prejudge me based on my last name. Sadly, the third option is the rarest.

Without lifting his head, he studies me. His finger draws a lazy circle on his chest. My attention wanders to where his t-shirt has scrunched up, exposing a narrow strip of pale olive skin and a thin trail of darker brown hair disappearing below his belt.

"Nah, I've met a lot of entitled people. Too many." He wrinkles his nose in disgust. "You're not one of them."

My lips curve into a smile. "Thank you."

He's wrong, of course, but I still enjoy the compliment.

"So you were with the influencer boyfriend to piss off your parents and get free stuff?"

Laughing, I shake my head. "No, I thought I loved him. The free stuff was a bonus. Nice but not expected. We had more in common. Both grew up in New York. Our families are friends and we traveled in the same circles. On paper, we make, I mean, made perfect sense."

He frowns. "Where were you when he broke up with you?"

Again, I dodge the details and the embarrassing truth of the viral video. I still have his expensive ring buried in the bottom of my pack.

"In the Berkshires near Mount Greylock."

"What a tool." Jay doesn't hide his disgust.

It makes me like him more.

"He dumps you and then what happens? Bear ate him? Attacked by leeches? Because he sounds like someone who needs his ass kicked by karma. Or some wildlife." He grumbles something else under his breath, too quiet for me to hear.

I'd love to witness any of the scenarios he's imagining. "For someone whose actual job is to stop bear violence, you seem to be advocating for it pretty strongly in this case."

"Fine," he drawls. "It doesn't have to be a bear. I'm fine with a wild boar. Karma takes too long."

"Maybe it's already gotten him." I can always hope. "I haven't seen or spoken to him since June. After we broke up, we went our separate ways. In hindsight, we weren't a good match. We had different priorities. Tye was only interested in the photo ops and bragging."

All true but not the whole truth.

"And you?" he asks, voice soft.

"Me?" I echo, distracted by his long fingers resting across his ribs.

"You managed to get yourself to the Great Smokies. What's the rest of the story?"

"Oh, right. How did I get here? I decided I could go home, mope about the breakup for the rest of the summer, or I could keep walking. I chose the latter, mostly fueled by spite and avoidance. When I got to Katahdin, I felt like a fraud. I was a poser, only half of a thru-hiker. So I went back to where I started and headed south."

He nods approvingly. "So you're a flip-flopper. No shame. You're still walking the miles. Probably smarter to split the trail and avoid the crowds."

For some reason, his approval matters. I grin at him. "This is why I need to get through the Smokies and into Georgia. I'm committed to finishing in two weeks. Otherwise, I'll add the AT to the long list of things I've started and never completed."

"Schedules are for meetings. Everyone hikes their own hike. Whether you make it to Springer Mountain next week or next month or next year, I have faith you'll get there eventually." He holds up his palm for a high five.

Smiling after slapping his hand, I nod. "I know, I know. It's about the journey, not the destination."

"Sounds like something hiker trash would say." He covers his head with a bent elbow, protecting himself from an assault that never comes.

"I used to think hiker trash was an insult. I know it's a slur against hikers, but I'm reclaiming it as a badge of honor. When we were slack-packers, I felt like a fraud, pretending to be something I wasn't. Now I can proudly say it's an honor to be considered hiker trash. Those are my people you're talking about."

He scratches his beard. "Own it, Snowbird."

I roll my wrist and give him a small bow. "I do."

In return, he nods. "How'd you get your trail name?"

"Same as everyone else. One day someone called me Snow and it stuck."

"Why Snow?" His brow furrows. "Like Snow White?"

"I'm not sure. T-Rex gave me the name, something to do with how naïve I was about everything. Could be he thought I was a delicate snowflake. The name evolved when I switched to southbound."

"Ah, like an old person who spends the winter in Florida?"

"That's me."

"It's nice to meet you, Snowbird." He yawns and his heavy-lidded eyes blink up at me. "Sorry, you're not boring me. It's been a long day."

I let out an echo of his yawn. "We should go to sleep. It's probably late. Hiking out of here in the snow tomorrow is going to be rough."

"Depends on how deep it gets overnight. Could be stuck here another day."

I grumble about being delayed.

"Better than dead." He yawns again and then stretches out like a cat.

"I'd think you'd want to get back to your station instead of being trapped here another day with me." Guess I'm still not over him using that word.

"I'm enjoying hanging out with you. I love hearing about AT adventures. I've only ever hiked the sections around here, so I'm living vicariously through you."

It hits me then: we've spent the majority of our time together talking about me—or more accurately, me talking about myself. I know very little about Ranger Daniels. He has a mom and a sister. He's been to Japan. What I know barely fills a small nutshell.

I make a promise to myself to turn the tables on him in the morning.

CHAPTER FOURTEEN

OLIVE

I'm not sure how we got here. Not the cabin itself; I know that part. I mean this place where there's a thick blanket of sexual tension wrapped tightly around us.

Just two lost souls spending the night in a murder cabin.

Jay's been friendly and kind. None of his actions have indicated anything more than professional courtesy mixed with genuinely-nice-guy friendliness.

I'm the one without boundaries and apparently zero respect for his. The things escaping my mouth and the constant stream of dirty thoughts aren't my usual norm. Evidently, the storm has turned me into a pubescent boy.

I'm more than mildly horrified by my behavior. Can't even blame alcohol or drugs for lowering my inhibitions and erasing my filters.

After we get out of here, I'll send him a nicely worded apology letter and a box of cookies from the local bakery. Least I can do considering I ate both of his last night. He offered and I was too rude to decline the second.

Jay's still asleep next to me. Curled on his side, he faces the door, a first line of defense should an intruder wander inside. Protective even in his sleep.

And me? I'm spooning him, invading his personal space even while unconscious.

I should remove my face from the middle of his back. Undrape my arm from his waist. Uncoil my knees from the shadow of his.

If I had a shred of decency, I would shift to allow enough space between us for the Holy Spirit, Jesus and at least half the apostles.

Do I scoot away? No, no I don't.

Obviously, my decency disappeared with my filter. Both are probably loitering inside a hiker box somewhere.

Jay is so warm, a human heater, and he's a better pillow than the floor or my smelly jacket wrapped around my dry, but even smellier clothes from yesterday.

In the dim light of morning, our once robust fire smolders over glowing embers, the ideal kind for toasting marshmallows to caramelized perfection.

At the thought of delicious, gooey goodness, my stomach rumbles loudly. In the silence of the cabin, the sound echoes, magnified into a roar.

Jay's breathing pauses.

Is he awake?

Did my stomach monster penetrate his sleep?

Should I move?

Unable to answer the first two questions, I take action on the last by slowly lifting my arm a few inches and angling my body away from his. I have no idea what time it is. Feels early.

One of us should get more sleep. If I can peel myself away, I might be able to sneak outside for a morning pee without disturbing him.

A large warm hand grips my wrist, catching me mid retreat. My breath hitches with guilt about getting caught so close to him

"Don't go," he whispers, voice thick with sleep. "Stay."

He must be dreaming, likely of a girlfriend who isn't me. A guy like Ranger Daniels must have a girlfriend, or a wife. He's too good not to. There's no ring, but some men don't wear them.

Oh no.

I'm big-spooning another woman's man, which makes me the actual worst.

"I'm sorry." I apologize and roll to my back. "I'm not who you think I am."

Without moving, his rough-hewn morning voice whispers, "You're the snowbird, aren't you? Unless someone else snuck in here while we slept."

"No, it's me. I'm sorry for invading your space." I sit up and gaze down at his profile.

Without opening his eyes, he softly says, "Fire died down and it's cold in here. You were just seeking comfort and warmth. Natural instinct."

"You're not mad?" I brush my hair out of my face. Most of it has slipped out of the braids and is a tangled mess.

"At your subconscious?"

"What if I did it deliberately?"

"Did you?" He squints up at me.

"No." I confirm this with a shake of my head.

He shifts to a sitting position next to me, his sleeping bag tucked around his legs and half his torso. Close enough to the hearth, he reaches for the fire-poker and jabs the ash-coated remains.

I notice he ditched his pants at some point in the night. The black band of his boxers peeks out when he leans forward and his bag slips. His t-shirt stretches over his back muscles and shoulders.

Opposing sensations take over my body. Hot and cold at the same time. The chill in the air creeping in, the warmth heating my cheeks from all the dirty thoughts I'm having about the park ranger.

Shivering, I tug my own sleeping bag under my arms and then hop to standing. With my back to him, I hope he can't see my flushed skin. "It's freezing in here." We're down to our last couple of logs and I add both on top of the embers. "I'll go outside and get more wood."

"Snowbird?" he asks from his spot on the floor.

I don't turn, instead busying myself with hop-walking to my pack. "It's okay. You collected it last night, I can supply the morning wood." I close my eyes and sigh. "I mean wood this morning."

Hearing a low chuckle and shuffling behind me, I know Jay is now standing.

"I'll do it," he volunteers, probably desperate to put some distance between us.

"No, it's fine." I swear he ghosts a hand down my arm.

His breath warms the back of my neck from his proximity. "How about we both go? Make one trip instead of two?"

He's too nice. All I want to do is corrupt him. Make him fall in love with me.

"Uh, nature's calling." I hop from foot to foot as if talking about it makes the pressure on my bladder worse.

"Same. We can take opposite sides of the cabin and meet back at the woodpile when we're done?" He dips his head, searching my eyes. "Should give us both enough privacy."

He's already pulling his jacket on before I get my shoes laced.

"Let's see how bad it is outside." Opening the door, he reveals a winter wonderland.

"It's beautiful." I inhale the crisp, bitter air.

A smooth plane of snow extends from the second porch step. Drifts of white powder create deep pockets near the bases of the trees. Narrow trunks and branches bend and arch under the weight of a multiple of inches of snow.

The wind has lessened but still whistles through the woods, blowing and twisting the snow in its path. Tiny pellets of precipitation fall from the heavy, gray clouds.

It's full-on winter out here. I wouldn't be surprised to see reindeer and talking snowmen decorating the fir trees.

"How long were we asleep?" I ask, attempting to cover my dread with humor.

His mouth forms a tight line. "This doesn't bode well for us getting out of here this morning."

"Maybe it looks worse than it is?" I step past him and onto the porch. A loud crack followed by a thump draws my attention to the right, where a large branch crashes into the powder, sending up a plume of white. "That can't be good," I whisper.

"The trees are still in leaf, which means their branches are full of sap. The extra weight of the snow is too much to bear. I'm guessing there are a lot of downed branches and trees between here and the station. Trails could be completely impassable."

"Not reassuring, Ranger Jay."

"Stating the facts. This is the reason we close the backcountry during the winter."

I want to point out that the calendar still shows October. Winter is more than two months away. However, I keep my thoughts to myself. For once.

"Don't stray far." His tone shifts from friendly to annoyed. Passing me, he steps into the deep snow off of the porch. It comes midway up his shins. "I'll bring in the wood since you don't have boots."

He stomps his way to the left side of the cabin and then disappears.

Really wishing I had a penis, I find privacy behind a tree. Thinking about frostbite and delicate areas, I finish and stand. My feet are already cold. The trail-runners that have served me well aren't made for snow They're already wet and provide zero insulation.

Retracing my steps in my existing footprints back to the porch, I debate going inside or helping Jay. Carrying a load of wood is the least I can do to help make a bad situation less awful.

He's trapped out here because of me.

"Marco," I call out from the corner of the cabin to give him a warning.

"Polo," he answers from nearby.

"I'm ignoring your instructions to go inside."

"I can see." His head pops above the messy, snow-covered pile of wood against the side of the cabin.

"Put me to work." I follow the large wells in the snow left by his boots. His stride is longer than mine and I have to extend my legs to match his footprints.

"I can manage." He still sounds annoyed. Or resigned. Both.

"I'm here. Load me up." I extend my arms in front of me.

"You're stubborn." His mouth curves into a small, brief smile.

"So are you," I say with a half-grin of my own. "Look at us finding things in common."

He stacks three medium logs and a few slender branches into a neat pile on my forearms. "Can you manage?"

With a nod, I turn to walk back to the porch. Laden with more weight, following his path is even more difficult, but I do my best.

Inside, I dump the wood in a pile and quickly remove my shoes.

"How are your toes?" Jay asks, dropping his own armful of logs on top of mine.

"Fine," I lie. "Dandy even."

He scowls. "Don't suppose you have boots in the bottom of your bag."

Sitting on the floor, I peel off my damp socks and replace them with the dry pair.

"Too heavy. I had a pair but I ditched them back in Massachusetts for hiking shoes."

He frowns. Again. "Would be better if you had boots."

"It wasn't supposed to snow in October. Blame Mother Nature."

"You should always be prepared."

"I thought you said you weren't a Boy Scout." I quirk an eyebrow.

"I wasn't, but common sense says you should prepare for the worst scenario." He crosses his arms.

I mirror his pose. "Why are you yelling at me about something I can't change?"

"I'm not yelling." It's true. His voice is low, serious. Bothered.

"Next time I'm in the backcountry and a freak storm hits, I'll be sure to thank you for the twenty pounds of extra gear I packed. Just in case. Boots, ice pick, crampons. A Dutch oven on the off chance I want to make chili or bake a cake." I list random things I've spotted in shelter boxes.

"Okay, who's arguing now?" He uncrosses his arms and shakes them out. "I apologize for sounding harsh."

"Accepted." I extend my hand. "Let's agree to not play the what-if game."

He stares at my fingers before meeting my eyes. "Not familiar with it."

"Something my sister and I made up. The simple explanation is we agree to avoid hypotheticals. Should-haves. Ifs. Maybes. For example, I should've foreseen the possibility of deep snow in Tennessee in October. If I had only heeded the warnings about the storm, maybe we wouldn't be stuck here. You get the idea?"

"I do." He shakes on it. "We'll play the hand we've been dealt. No point in exploring alternate timelines."

With a nod, I give him a happy grin. "Agreed."

My stomach monster grumbles again. I attempt to quiet it by pressing my hand to my abdomen.

"Hungry?" he asks. "I don't imagine you have bacon and a waffle iron in your bag of tricks."

"Stop. I'd murder for Belgian waffles right now."

He steps away and holds up his hands facing me. "Whoa. That escalated quickly."

"Figuratively speaking. Although, I really have nothing to lose. I'm already the black sheep of my family and probably disowned after this crazy trip."

"Not comforting, Snowbird. For all I know, 'family,'"—he makes air quotes around the word—"is code for cellmates. You could be a felon on the run."

The idea makes me laugh. "I can think of better places to hide out. Brazil. Lake Cuomo. The beaches of Thailand. Or Australia. Huge country, really far away. I could blend in easier, and they breed Hemsworths there."

He snaps his fingers to draw my attention. "I think you're playing the what-if game."

"Oops. Sorry." I mentally wave goodbye to my imaginary life surrounded by minor Hemsworths. I might have a small obsession. "To answer your question, no, I'm not a felon. Got one or two parking tickets in college. Not an issue now because I never drive."

"Ever?"

I smile at his surprise. "City girl. No need for a car when there's car service or Lyft or public transportation. Or you know, walking."

"I imagine you've had your fill."

"True. I should probably travel by roller skates or scooter while enjoying the joy of pavement and gentle inclines."

"Should?" He arches a brow.

I slap my forehead. "Dammit."

He chuckles and then rolls his lips together like he wants to resist finding me funny.

"Now that I no longer have to worry about you shanking me with your spork over the lack of waffles, what should we have for breakfast? I still have my delicious and nutritionally balanced protein bars." He holds up the evidence.

"I think we should save those for when we're really desperate." Like a game show hostess, I gesture at the floor where my stuff is scattered. "I have more Pop-Tarts, and tea. Or, if you like none of the flavor or kick from real coffee, this stuff is for you." I toe a pile of instant coffee packets.

"Sounds great," he says flatly.

"You're a terrible liar."

We filter and then boil water on my pocket rocket stove. Sitting on my sleeping pad near the fire, hot English breakfast tea in my water bottle, I say a little thanks of gratitude for being safe, warm, and dry.

Jay drinks his coffee out of the pot like he's in Paris sipping a bowl of cafe au lait. From our conversation last night, I didn't get the feeling he's seen a lot of the world outside of Tennessee and his trip to Japan. I'm curious and want to know more about the reticent ranger.

Prepare yourself for twenty questions, Ranger Daniels.

"Did you grow up around here?" I ask.

"Not in these mountains, no."

"Funny." I gently kick him with my socked foot. "I meant in Tennessee or North Carolina. The general area."

"I spent most of my childhood in the suburbs of Knoxville."

"Was it nice?"

He shrugs. "It was all right. I don't have anything to compare it to, so I guess it was fine. And you? Is your family from New York?"

He's a master at shifting the conversation away from himself. I play along for the moment.

"My parents moved there before getting married and having kids, so I guess so. Neither of them grew up there. Their families are spread out all over the country." Vague but true.

"Both my mom and sister still live in Tennessee. Jenni is in Nashville."

"Is that far from here? I'm terrible with distance if I can't count it in blocks or subway stops."

"A few hours' drive. Far enough but still close." He sips from his giant coffee.

"What about the rest of your family? You didn't mention your dad."

"He died when I was eleven." He says the words like he's talking about a random historical figure, not his own father. "Car accident."

"I'm sorry." I'd assumed divorce and feel terrible for bringing up a tender subject.

"It's okay. Happened a long time ago. I've lived twice as long without a father as I did with him alive." He stares at the fire.

"Must be tough." Brilliant observation, Olive.

"It was. My mom isn't from around here. I mean Tennessee and North Carolina." He smiles, echoing my definition from earlier. "No family close by to support her with two kids on her own."

"She didn't want to move closer to her parents?"

"Wasn't an option." His blunt tone cuts off further questions.

Observing him, I sip my tea for a minute. "She must be so strong to raise you and your sister all by herself."

"You have no idea. She's a music teacher and we didn't have a lot of extra money on her salary. She taught piano and violin lessons after school and on the weekends, always working to make the money stretch a little farther than should've been possible. My father had life insurance, but she never touched it. Saved every penny for our college funds so we wouldn't have student loans."

His admiration for his mom is heartwarming. "She sounds remarkable."

"She is. One of the strongest people I know. Her life didn't turn out the way she'd imagined. She took a huge gamble when she married my dad and uprooted her life to come to Tennessee. Some think she lost more than she won. She says she got everything she ever wished for and more."

He takes a long drink of his terrible coffee.

Sensing I should change the subject, I say, "I studied piano and violin, too. I mean, I used to play. Haven't in years."

"Were you any good?"

"I didn't practice enough on the piano. I'm better on the violin, although I stopped playing in high school."

"According to my mom, you never lose the skill, only the finesse. I'm sure it would come back to you with practice."

"Did you play an instrument in school?" I ask.

"Percussion in band." He taps a quick beat on his knee before hitting a rim shot, complete with sound effect.

"Why did you choose drums?" I'm trying to picture him as Dave Grohl, thrashing on a drum-kit.

"There was a shortage and it meant I could hide in the back."

"Were you shy as a kid?" I'm trying to unravel him. His shyness could explain his discomfort around people. Social anxiety presents itself in a myriad of ways. Some people retreat. Others overcompensate.

I'm in the latter group.

He clears his throat. "I didn't like standing out."

"And what did your dad do before he passed?"

"He worked in car manufacturing."

"Sounds like you get your strong work ethic from both of them." Great, now I sound like I'm interviewing him for a job.

"His job brought them to Tennessee. He got transferred shortly after they met. She moved to be with him."

"Wow. So romantic. New city, new love. Big leap of faith." I'm not sure I could do it. Move across town, maybe. Give up everything I know to follow a guy? Unlikely.

Except that's what I did with Tye—walked away from my perfect life in the city. For what? Blisters, chafing, and social media likes.

Clearly, I'm not in any position to sit in judgment of Jay's parents.

"Not everyone agrees with you. I think they both sacrificed a lot for their love." He looks wistful, almost sad.

"Doesn't everyone compromise? Isn't that part of the bargain?" I think of my grandmother, who basically gave up her life for my grandfather's career, my mother who married into the family and accepted all the responsibilities of the Perry name.

"Sacrifice," he says, tearing his Pop-Tart into smaller pieces.

"Isn't it the same thing?" I give him a sidelong glance.

"You said compromise. Big difference. One means meeting in the middle. The other can equal losing everything." He takes a bite of his pastry, letting the words linger in the quiet.

The fire crackles while the wind battles its way through the forest.

His words float down and settle over me, soaking into my skin and burrowing into my bones.

How many times have I bargained too much of myself in exchange for love and a relationship? Is this why I've never been able to go through with an engagement? Deep down, my heart knew. Even when my brain said yes, I knew I meant no.

"Wow." I set my tea down and stretch my legs. "I've never thought about the difference. Ranger Jay, you're deep."

He finishes his coffee and leans back on his hands. "I'm observant. It's the secret power of the outsiders and misfits."

A laugh escapes me. Rugged, smart, kind, and hot as hell handsome are words I'd use to describe Ranger Jay, not oddball.

"You? You look like you were captain of your football team, or maybe the star soccer player. Admired by guys, crushed on by all the girls. Liked by teachers and parents. A golden boy."

His scowl returns. "I hate team sports and I was never a big man on campus. Want to guess again?"

I study him. The wary energy behind his eyes, the way his foot bounces with directionless energy. "Likable outsider?"

"Bingo." He straightens up. "If we're playing this game, I'm going to say you were prom queen."

"Wrong. Kelsey Markham wore that crown. Campaigned for it starting in ninth grade."

"Hmm," he hums, stroking his beard. "Tennis star? Wait, a cross country runner. Yearbook editor. Serial dater."

I laugh at his ridiculous guesses. "You're right about only one of those."

He squints at me. "Cross country?"

Cackling, I tip over and nearly spill my tea on the floor.

"What's so hysterical? You're obviously fit enough to endurance hike. I made the leap that you'd also be a runner. Cross country is the closest thing I could think of."

"I *might* be able to break out into a jog if a bear were chasing me, but no guarantee." I wipe away the tears on my cheeks. "If you calculated all the deliberate exercise I've participated in over the course of my twenty-nine years, it wouldn't add up to a month on the trail. I've never been active, or fit. The closest I came before this would be wearing a cute athleisure outfit to brunch."

He doesn't laugh at my attempt at self-deprecating humor. For some unknown reason, I take this as a cue to continue my confession.

"Growing up, I was what society likes to call chubby, because chubby was a more acceptable word than fat. Stocky worked too. Whatever the term, I was far from the willowy, waif ideal my mother hoped for and my sister exemplifies. Shockingly, not every girl can live off of plain lettuce and water and pretend she's satisfied.

"I went to my first fitness camp at eight, had my own nutritionist at ten, followed by a decade of therapy to undo the damage of both. Much to my mother's disappointment, I never grew out of the chubby phase. So no, I was never the star of the tennis team or a cross country runner. In middle school, I staged a protest over running the mile for time and a grade. Refused to do more than walk it. Recruited others to join my movement. We almost failed P.E."

"I don't know what to say." He meets my eyes, kindness in his expression. "I'm sorry you went through that."

"Society's expectations for girls are toxic. Women, too. We're expected to look a certain way so we fit neatly into our boxes. I can't tell you how many times I've had men question me doing this hike. Some doubted my daily miles. Some openly asked what made me think I was capable of finishing."

"Is this where the spite comes from?"

"A little bit, but really I want to prove to myself I can do this more than I want to prove them wrong."

CHAPTER FIFTEEN

JAY

*H*ow I'm feeling in one word: captivated.

I think I hurt Snowbird's feelings yesterday when I used the word trapped to describe our current situation. She reacted like I said I'm being tortured by being forced to spend time with her.

Under normal circumstances, she'd probably be right.

Yet, I'm having a nice time.

We spent last night and early this morning in easy conversation. Sure, there have been a few awkward pauses, but overall, we've been at ease with each other, as comfortable as two strangers can be in a decrepit cabin.

If I'd believed Guy's warning about the snow, I might have pressed us to keep hiking last night. We're about four hours walk back to the valley and another hour to the station. The lower we go in elevation, the less likely there will be snow. We probably could've made it.

Shutting down the what-if game I'm playing in my head, I try to focus on the present. We're dry, we're warm, and we're safe.

Accepting the fact we're not going anywhere, we restock the wood during a break in the sleet and frozen rain. At least there isn't more snow accumulation. Hopefully by tomorrow, the temperatures will warm enough to allow us to hike out of here.

Like last night, we spend the morning talking. We stick to safer topics. I must be a masochist to want to know about her ex. He sounds like so many of the guys I've encountered on the trail over the years; cocky mixed with a large dose of hubris. Expensive gear won't drag your ass up a boulder-strewn mountain. They're lucky his ignorance didn't get them injured or worse. Stupidity will get you killed out here.

I try my radio again after breakfast. "350 for dispatch." I add, "Over," just in case Guy is listening.

An unfamiliar voice responds. "350, this is dispatch. What's your location?"

I give our GPS coordinates. "Everyone is safe, but we have about half a foot of snow up here. Wondering how the valley is doing. Heard we lost a tower in the storm last night."

"Correct. Possible tornado touchdown. No confirmation of a funnel cloud. You need a rescue up there?" Dispatch is all business.

"No. We're fine. Use the resources where needed. Can I get a weather update? Planning to hike down tomorrow."

"Should be all clear by this evening," she confirms. "No snow below 3000 feet."

Good. Means we'll only be hiking through snow and slush for the first half of our descent.

"Can you give the Cades Cove station an update on my location and planned return tomorrow? I'll be bringing a thru-hiker down with me. No health issues."

The dispatcher repeats my coordinates, call number, and information. "All set. Stay warm up there."

I thank her and set my walkie-talkie down on the table.

"We're getting out of here?" Snowbird asks, hope in her voice and a grin on her face.

"I think our best bet is to spend one more night here and start in the morning. Gives us the most daylight should we have to detour around storm damage."

She nods in agreement. "What should we do with our day? Snowball fight? Snow angels? Igloo building?"

"How about we check our food supplies and make sure we have

enough to get us through the next thirty-six hours?" I suggest, grabbing both our packs with the plan to dump all the contents on the floor.

Snowbird jumps up and takes hers out of my hand. "I have an organized system. All my food is in the bear bag, and I did a gear shakedown back in Virginia. Trust me when I say I only have the minimal essentials."

Her tone is defensive, which makes me suspicious. What's in there that she doesn't want me to see?

"Fine." I upend my own pack and its meager contents drop to the floor. An extra pair of socks I forgot I stuffed in the bottom is the only surprise. It feels like Christmas when I see them.

She opens her bear bag and spreads out her food supply on the floor. "Sorry it isn't more exciting."

I take inventory. Pouches of tuna and cooked chicken, small packets of mayo and relish, more soup mixes, almonds, olives in a pouch, peanut butter, Pop-Tarts, a package of mac 'n' cheese, and a small bag of cheese balls. Plus, the instant coffee and more tea bags.

"We can work with this."

"I feel like this is a challenge on Top Chef." She studies the random products. "If it didn't make me want to vomit, I could make a tuna casserole for us. Without the casserole part. I guess it's tuna pasta, which sounds worse."

"Tuna sandwiches on Pop-Tart bread?"

"Stop." She pretends to gag—at least I think she's faking it. Her skin's gone pale.

"Okay, how about peanut butter Pop-Tart sandwiches for lunch? Better?"

"Sounds good." She sets those ingredients to the side.

"Dinner can be mac 'n' cheese with chicken and a crunchy cheese ball topping. Fake cheese two ways," I declare, thinking myself brilliant. "We can have my jerky as an appetizer."

"Add the olives and it'll be like a charcuterie board."

I find myself disappointed when she doesn't make a joke about my meat stick.

"Fancy." I organize the food by meal. "We're left with the tuna and soup. You can keep the mayo, AKA the devil's mucus."

Her eyes widen. "No, you're one of those people."

"Exactly which kind of person am I?" I challenge, my tone playful.

"The kind who hate mayonnaise."

"I believe you mean the right people." I smirk.

"How do you eat tuna salad? Or egg salad? Chicken salad? Potato salad? Macaroni salad?"

"I don't eat any of those so-called salads." I stick my tongue out in exaggerated disgust.

Her entire face scrunches up with confusion. "Sorry, your words don't make sense. You live in the South. You have access to Duke's Mayonnaise whenever you want. Every Southern picnic and funeral, birthday and holiday in the movies has one of the aforementioned salads."

She's apoplectic with disbelief.

"Propaganda by the mayo cartel. Don't buy into the lies." I close my eyes and exhale to keep from bursting out in laughter

"But it's the secret ingredient to moist chocolate cake."

"Please don't ruin my favorite dessert."

"Okay, fine. I'm not going to try to convert you. I don't need or want your kind of negativity in my life. We'll just have to agree to disagree to maintain the peace."

"Fine," I echo her.

She continues to cast sidelong glances in my direction.

"Stop judging me," I tell her after the fifth dirty look.

"Are you sure you're really Southern?" she asks, joking, not knowing the land mine she's stepped on.

"Born and raised in Tennessee." I give her my standard answer followed by a wide grin. "Want to see my birth certificate?"

"Do you carry it with you?" She looks and sounds confused.

"No, but sometimes I wonder if I should." My default state of grumpiness returns.

"Your accent gives you away. Once you speak, there's zero doubt you're Southern."

"Mine? You're the one with the northern, Yankee accent." I drawl out the word yankee, mimicking her awful southern imitation from yesterday.

Hold up. I only met her yesterday afternoon? How is that possible? Time's funny, stretching and curving in on itself. The sixteen hours I've spent in her company definitely feels like longer.

* * *

"When I was six, my dad brought home a puppy for my sister and me. Mom wasn't a big fan, probably because she got stuck cleaning up after Akebono. She used to say he peed on or destroyed everything she loved." I laugh at the memory.

We're sprawled on the floor near the fire, me with my back against the crate and her lying on her stomach on top of her sleeping bag. Without games or books to read, the only things to do are talk, sleep, eat, and tend to the fire.

She repositions herself to sit cross-legged. "Akebono is an unusual name for a dog."

"I named him after a famous sumo wrestler from Hawaii. He was a lab mix, built like a tank. Still miss him. He was a good dog. The best." A swell of emotion leaves me feeling vulnerable.

"A man who gets all soft-eyed and sentimental about his childhood dog is a good man. Ranger Daniels, you might not be the cantankerous grumpasaurus you want the world to believe you are."

Ignoring her comment, I ask, "Did you have dogs or pets growing up?"

"When my sister and I were little, we had a very limited run of guinea pigs. My mother had Norwich terriers, but they were show dogs, not really pets. They only loved her, followed her around like the queen with her corgis. I always wanted a cat, but my dad is allergic and my mother wasn't a fan of litter boxes and having her furniture destroyed. I mean, is anyone? My grandfather has horses and some cattle, but they're not exactly pets."

"Is your grandfather a farmer?" I ask. She hasn't shared much about her family other than being from New York, which might as well be the moon.

Her pause stretches longer than it should, like she's editing her response. "Not really. He's retired and lives on a bunch of acreage in the middle of nowhere in central California. Doesn't like having neighbors."

"Hmm, sounds nice."

Her gaze finds mine. "I get the feeling you're not a big fan of people."

"Really?" I smirk. "I think I hide it well."

"No, you don't." Her laughter draws out a chuckle of my own. "You wear it as a badge of honor, right next to your NPS patch and name tag."

"I have friends—colleagues who I enjoy working with, a few locals in town I'm friendly to when I see them. I'm not a complete troll who lives under a bridge" Laughing, I try to defend myself. "I can have them write letters of recommendations on my behalf."

"Somehow I believe you would. Unnecessary. However, I was imagining you as more of an ogre living alone in the woods. In fact, how do I know this isn't your cabin?" Her eyes bug out. "How do I know you're really even a ranger?"

"I'm a ranger," I say, humor gone. "And if this were my cabin, it would be a helluva lot nicer. Might even have furniture. Would need to add a bathroom and electricity. Solar panels would work given we're off the grid."

"No bed?" she asks, her eyes focused on the corner behind me.

"Falls under the furniture category. Small couch and a table with chairs near the fireplace. A bed would fit over there." I point my thumb over my shoulder. "Nothing fancy. Wouldn't need much to be happy. There's only one hitch."

"The risk of isolation and loneliness?" Her voice is soft, the question revealing more about her own fears than she might realize.

"No. I prefer my own company to being around people for the sake of avoiding being alone."

"So what's the hitch?" she asks.

"Cabins like this were built in the twenties and thirties back when the national forests were less regulated. If you could locate the owner and get them to sell, you'd only be buying the building. The US government owns the land, which you'd have to pay rent on, as well as taxes."

"Sounds way too complicated for a shack. Wouldn't it be easier to purchase land outside the boundaries? Construct your dream cabin without all the added paperwork?"

"Suppose I could. Been saving up to do something similar. Someday." I've been dreaming of my own place for years. I wasn't joking about not needing much in terms of square footage and furnishings.

"Land has to be cheap around here. Besides working for the NPS, what do people do for jobs?" Her tone edges on snobby, and I don't think she realizes it.

"There's a timber mill down valley. Schools, a decent library. Lots of private businesses, tourism, service industry. You might be surprised how vibrant small towns can be out here in the middle of nowhere."

She cringes. "Sorry. My big city privilege was showing there, wasn't it?"

I hold my thumb and forefinger an inch apart. "Just a little."

"My grandfather always says we'd realize we're more alike than not if we spent more time visiting different parts of the country. I should take his advice."

"He sounds like a wise man."

"Smartest man I know and one of my favorite people. I think he'd like you. He's always been a big fan and supporter of the national parks."

"That's good to know. With the current administration cutting our budgets and funding, we need all the private patrons we can get."

"Are you directly affected? I don't really know what you do, besides boss around hikers." She flashes her flirty grin.

"Given how stubborn you are, I'm failing at my one job." I mirror her expression. She's adorable and she knows it. Who am I to try to resist her?

"No, seriously. I'd like to know."

"I'm one of the resident wildlife ecologists."

"What do you do exactly? Deal with bears?"

"I have my doctorate in ornithology. Day to day, I spend a lot of my time out in the field, studying our local bird population and monitoring the migration patterns of our seasonal species. I give educational talks to school kids and visitors. I'm also routinely asked to do trail sweeps for hikers. Most of the time I don't mind doing those because it means time on my own."

With an excited squeak, she jumps up so fast, she gets herself tangled in her sleeping bag and almost faceplants on her way to her pack.

"Was it something I said?" I ask, watching her turn into a human tornado as she searches for something in her bag.

CHAPTER SIXTEEN

OLIVE

"*L*ook!" I shove my battered copy of *Peterson Field Guide to Eastern Birds* directly in his face.

He places his hand over mine and moves my arm back so the book is no longer touching his nose. "Nice."

His low-key reaction is in direct opposition to my enthusiasm. "Nice? Aren't you excited to meet another bird lover? One more thing we have in common. It's fate."

"What is?' he asks, dragging a hand over his beard to cup his cheek.

"The two of us meeting. You can be my Yoda and I'll be your young Jedi protégé—only with birds."

"Sounds like weird role-play involving costumes and magic hat birds." He cracks up.

"How do the doves get involved?" I join his laughter. "And I'd like to point out that for the first time, I'm not the one with the dirty mind making things awkward."

"Just because I said it first doesn't mean you didn't think it."

"I was excited about the birds. Tell me everything you know." I pat his leg above his knee.

"Everything? Well, we have over two hundred species in the Smokies. Among those are the migrant and resident populations, which vary depending on season, altitude, and location." His eyes remain on my hand, which rests midway up his thigh.

I remove it and fumble with what to say next. Once again, I've crossed some invisible fence around him. "Okay, right. We don't have enough time for a master class. What do you know about warblers?"

"Within the *Parulidae* family are about eighteen genera. Out of those, we have about forty species in the Smokies. Can you narrow it down for me?"

"Whoa. I had no idea." In my head, I repeat the old mnemonic I learned in biology: Karen, please come over for good soup. "Okay, so what can you tell me about the Black-throated Blue Warbler?"

"Why do you ask?" His voice is wary and his eyes crinkle with uncertainty, like he's suspicious I'm setting him up.

When I open the book, a few of my postcards slide out.

"What are these?" He picks up the Shenandoah one and flips it over.

"Journals are too heavy. Every ounce adds up when you carry it on your back, so I decided I would keep track of my trip and deeply philosophical musings by writing myself postcards. I send them whenever I find a mailbox. When I get home, I'll have a record of the hike."

He nods, impressed. "Very clever."

"I know." I beam at his compliment.

Flipping through the book, I search for the page with the double-dog-eared corners. Out of the corner of my eye I catching him cringing.

"Why are you looking at me like that?"

"Remember our conversation about mayo and how offended you were I could loathe something you like?"

"Uh-huh." I continue flipping.

When he doesn't say anything more, I glance up. He's focused on the paperback. "There are two types of people in the world: those who use bookmarks, and monsters."

"Are you a librarian spy? I found it like this." I spread the pages for him to see all the bent corners and notes. "It's a field guide, not a first edition of Shakespeare's plays. If anything, I rescued it from a life of neglect."

"Let me see." He places his hand over mine.

I reluctantly release my grip on the spine. "Not all the notations are mine."

He opens the book and slowly turns a few pages, reading the scribbled comments in the margins. Finally, he glances up, his eyes searching mine. "Is this a new hobby?"

"I stumbled into it accidentally. It started with the story about the bear trampling the hiker."

"The guy with the earbuds?" he asks before adding, "Idiot."

I leave out the part about listening to podcasts while walking during the early days of solo hiking. Instead, I roll my eyes and sigh. "Right? Totally."

His presses his thumb and index finger against his bottom lip. "What does that have to do with *Peterson*?"

"Well, during the early days of hiking, I began listening to the birdsong, you know instead of music or podcasts through earbuds. Because, as we've established only idiots would do such a thing." I widen my eyes and bob my head to show I now see the error of my ways. "I became fascinated with birds, and soon it wasn't enough to hear the songs, I needed to identify the individual species."

Can I kiss up anymore? Let's see.

"You became a bird spotter." He states this as fact without judgment. "Ah, now Snowbird makes even more sense. The best trail names always have layered meaning."

"You could say I'm obsessed with identifying as many species as possible."

"And the Black-throated Blue Warbler plays into this how?"

"I decided I want to see all the bluebirds I can on this trip. It's my thing."

"Chasing the bluebird of happiness?" he jokes.

"In a way, yes. Like finding a penny, only instead of luck, they're a sign of upcoming joy and happiness. Who doesn't want more of those?" Worried I sound silly, I peek at him from the side before continuing.

"Blue jays were easy up north. They're so loud, large and in charge, it's hard to miss them. Saw Eastern Bluebirds hanging around a birdhouse in New York. I thought I saw a female warbler the other day, but the real prize would be finding a male."

He nods slowly like he's really listening to my ramblings. "They're fairly small and easy to miss."

Excitement gathers in my belly. "Would you help me? I just need to see one. Then I can leave happy."

"Your timing is off. The majority of the migratory pairs leave the area by September."

"Some years it can be as late as October. Birds don't have planners and calendars," I argue back. "There could be a few still in the park."

"Not with yesterday's storm. They prefer warm Caribbean winters to cold temperatures. There's zero chance of finding one hanging out in the snow. Unless it's dead."

The thought of a tiny, frozen bird punches me right in the heart. Tears pool in my eyes. "You don't think they got caught in the bad weather and all died, do you?"

He must see the sadness on my face. His voice softens. "They're resilient and come with their own down coats. I bet they found a protected area."

"So there's a chance I might spot one?" I hate how my voice wavers when I speak.

"I wouldn't set your heart on it." He frowns at me. "Are you crying?"

Embarrassed by the flood of emotion over birds, I wipe under my eyes with the backs of my index fingers. I wave my hands in front of my face. "No, of course not. That would be silly, and as you have probably figured out, I'm a deeply serious and rational person."

"You're kind of a mess." With a closed mouth, he gives me a sympathetic smile.

"Are you complimenting me? Because it doesn't sound like it." I flinch at the label. Hits too close to home.

"Does everything have to be a compliment?" He does the thing where he holds my gaze, peering behind the curtain to where my true self is hiding.

"Guess you don't believe in positive vibes only?" I break eye contact first.

"It's bullshit," he loudly grumbles, running his hand through the thick hair near the nape of his neck. "Everyone has bad days and rough patches. I hate those quotable sayings people throw on t-shirts like they're 'Woke.'"

"I think I saw 'woke' on a shirt at Target in Virginia, next to the 'Mermaid Goals' and 'Rosé all day' gear."

"Ahhh." He tosses his head back and groans in frustration. "Exactly the problem. Why does every girl want to be a mermaid? Or a unicorn? They don't exist. Be a narwhal if you want to have a horn. Or a rhino. They're super cool and couldn't care less about what other people think of them."

"Trust me, no girl wants to compare herself to a horned whale, or a rhinoceros. Or a manatee."

He opens his mouth to interrupt me and I hold up my hand before continuing.

"Yes, they're all cool animals, and some might even say adorable, especially the manatees, but thanks to society and body shaming, they're equated with being fat, which is the absolute worst thing a girl can be. Dreaming of being a mythical creature allows us to escape the pressure. Nobody is going to hate on a magical horse shooting rainbows out her ass."

With his eyes closed, he shakes his head. "Society is fucked up. This is why I don't like people."

"You're lucky you don't have to worry about any of this. You basically won the lottery—smart, educated, white, male, handsome."

He physically jolts at my words. I wasn't expecting my attempt at a compliment to affect him so strongly.

"Is that what you see when you look at me?" He practically whispers the question.

I guess I shouldn't have brought up his appearance. It obviously makes him uncomfortable. "Sorry, I was being superficial. You're adequately not hideous. Better?"

"Don't placate. Women aren't the only ones who find themselves trapped by expectations." Using both hands, he rubs his temples with vigor. "People see the world through their own biases. We can't control how others perceive us, yet we are unable to stop those opinions from shaping our identity."

In the quiet that follows, I mull over his words. We keep finding ourselves in these deep, uncomfortable corners of conversation. It's the opposite of my time with Tye, who lived life happily skimming the surface of the shallow end of the pool.

On the opposite end of the spectrum, Jay dives right into the deep end without hesitation.

"How did you get so wise?" I mean it as a compliment. I'm not sure he takes it as one.

"Sorry, I just wish people could be themselves without all the bull-shit." He apologizes and clears his throat. "Do you have more questions about the blue warblers? Maybe we should stick to talking about birds."

"Better than the birds and the bees, because I'm guaranteed to make that sexual." I lob a joke into the air and hope it lands.

It doesn't.

It does earn me an exaggerated eye roll. "You're worse than any twelve-year-old boy, and I should know from firsthand experience."

"Everyone says so, but girls are huge perverts too. We're just better at keeping it amongst ourselves—except when we're fangirling over boy bands and cutie-patootie actors." And hot rangers.

Hey, I didn't say it out loud!

My filter might be regenerating. Or I'm building immunity to Jay. Doubtful.

I keep flashing back to earlier this morning and his warmth. We barely had skin-to-skin contact, my arm against his, and yet … and yet I can't stop remembering how he felt, strong and solid beneath my touch.

Our conversations have been a series of advances and retreats. One step forward, a dozen back. I blame myself for making it awkward.

He cracks up. "Did you say cutie-patootie?"

Grinning, I nod. "Blame my grandmother and her friends. If the expression is favored by Abigail Perry, it's certainly good enough for the rest of us."

The name floats above my head. If I could, I'd snatch it back and shove it down my throat. I brace myself. Once he figures out who I am, he'll look at me differently. Our bubble will be gone.

He doesn't react. The follow-up question I dread never comes.

His walkie-talkie comes to life with a woman saying his call number. He stands to grab it.

"Hey, Guy." A wide, happy grin splits his face. "Good to hear your voice."

"You too. Heard you're stuck at elevation. Everything okay?"

"We're fine. Hanging out at the old moonshiner's cabin off the spur past Thunder."

"Still snowing up there?" she asks.

"Let me check." He ducks to peer through the filthy window. "Looks like it's stopped."

"We have patches of blue sky down here."

"Bragging doesn't suit you, Guy." He chuckles, displaying an ease with his co-worker that borders on flirting.

I wonder if they've had a thing, past or present. I can also see him dating a local girl, maybe a reference librarian or the baker who makes extra of his favorite kind of cookie. Someone smart and sweet without generations of baggage and a messy romantic history. He deserves someone nice in spite of thinking he doesn't.

Attempting to avoid eavesdropping on his conversation, I decide to step outside for fresh air and a wee. I pantomime my plan to him and step outside after shoving my feet into my shoes and zipping my puffy jacket.

I could bring in more firewood while I'm outside. Not sure how long Jay's call will take, I decide to check out the far side of the cabin.

* * *

In the hours we've been inside, the rain and sleet have shrunk the snow, compacting the powder into a denser layer, making it both easier and more difficult to navigate in my trail shoes. Snow slides between my skin and my socks, an unwelcome invasion.

The stone chimney puffs white smoke into the chilly air while water drips from the roof as snow melts. There's no porch on the back of the cabin. Brush and saplings crowd the ground, possibly hinting at there once having been a clearing out here.

With the wind no longer howling, the sound of running water catches my attention. A creek must be close by.

With a glance at the cabin, I decide to explore the area. Despite Jay's declaration about the warblers, I'm still not convinced all of them have left.

Snow and ice crunch underfoot as I weave a path through the shrubs and narrow tree trunks. Every now and again, I pause to listen for the familiar chirping of birds, hopeful for a sign they're still here.

The chimney barely visible behind me, I discover the creek, a narrow black line curving its path through the white snow. Various rocks line the edges and the occasional boulder breaks the surface of the water, forcing the current to split around its mass.

Movement on the opposite side catches my attention. I stand still, straining to hear a bird call or the rustling of an unseen animal. Fallen logs and the aforementioned shrubs provide protection for the birds from aerial assaults by the local raptors. If I were a bird, this would make a lovely place to ride out the weather.

While not promising to be warm or dry, a partially submerged boulder at the edge with a flat top seems like a nice place to hang out and spy on the neighbors, AKA birdwatch.

Thankful Jay isn't around to witness me scrambling over the rocks, I use my hands to keep my balance. After removing a thin layer of snow, I settle in my spot. I brush the dirt from my palms and regret not bringing my gloves with me. At least my jacket has pockets. Everything should, and it's a crime when they don't.

The dark water of the creek stretches about a dozen feet from bank to bank. Given all the exposed rocks and swirls of current, it doesn't appear to be more than a few inches deep in most spots except in the pools closer to the boulders nearest me. My hiker brain looks for an easy path to cross it.

A crow caws from overhead and my head automatically jerks back as I try to spot the dark feathers. Gold and rust tones of fall foliage color the landscape like confetti against the white backdrop of snow.

The crow flaps its wings as it continues its flight and disappears. Hoping this means other birds are resuming their activity, I scan the woods for other movement.

"I know you're out there somewhere," I say to the quiet burble of flowing water. The wind answers with a gentle rustling of dying leaves.

Below my foot, a collection of debris swirls in the icy water. In the center floats a slim blue feather.

Taking it as a sign, I lean to the side, stretching my arm and fingers to reach for my prize. No matter how much I will my bones to lengthen another inch or two, I come up short.

Determined to collect the feather to show Jay, I shift position to lie on my stomach. Now dangling over the side, my hips anchored and my toes dug into the surface to brace myself, I extend my arm into the flow.

"Careful!" Jay's voice calls out, close by. "What are you doing?"

In triumph, I grasp the feather.

Right before I slide into the water.

CHAPTER SEVENTEEN

JAY

*O*ne second Snowbird is lying on a boulder. The next she's sliding headfirst into the shallow creek like she's diving into a lake for a swim in the summer instead of potentially knocking herself out on a rock and drowning.

"Snowbird!" I shout, already running toward the boulder, the nickname sounding ridiculous to my ears given the gravity of this situation.

I caused this by startling her. I should have waited longer to let her know I'd followed her.

My conversation with Guy ended shortly after Snowbird went outside, and I expected her to come back inside within a few minutes. When she didn't, I tracked her footprints through the snow to here.

I reach the muddy bank as she scrambles to right herself in the creek bed. On her hands and knees, water drips down her face as she sputters for breath.

"Are you okay?" Without thinking, I step into the water to help her. I hiss when the frigid temperature wraps around my shins, immediately numbing my skin.

"I was fine until you scared me." Her foot slips as she attempts to stand.

We're in about half a foot of depth, the bottom covered mostly with rocks, polished smoothed by the current. In other words, they're slippery as hell. Carefully stepping my way closer to her, I nearly fall twice.

She's upright when I get to her. My fear for her safety comes out as frustration when I ask, "What the hell were you doing?"

"I *was* having a quiet moment, communing with nature, thank you very much." She shivers, her teeth chattering.

"Let's get out of here before you get full-blown hypothermia." I touch her elbow. "Give me your hand." When she doesn't budge, I add in a pleasant, but pleading tone, "Please."

Shaking now from the chill, she grips my hand and allows me to pull her closer to the bank. My foot slips on a rock and I tip forward. Her weight provides a counterbalance, keeping me from taking a face-plant of my own. Unfortunately, I still stumble enough to get my pants wet up to mid-thigh. I can no longer feel anything below the knee.

Once we're back on solid, albeit snow-covered, ground, I visually inspect her for cuts and bleeding. She holds her right hand curled tight against her chest, definitely favoring it like she might have fractured her wrist. "Did you hit your head? Is anything broken?"

She dismisses my concern with a shake of her head. "I'm fi-fine."

Her teeth chatter to the point that I can hear them.

"No, you're not. What's wrong with your right arm?" I'm stripping off my jacket to wrap around her shoulders. We need to get back inside to the fire as quickly as possible.

Extending her clenched fist, her arms shake with tremors. Slowly unfurling her fingers, she reveals a crushed blue feather. "I saw this in the water and was reaching for it."

A quick glance doesn't give me much information, but I blurt out the first thought in my head. "Could be from a cerulean, not the Black-throated Warbler."

I know I've said the wrong thing as soon as the words leave my mouth. Logically, I'm right, and a feather doesn't mean there are warblers close by. It could've come from anywhere or floated downstream from miles away.

Her eyelids close and she exhales audibly through her nose, reminding me of a bull about to charge.

"I'm probably wrong." I gently lift it off of her palm and straighten the crooked shaft. "Definitely from a Black-throated Blue."

I'm lying. There isn't enough black on it and I'm ninety-percent confident it's a wing feather from a cerulean. I don't want to disappoint her, though. What's the harm in a little white lie?

"You think?" She takes the feather back, returning it to her jacket pocket, her hands shaking from the cold. Her entire body trembles.

With a nod, I avoid extending my fib. "Let's get you back inside. Want me to carry you?"

She balks. "No, I, I'm fi-fine."

"Not buying it." Before she can protest, I bend to get my arms behind her knees and scoop her into my arms.

With a yelp, she tries to wiggle herself down at first. "Jay, I can walk."

"I know—so can I." To prove my point, I stride through the woods.

Teeth still clicking together and her body shivering, she rests her head on my shoulder with her arms looped around my neck.

I accept the small victory with a silent cheer. She's so stubborn. Then again, so am I.

We don't talk on the short hike to the cabin. I mull over why I lied to her about the feather. Was it because she was hopeful and I didn't want to disappoint her? Or was it because she was half-frozen and I didn't need to stand there and argue with her? Either way, I don't feel good about the dishonesty even though my life is one big half-truth.

Keeping it simple is the first rule in deception. Don't overcomplicate the story or you'll be more likely to get caught. Learned that lesson when I was a kid and didn't want people to know I'm half Japanese.

Silly now, but back in high school, I was focused on fitting in and surviving. Anything different was weaponized and used against you by other kids at school. Divorce. Sibling's reputation. Where you lived. What kind of cars your parents drove. If you had the right kind of video game console or sneakers. Being an outsider only made navigating the school politics harder.

At least in my experience. I'd like to think—or better yet, believe people are inherently good. I want to believe this with my heart, soul, and body.

However, I've seen too much racism and bigotry to ever fully believe in equality. I'm sure Snowbird is lovely, but I don't know her well enough to reveal my background. A few of her comments reveal she assumes I'm white like her.

I loathe the word and concept of "passing" but I'm not fool enough to believe my looks haven't helped me. Growing up, my sister bore the weight of her difference on the surface. I carried mine bundled in fear of being found out and labeled, not proud. Most kids yearn to fit in and belong. I was no different.

* * *

"Don't carry me over the threshold," Snowbird instructs. "Too weird. Drop me on the ground anywhere before you get to the door. Here is fine. Or here." She continues pointing out drop zones as I walk up the porch stairs.

"How about here?" I release my support of her knees and her legs dip to the ground.

"Thanks for the lift." She manages to speak without stuttering from cold. However, despite being wrapped around my neck and shoulders, I know her fingers are still icicles.

"You're welcome." The words come out a whisper as we stare at each other. "I'm glad you're okay."

"Me too," she whispers back. "Thank you."

Standing on her toes, resting her hands on my chest, she plants a kiss on my mouth.

Her lips are cold but soft. Acting on primal instinct, my body takes over, sucking her full bottom lip into my mouth. I could drown in her kiss.

When her cold fingers slip into my hair and she presses herself against me, I'm reminded of why we're out here. Holding her by the upper arms, I push her away.

"We shouldn't," I tell her, firm.

"Why not?" She blinks up at me, hurt in her eyes.

"You're in shock and clearly not thinking straight." The excuse sounds lame to my ears.

"I'm fine. I keep telling you and you don't believe me." Contradicting her defense, she tucks her hands into her soggy jacket sleeves and hops from foot to foot

"Inside, now." Still concerned about frostbite and hypothermia, my words come out harsher than I intend. "Please."

"Well, since you said please." Snowbird glares at me.

Her dawdling drives me to frustration. "You lose a toe, you'll only have yourself to blame."

"Seriously?" Staring down at her soaked shoes, she points and flexes her feet.

With only the best intentions, I give her a gentle shove through the open door. "Get out of your clothes and socks."

Apparently, I have to be gruff and mean for her to listen to me. What does that say about the kind of men she dates?

"Hey, you used my line!" she pouts.

"You're still shivering and in wet clothes." My patience is running out at a quick pace.

"Fine." Unzipping her jacket, she removes it first. Next, come her shoes and socks. I gather the discarded articles to lay out in front of the fire. "I'll keep my back turned."

"You don't have to," she practically purrs.

"Yes, I do. I'm trying to remain a gentleman." Normally this isn't a challenge for me, but Snowbird is pushing my buttons. She isn't being coy about it either.

Busying myself with stoking the fire, I try to ignore the shuffling and soft cursing behind me.

"Brrr," she mutters. "It's cold in here."

I tell myself not to picture her naked. So naturally, my mind promptly does the opposite. Minds are funny. They like to ignore the word not.

"Are you dressed yet? You should also get inside your sleeping bag."

"I'm not shivering anymore. I'll be fine."

"Snowbird, please just do what I ask. Which one of us is the trained EMT?" I don't bother to keep the exasperation out of my voice.

"Since it isn't me, I'm guessing it's you." Behind me, I hear the long pull of a zipper, followed by a strange thumping sound.

She stands beside me, fully enclosed in her sleeping bag with only her face peeking out.

I laugh. "You look like a blue Teletubby."

"More like a friendly worm. I don't even have use of my arms." She wiggles around in a shimmy.

"Are you warm?" I smirk down at her.

"Yes." She sighs. "Much better."

"Good. I'll make some tea. Or would you rather have soup?"

"Tea is fine—with Pop-Tarts on the side." She grins, but it fades quickly. "Sorry I kissed you."

"No need to apologize." I rest my hand on the back of my neck, feeling rotten for rejecting her.

"I promise to never do it again. I'm sorry for making you uncomfortable." Her eyes flit between mine.

The word never settles heavy on my chest. I'm not even sure why I stopped the kiss. Do I really think she's in shock? No. Does my reasoning have anything to do with the stories about her ex? Maybe. This isn't her real life. Any event on this hike is only a blip in her adventure. She's passing through, and in a day or two, she'll be gone.

Some men might take advantage of the situation, enjoy a quick, semi-anonymous romp. Fortunately, or unfortunately, I've never been that guy. I like to know the real names of the women I sleep with.

Cranky, I dismiss her apology. "It's fine. Sit by the fire."

"You're bossy when you slip into ranger mode." With a sigh, she shuffles closer to the fireplace and then sits on the crate. Or almost sits on it—she falls off to the side because she lands too close to the edge. Quickly recovering, she unzips the top of the bag. "I can't breathe."

Finally settled, she sips tea and munches on a pastry.

Relief softens the defensive quills that appear when I'm worried, stressed, or threatened. She's fine and doesn't seem to have any lingering injuries.

"What made you decide to become a ranger?" she asks, sitting above me as I rest on the floor.

"I've always loved the woods and the national parks. I like science. Seemed like an obvious choice. Not a ton of jobs out there for ornithologists other than research or teaching, and dealing with college students sounds like my own personal hell."

"Too much peopling?"

I nod. "Way too much."

"I get that."

"What about you? What do you do for work?" I ask because I'm curious. She's given me so little information about herself.

"Guess."

"Teacher?"

"Ack, no. I'm not a saint, and you definitely need to be one to work in the classroom."

"My mother falls into the same category, in terms of teaching. Though I don't think she's an actual sainted angel because she's my mother."

Her musical laugh floats around the room. "Thanks for clarifying."

I wait for her to tell me about her job.

"No more guesses?" she asks

"I didn't think you were serious."

"Always."

"Okay, you're a game show hostess. No? How about home organizer? App designer?"

Each guess is met with a shake of her head.

"How about you tell me?" I prod.

"None of the above. I'm gainfully unemployed."

"I figured since you've been hiking for five months. What did you do before?"

"It's a long list, but a lot of different things. There wasn't a lot of pressure in my family for me to have a career. My mother didn't. My grandmothers didn't. Get married. Have kids. Support my husband. Do charity work. That's about it. So in college, I studied documentary filmmaking. I've been a grant writer for an NGO. Fundraiser. Blogger. Nothing seems to stick." She frowns. "Obviously true for relationships too."

"You sound like my sister. I think I'm probably the freak to have decided what I wanted to do when I was thirteen and never deviated."

"Is your sister a mess?"

"No, and I doubt you are either." I try to reassure her while wondering why she thinks of herself this way. To me, she comes off as smart and strong-willed, not some lost lamb without a clue. "The fact you're on the AT means you can do hard things."

"Is she gainfully employed?"

"Yes, she works for a small fashion company up in Nashville." I finish my tea. "What kind of work will you look for when you get home?"

"I have no idea. It usually finds me. I stumble into jobs the way some people walk into walls. One minute I'm minding my own business, and then boom, I have a job. Not sure why, but that's how it happens. Kind of like relationships."

She shrugs off the randomness of this pattern. "I think I'm thoroughly thawed out. Can I remove my bag now?"

"Sure. You don't seem to have any issues."

"Then you're not looking close enough." She laughs at her statement. "You'll need to turn around again unless you want to check out my ass."

"Huh?" I lose my train of thought.

"I'm not wearing any pants. Figured I'd warm up quicker without them. Skin-to-skin but just mine."

Groaning, I close my eyes in an attempt to erase the images in my head. Doesn't work.

"Everything okay, Ranger Jay?" Her tone is concerned but also self-satisfied.

"Fine. Go put on the rest of your clothes, Snowbird."

"Interesting," she whispers to herself as she retreats across the small room.

I ignore her as best as I can.

She's sneaky, dangerous, slowly slipping past my guards and defenses, and worming her way into the place I allow few people to enter.

CHAPTER EIGHTEEN

OLIVE

*J*ay is very sweet after he scared me, saved me from freezing to death, and then rejected me.

It's only a partial exaggeration about dying, given his concern about me catching hypothermia from a quick plunge into a shallow stream. In reality, my form was closer to a belly flop, and I was barely submerged before scrambling out of the water. I was always going to be fine.

Speaking of fine, being carried back to the cabin in his remarkably strong arms is definitely a highlight of this week and possibly the entire trail.

This must be why romance books in grocery stores always have the hero sweeping the heroine off her feet—because it works wonders on the libido. Evidently, it makes the man irresistible, causing the woman to lose all sense and sensibilities.

I kissed the ranger.

And while he kissed me back, it's painfully obvious the dear man doesn't think of me as anything more than a professional duty.

Which would be okay if he weren't so handsome, smart, and charming.

And if his kiss wasn't seared on my memory for life.

He's not the first to reject me. If my past is any indication, he won't be the last.

When it comes to men and freezing creeks, I tend to fall hard and fast. Luckily, I'm also good at compartmentalizing my feelings and moving on.

After another semi-edible meal from the pack pantry, we're spending the time before sleep arguing about all the other ways to die in the park.

Besides hypothermia.

And mortification from rejection.

"You're more likely to die in a car accident or by drowning in the parks than getting mauled by a bear." He stares me down, challenging me to argue with his facts.

I purse my lips. "Sounds like propaganda to reassure nervous visitors. Wild animals are notoriously vicious killers. We've all seen the nature videos."

He sighs. "You've spent how many months walking the trail? And how many bears have you actually seen in person?"

"Two."

"Close up?" The way he cocks his head is both arrogant and charming.

"At the time, I thought the first bear was a boulder in the distance and the other I could only see by zooming in on the picture Tye took with his phone. That one also looked like a black rock."

"So, you're saying no."

"Okay, from a far distance. We saw a giant moose in Maine and there were also a few mountain goats with murder in their weird sideways pupils."

"Actual mountain goats?" His eyes narrow. "Pretty confident those aren't native to anywhere east of the Rockies."

"Well, they were goats and I was in the mountains," I say, sheepishly avoiding his eyes.

"Good thing they were domestic goats. There was an unfortunate death by mountain goat about a decade ago out west."

My mouth pops open as I stare at him.

He bobs his head, serious. "I wish I were kidding. Isolated incident in the Olympic Mountains, and no one knows what provoked the goat. Luckily he didn't become a serial killer."

"Serial killing goats—I knew it." Smugness rarely looks good on anyone, but I think I wear it well.

"The whole taste-for-blood issue? Once an animal kills, they'll kill again."

From his blank expression, I can't tell if he's serious, but I go with it. "Ted Bundy goats."

Watching the Netflix film during a zero day at a motel probably wasn't the smartest idea. I only have myself, Zac Efron, and my childhood obsession with High School Musical to blame.

"Not limited to goats. Mostly bears, the occasional moose, or mountain lion." Ignoring my disturbing line of thinking, Jay continues giving me nuggets of factual information. His tone remains level-headed and unamused by my detour into psychopathic ruminants.

He's unflappable and it fascinates me how he's apparently immune to my charms. I must be off my flirty game. Or he's just not interested.

"You know a lot of random facts about death and dying in the park system." I arch an eyebrow. "Standard operating procedure to inform your guests of their odds of not making it out alive?"

"Part of the job, ma'am." He tips an invisible hat brim. "People who visit the park want to know these things. Most common question is about the odds of a bear attack."

"Then why do we need bear cans and bear bags?" Check and mate.

"Who doesn't like a tasty snack? Blame your fellow humans." The way he says it makes it seem like he's defending the bears.

"You've never had any issues in the park?" I keep pushing, wanting him to be on my side.

"A few years ago, a Sienna Diaz movie filmed here and we were in charge of bear control. Moved several of them out of the area for the duration of the shoot, more for the insurance than a real fear of attack. Hollywood." He shrugs. "Normally, we don't get so fancy around here."

"I think I remember reading about her falling in love with a park ranger and getting married. Guy had a funny name. Like Arlo or Judah. Jebediah? Something biblical. Although from what I remember of the pictures in *People*, the only thing Old Testament about him was the beard." I remember the guy was hot in a natural, God-given way. Nothing metro about his sexual.

Kind of like Jay.

I doubt he owns two face serums and three hair products like Tye. His light brown hair brushes his collar and his beard could use a trim, but he doesn't look scraggly.

Not at all. Jay is ruggedly handsome.

"You're talking about Jethro," he corrects me.

Because of course he's named Jethro.

"No last name?"

"Winston."

"Rings a bell. Is he still a ranger?" I ask, purely out of curiosity, not because I'm going to go after another woman's man. How many hot rangers are there up here in the Smokies anyway?

"Not anymore."

"Makes sense, I guess."

"Why?"

I repeat his words from last night. "Hard to make a relationship work when you're from two different worlds unless one of you is willing to sacrifice everything."

CHAPTER NINETEEN

OLIVE

*W*e're up early with the sun the next morning to hike out of here.

My body gravitated to his again in my sleep, but this time he was the big spoon. Not mad about it at all.

Jay radios our plans to his station so they don't send out a search party.

The snow has shrunk as it's melted, which bodes well for us successfully getting down the mountains to the valley where the main ranger station for this area of the park is located.

In spite of us waking early, we're still walking in the late afternoon as dusk approaches. What should've been four or five hours of hiking has turned into seven due to storm damage and obstacles on the trail.

Jay assures me we'll be fine and regales me with fun nature facts to keep me from worrying. Or to horrify me. The jury is still out on his true motivations.

Still no sign of my Black-throated Blue Warbler, but I'm optimistic they're around. I asked him to tell me more about birds, and he's all in with the information. All. In.

"Unlike us, birds can see UV colors because they have four cones in their eyes versus our three."

"I actually knew that. *Peterson* talks about avian anatomy." I give myself a mental thumbs-up.

Walking slightly behind me, he continues, "There's more. Were you aware rodent urine shows up on the UV spectrum?"

"I was not."

I'm not sure what he wants me to do with this information other than to imagine birds spotting all of the bodily fluids, animal and human, along the AT. Must resemble a Jackson Pollack painting. *The horror.*

"Owls and other birds of prey are able to spot rodents by following their pee trails."

He must be a hit at dinner parties.

"Ew. What a relief we don't have permanent blacklight vision. I'm happier not knowing everything I see is covered in urine and ..." I want to say semen, but instead edit myself to say, "Other things."

Strangely enough, this isn't the weirdest conversation I've had while hiking.

Daylight is fading when we come across a pasture surrounded by simple split-rail fencing.

"We can cut through here and shave forty-five minutes off our time." Without hesitation about getting shot for trespassing, Jay ducks under the top rail and then extends his hand back for me to use as support.

"Are you sure this is a good idea?" I ask, studying the dim twilight for movement. With blue mist thick this time of day, it's almost impossible to see anything farther away than a few yards. Since it's not truly dark out, my headlamp doesn't provide any help whatsoever other than to make me look like a miner or cool archeologist.

"Trust me, the point of these fences is to keep animals out of the fields so they don't eat the crops. We're fine. Remember my list of deadly hazards? We're more likely to be killed in an automotive accident. Do you see any cars out here?" His reassurance fails to have the desired effect on me.

"If you say so." I grip his palm and slip under the top rail without snagging my pack.

Across the open space, something makes a low, moaning sound.

"What was that?" I ask, pausing near the fence with my hand on the lichen-covered post. "Bear? Bobcat? Bull?"

Jay also stops, cocking his head as he listens. "Could be the wind."

I scoff. "If the wind has a deviated septum and a head cold."

He glances over his shoulder at me. "Seems very specific."

I shrug. "A lot of girls in my class developed a deviated septum around ninth or tenth grade."

He stares at me, confused.

"Rhinoplasty was a phase." I point to the bridge of my own nose. "It's the gateway to plastic surgery. Saying you have a deviated septum makes it sound like it's medically necessary when in reality, it's a matter of vanity."

He blinks and then nods. "Interesting."

Is it though? "I think you're humoring me."

"Did you?" He points at the center of his face.

"No."

"I don't think I know anyone who has had plastic surgery except maybe Kevin Mane after he broke his nose on my fist." He shrugs and flashes a sheepish grin.

I gasp and press my hand to my heart. "Ranger Daniels punched someone?"

"More than once. I had a problem with fighting when I was younger."

Trying and failing to picture him as a bad boy bruiser, I squint up at his face. Jay with a split lip and a purple bruise on his cheek might be kind of hot, especially if he were fighting to defend me.

There's obviously something wrong with me. Maybe I hit my head harder than I realized when I fell yesterday.

The low, animal sound repeats.

I freeze and whisper, "Is it getting closer?"

"The wind?" Jay asks, but his attention is also focused across the field.

"Can we drop the pretense of not being trapped on the wrong side of the fence with whatever bloodthirsty beast is making such a sound?"

I squint into the distance, hoping narrowing my eyes will give me super strength vision.

It doesn't. I step behind Ranger Daniels for protection.

"What are you doing?" He twists his neck to look down at me.

"Hiding. I believe you took an oath to protect and serve."

"Pfft. You're confusing me with a police officer. I'm here to engage, educate, and empower." He moves so he's beside me.

"You carry a gun, don't you?"

"Sometimes. Do you see a holster now?"

I scan his hips and shake my head, allowing my eyes to linger on the tight fit of his uniform pants over his strong thighs and the thick belt at his narrow waist. Ranger Daniels is packing heat, but not of the pistol variety.

Is it hot in here, or is it just me?

A distinct braying reaches my ears.

"Is that a donkey?" I tip my head.

"What would a donkey be doing up here? Makes no sense."

"Ask him. Or her." I point at the gray beast moving toward us. "I'm a city girl, but I'm pretty sure that's an ass."

"Well, I'll be damned." Jay removes his hat.

Maybe he plans to shoo away our attacker with it?

The gray form ambles toward us, letting out a loud bray and revealing large teeth.

"Should we be worried?" I'm standing behind Jay again.

"About a donkey? They're mostly docile. He's probably just curious." Shifting his attention forward, he addresses our new friend. "Hey there. Where'd you come from?"

The donkey halts.

"See? He's fine. Probably thinks we're bringing treats."

"And what will he do when he realizes we're showing up to his house empty-handed?" I'm half mocking. In my world, not bringing a hostess gift is an unthinkable breach of etiquette. I have no idea about the social decorum for equines.

"Let's go." Jay encourages me forward with a sweep of his hat.

We take several steps and the donkey does the same without

breaking eye contact, like we're about to duel. There's definitely a challenge, a mild threat in the eyes of our new foe.

"Should we slowly retreat to the fence?" I whisper at Jay's back.

"Nah, we're fine."

"Maybe he's a guard donkey." I slide a glance over my shoulder toward safety. We're a dozen or so yards away, but it isn't too late to make a quick escape.

Jay's eyes meet mine. "You know guard donkeys aren't a thing."

"I'm a stranger in a strange land—anything's possible." I wait until he faces forward to stick my tongue out at him.

He's shaking his head and clearly not paying attention to me anymore as he stomps across the squishy field.

Left with no choice, I follow after him.

My boot slips in the mud, or donkey poop—it's impossible to tell the difference. I squawk and flail my arms as I tumble forward in an awkward motion resembling the mating dance of an emu.

The donkey's ears prick up before flattening against his head.

"Uh oh," I murmur as I straighten up.

"It's fine," Jay says for the dozenth time.

Only he's wrong.

Our new friend trots for a few beats and then *charges* toward us as fast as his (or her) short legs can go.

Ranger Daniels doesn't move. Probably frozen in shock.

However, I take off in a sprint, which is not easy given my large pack and the muddy, uneven ground sucking at my shoes.

With no idea how big this pasture is, I run in the opposite direction of where we entered. Donkeys are pack animals, not race horses, but I have no clue about their sprinting endurance. If only I had carrots or sugar cubes I could throw at it as a distraction.

Running is a bad idea, and pointless, as emphasized by the steady thump of hooves behind me.

With a glance over my shoulder, I realize Jay is standing stock-still, observing the chase.

"Why aren't you running?" My voice is breathless, the words choppy.

One thing I've learned on the trail is to not run from bears. Does that apply to other animals too? What does Jay know that I don't?

He chuckles. The man actually laughs while I'm being chased by a murderous beast that's clearly crazed with bloodlust.

"The better question is why are you?" he shouts, amusement shading his question.

I'm not going to stop to prove his point. Too risky.

The old adage about not having to outrun a lion, only outpacing the other guy comes to mind. As long as this hell horse is chasing me, Jay knows he's safe.

Clever asshole.

A large tree stands in the field up ahead and behind it is what appears to be another fence. Only a few more yards until safety.

Panting, sweat beading on my brow and on my back where the pack rests, I zigzag around the tree and throw myself at the fence, hoping I'll slide under like a baseball player diving for home.

The muddy grass gives more resistance than I'd hoped. I don't so much glide to safety as stumble and flop.

Braying, the donkey clomps to a stop behind me as I scramble under the top rail to freedom.

Once I'm on the other side, I lie back, a turtle resting on my pack. Out of breath but alive, I lift my muddy fist in triumph.

"You're on your own now, Ranger," I shout.

In my awkward position, it's difficult to lift my head to search for him in the field. Shoving myself up on my elbows, I make eye contact with the donkey, who is stretching his head over the fence.

"Not today, Satan." I wag my finger at him.

"I hope you don't mean me." Grinning, Jay pats the donkey on his head the same way you would with a dog, giving it a scratch by the ears. "Or this sweet guy."

They're both adorable, which only makes everything worse.

"I hate you both," I mumble, rolling to the side in an attempt to stand. From my spot on the ground, I have a good angle for watching Jay slip under the fence and walk toward me. It's a very nice vantage point.

"Can I help you?" His hand appears directly in front of my face, blocking my view.

"I've got it." I switch to hands and knees to shove myself to a vertical position.

"You have a little something here." Jay gestures at his own cheek.

With a glance at my dirty fingers, I decide to use my jacket sleeve to wipe my face. Bad idea. It's also filthy. Taking notice of my body from the neck down, I realize all of me is splattered with mud. Grass sticks to my leggings like I'm a scarecrow losing my stuffing.

By the time I finish my inspection, Jay bends over with laughter.

"I hate to tell you, but it's worse on your back." He tries to make a straight face, willing the corners of his mouth downward.

He fails.

With all the pent-up adrenaline rushing through my body, I shove him.

Like that story of a mother who lifts a car off of her toddler, my strength is superhuman.

Jay stumbles, catches his foot in the mud, and tumbles back, landing on his ass in a puddle.

I'm not sorry at all.

CHAPTER TWENTY

JAY

We made it through the pasture without being trampled by the donkey or running into its owner, who might not be pleased about us traipsing through his fields.

I shouldn't have laughed at Snowbird's antics, or how muddy she got herself. Wasn't polite or kind to find amusement in the misfortune of others.

I'm certainly not amused now with my ass in a puddle.

Didn't see that coming.

"Now who's laughing?" she asks, smug and clearly pleased with herself.

"You pushed me." My mouth drops open with surprise.

"Turnabout. Fair play. All's fair in love and war and muddy fields." She extends a hand to help me up.

I accept the gesture. "Thanks. You're not forgiven."

"Then we're even." Wiping her hand on her leggings, she frowns. "I'm pretty sure this isn't all mud."

Wrinkling my nose, I take a long step away from her. "I preferred it when you fell in the stream. At least you were clean afterward."

"How soon until I can take a shower?"

"We're about half an hour from the campground."

She lifts her gaze to the misty sky. "Thank heavens."

"Unless we run into a gang of alpacas looking for trouble."

"Can we not talk about the thousand ways to die in a national park again? I'd like a quiet moment to dream about my shower and the real food I'm going to eat for dinner."

For the short duration of our hike, I keep myself from sharing more random facts about the Smokies. Normally, I'm not the kind of guy who prances around, displaying my knowledge like brightly colored plumage to impress human females.

Snowbird is obviously not impressed.

Not surprising.

There is more than one reason I'm perpetually single.

* * *

The campground is a welcome sight when we round the last curve of the trail. Tents and RVs occupy every visible spot.

Snowbird's expression morphs from excited to disappointed as we walk through the rows of occupied campsites, headed in the direction of the ranger station.

"Looks full." She worries the strap on her pack.

"I'm guessing a lot of people rode out the bad weather here rather than be on the road, but there's no way we're fully booked. I'm sure we'll find you a spot." I reassure her even though I'm surprised at how crowded the campground is.

We pass a bathroom and she makes a beeline for the women's side.

Outside, I debate whether or not to wait for her. There's no reason I need to escort her to the office, or loiter around to make sure she gets set up for the night in the dark. We're not friends. My obligation to her was fulfilled as soon as she was safely off the trail.

Still, I linger. Rather than stand around the bathroom entrance like a creeper, I decide to sit at a nearby picnic table. Other than a few puddles, there's little evidence of the storm. Crazy to think we hiked through snow only hours ago.

The air has a chill to it. I dig out my phone to check the low temperature for tonight. Turning it on after being in the backcountry for three days, I notice a bunch of texts in my family group chat.

Forty-seven to be exact.

I scroll through the conversation to make sure everything is okay with both my mom and my sister. It would appear everything is fine, but the planning for their annual trip to Japan is in full swing. I don't know if they discuss everything in this chat to keep me in the loop so as to not hurt my feelings or if it's to apply gentle pressure to get me to change my mind.

Frowning, I tuck the phone in my jacket pocket. Snowbird stands a few feet in front of me, observing me. Her face is clean, as are her hands, but the rest of her is a wreck.

"You stayed?" She sounds confused.

"Why wouldn't I?" I shrug. "Figured I'd make sure you get a spot for the night or give you a lift into town if you needed."

"That's nice of you," she says, genuinely pleased.

"It's nothing." I jump down from my seat on the picnic table.

"I do appreciate your kindness," she drawls.

"Your Scarlett accent again?" I nudge her with my elbow.

"I already told you—Miss Julia Sugarbaker. Sheesh. It should be obvious." With an exasperated sigh, she rolls her eyes.

Her happy mood fades when we reach the campground office. The sign on the locked door explains they're full for the night.

"It's okay. I'll sniff out some hiker trash and share their site." She covers her disappointment with a smile. "No big deal. I can always stealth camp in the donkey pasture. Shh, don't tell the rangers."

"In the mud? Sounds like a terrible idea." I scowl at her suggestion, and not because she's teasing me about breaking rules.

"If the showers are hot and the laundry room is still open, I'm all good."

This feels like goodbye, and I'm not ready to watch her walk away.

"Or ..." I hesitate.

"Or?"

"You could come back to my quarters. We have hot showers and a laundry room so you don't have to worry about having change for the machines. And ..."

"Yes?" Her eyes hold wary anticipation.

"I have a bed and a couch ... if you wanted to stay over. Better than squeezing your tent into an overcrowded spot with a bunch of strangers. Might be nice for you to have another night inside. I'm happy to take the couch."

"Jay?" she interrupts.

"Or, I'd be happy to drive you into town and find you a room. Although, I'm thinking if the campground is full, it means there aren't any vacancies nearby."

"I said okay."

Lost in my head, I missed it. "To what?"

"I'll stay with you."

"You will?" I ask, surprised.

"I like hanging out with you, too."

My answering smile feels too wide, too happy. I temper my expression, or at least attempt to. Not sure how successful I am. "Okay, sure."

"And Jay?"

"Yes?"

"I'm fine with sharing a bed."

CHAPTER TWENTY-ONE

OLIVE

I'm totally playing it cool with Jay, impressively nonchalant about his sleepover invite.

He didn't even run back into the hills when I brought up sharing a bed. We've proven we're mature adults who can sleep together without *sleeping* together. If he balked, I was going to suggest a pillow wall or hanging a blanket between the two sides. There is no way I'm not sleeping on a real mattress with sheets and blankets and maybe even a comforter tonight, but I'd feel bad making him sleep on his couch. Jay's tall, and unless he has a long sectional in his tiny ranger pad, I doubt he'd fit comfortably.

He leads us down the road behind the station to a group of small cabins and a long, single-story building. Or bunkhouse. Not sure what to call it.

"Seasonal employees stay in the dorm." He points to the long building. "It's exactly how you're imagining it, complete with bunk beds."

"Do you have bunk beds?"

He glowers at me. "No, I have my own cabin."

"Fancy," I kid.

"Simple, but it suits me." He bends to unlace his muddy boots. "Uh, do you mind taking off your shoes before we go inside?"

"Don't want me to track dirt all over your floors?" I toe my shoes off.

"Habit. My mom always had us do it at home." He places his shoes neatly next to the front door.

Inside, the cabin isn't much larger than the moonshiner's retreat, except his has a living room with a green couch and a plaid armchair, a bathroom, and a bedroom. His kitchenette features more than a sink. Feels like we've upgraded from the bedbug-infested motel next to the highway to a Marriott. It's not the Four Seasons, but I'm not complaining.

Dropping his pack near the threshold, he removes his hat and jacket. "I'm starving and I can't even offer you a toaster pastry. We both need to eat—what do you say about grabbing dinner together?"

I watch him, trying to determine his motivation. Ranger Daniels is an expert in sending mixed signals. My ego still stings from his rejection of my kiss. Yes, it was forward of me. Yes, it might have been unexpected. No, I won't be sticking around to develop any sort of relationship. Still. It stings.

Yet, here we are. He could've let me disappear into the night with a tip of his ranger hat and a fare-thee-well. Instead, he's invited me over and asked me to dinner.

"Would this dinner include real food that doesn't come out of a package?" I can feel the drool pooling in my mouth at the thought of an actual, never-freeze-dried meal.

"Uh, sure. Although, your package free requirement rules out the grill at the camp store. Their burger patties come frozen." His forehead wrinkles in an adorable way when he's confused or thinking. "I'm pretty sure both Daisy's and The Porch cook everything in house. Daisy's is known for her pie. The Porch has steaks, but it's kind of fancy."

The way he says it means it's expensive and likely out of his budget.

I swear my knees buckle and my voice shakes when I ask, "There's pie?"

"If we get there early enough. They often sell out."

It's dark out, but it's also Daylight Savings, so it could be nine o'clock or five right now. I have no idea what early means around here. Four-thirty? It could already be too late.

"What are we waiting for?" I open the door and sweep my arm outside. "Let's go."

His eyes scan down to my feet and back up to my head as he remains silent.

"What?" Why is he stalling when there's pie at stake?

"Maybe you want to, um ..."

"What?" I roll my wrist in hopes it will encourage him to spit it out.

"Well ..." I swear the tips of his ears go red.

Impatiently tapping my socked foot, I cross my arms and wait.

He blows out a slow, extended exhalation. "You've been on the trail a long time and maybe ..." He scratches the back of his neck. "No offense or anything, but ..."

"Whenever anyone says no offense or anything followed by a but, it's going to be offensive." Dipping my chin, I pin him with a look. "Spit it out."

"You might want to shower and change your clothes." His words tumble over each other in a crowded rush. One of his eyes scrunches closed as he grimaces. "Sorry."

Right, the mud and grass and let's not think too hard about what else covering my clothes. How could I forget?

"Why don't you shower first? I'll put the muddy stuff in the wash for you."

Domesticated ranger? "You do laundry?"

He gives me a funny look. "Of course. My mother doesn't live with me."

I think he's joking. I hope he's joking.

He laughs. "Single mom, remember? We took turns doing laundry. So yes, I do my own. Kind of sexist for you to assume I don't."

163

He's right. "Okay, you have a deal."

After showing me to the bathroom and giving me a clean towel, he leaves. I strip out of my clothes and, extending my arm past the barely open door, drop the filthy and stinky pile outside.

The shower is everything, and Jay has decent bath products. Shampoo *and* conditioner. Manly fresh body wash. The only thing missing is a razor. With the beard, he obviously doesn't shave his face. I don't need to shave anything either. We're having dinner and a platonic sleepover. Like I would with Campbell.

Shit. I need to text her a proof-of-life pic. It's been over three days. She's probably worried.

* * *

Clean and fresh as mountain snow, skin pink from the heat, I step out of the shower and grab my towel. Drying off, I realize I don't have a stitch of clothing to put on. Not even underwear. Jay took it all.

The horrible scene in *Sixteen Candles* where the nerd holds up the girl's panties to a consortium of fellow geek boys flashes into my mind. For a brief, horrifying second, I imagine Jay showing off my underwear as some sort of trophy.

Thankfully, life is not an eighties teen movie and Jay isn't a pig.

My pack is next to the door in the living room. Down the hall.

The towel covers the important bits. Barely. I've joked about Jay seeing me naked, but it's all been bravado in the name of flirting.

I crack the door and listen for noises. His little cabin is still. Carefully clenching the towel around my breasts at the top and holding it down in front of my nethers, I call his name.

When there's no response, I tiptoe down the hall. No Jay.

Like a cartoon burglar, I creep across the room to my pack. I should have one pair of "clean" leggings along with underwear and my other sports bra. The only top I have doesn't pass the sniff test, but I don't have any other … options.

I glance over my shoulder at Jay's bedroom.

If I were Ranger Jay, would I mind if some random hiker chick snuck into my dresser and borrowed one of my t-shirts?

Definitively yes.

Teeth worrying my bottom lip, I balance the tiny pouch containing my toothbrush and toothpaste on top of the pile of clothes and head to the bathroom. Still thinking about how it's unfair he probably has dozens of clean shirts just going to waste in there, I brush my teeth.

I totally use his deodorant. He'll thank me later when we're in public.

The exterior door opens and shuts. Heavy footsteps make their way down the hall and stop outside the bathroom.

"Snowbird?" He knocks twice.

I swing the door open, and he averts his eyes. "I'm decent."

He glances at me then sweeps his gaze down my body to my feet. "You're dressed."

"I figured Daisy's wasn't a clothing-optional pie shop. Sorry I'm not wearing something nicer. This is all I have."

"No, people around here aren't fans of naked pie consumption." He shakes his head. "I bought you these. In case you wanted fresh clothes."

I snatch the bag from his hands quicker than a tourist snagging a fake Birkin bag on the streets of New York.

"Nothing fancy. I had to guess your size."

"Where did you go shopping so fast?" I peer into the bag. All I see is dark green fleece.

"Campground store. They have souvenir sweatshirts and tees for the visitors."

"Thank you!" I hug him.

He half-hugs me back. "I'll leave you to it."

"If you don't mind me changing in your room, you can use the bathroom now." I slip past him.

"Okay, sure. Make yourself at home." He closes the door.

With my bag of loot in hand, I enter Jay's bedroom and flip the light switch near the door. I don't know how I expect his room to be decorated. Maybe a Smokey Bear blanket or moose sheets.

His bed is neatly made with light gray sheets and a navy tartan comforter. There's not a bear or buck or moose in sight. Straight up LL Bean-approved tasteful decor.

A simple dresser sits on the wall opposite his bed. On the top are framed photos. Having no idea how long Jay will be in the shower, I do my snooping first. Is it really snooping if he knows I'm in here? What else am I going to look at? The old-school poster of the Smoky Mountains on the wall?

The largest frame holds a color photo of a little boy with a man with the same hair color. They're at a car show and the man has the boy on his shoulders. Their smiles are identical. This must be his dad.

Next is a smaller silver frame. In it is a picture of a more recent Jay hugging a petite brunette in glasses. Her arms are wrapped possessively around his waist and he's resting his head on top of hers. They look happy.

My stomach sinks.

Is this his girlfriend?

Feelings of guilt and regret propel me away from the dresser and the snooping. I dump the contents of the bag on his bed. A pair of gray sweatpants with GSM on the side and a coordinating green sweatshirt with a bear on it slip out onto the comforter.

I wouldn't be caught dead in this outfit in New York. Luckily, I'm not in the city right now. Clean, fresh, unstained clothes are the sweetest gift.

Even if he has a girlfriend, I like Jay, really like him. Beyond the rugged good looks and whole birds-of-a-feather thing in common, he's smart and kind, makes me laugh, clearly thinks I'm hysterical.

If nothing more, I think this could be the start of a friendship. We can be pen-pals. The thought of being "just friends" with a guy like Jay pings of disappointment in my chest, but I also know I'd be okay with it. Better to be friends than say goodbye in a couple of days and never speak to him again.

Quickly, I switch outfits. The sweatshirt is too big, the pants tight over my hips and too long in the legs. I roll the length into cuffs and tug the hem of the top to mid-thigh to cover my butt.

I'm not sure about the dress code at steakhouses in the Smokies, but this outfit wouldn't get past the maître d' at a single high-end restaurant in the city. Maybe Gray's Papaya, the hot dog chain.

Jay doesn't have a full-length mirror in his bedroom, so I have to imagine what I look like in this moment.

A Spanish olive comes to mind.

To avoid the temptation for more snooping, I decide to send my overdue selfie to Campbell.

Water still runs in the shower as I pass the bathroom.

Reaching deep into my pack, I extract my phone and turn it on. For self-protection, I've turned off all notifications. Tapping Campbell's name, I bring up our texts, snap a selfie, give her my location, and hit send.

Done. Time to once again unplug myself from the Matrix.

"I thought you didn't have a phone," Jay accuses.

He's standing in the opening between the living room and the hall. In a towel.

Okay, who's the one without boundaries now?

Sweet Keanu, his chest. Water rivulets chase each other over his pecs, down his abs, disappearing beneath the white terrycloth towel. I'm envious of fabric. Life isn't fair.

I hold up my smartphone. "I have a phone."

"The guy on the trail said you didn't."

"What guy? Oh, Bronchialasaurus? The older guy with a cough?"

He nods.

"I told him I didn't have a phone. He wanted to exchange photos or numbers or send me dick pics. Probably. Whatever his motivations, I lied and told him I've been traveling without one. No big deal." I shove the phone into the small zippered pocket on the front.

His brows draw together above the bridge of his nose. "Did you ever think to check the weather warnings with it?"

"I only use it to send proof-of-life photos to my best friend so no one sends out a search party. Then I turn it off to avoid the rest of my life." Having no reason to be ashamed or upset, I remain calm.

He grumbles and brings one hand to the top of his head.

I'm not opposed to what this position does to his muscles, but I don't like how he's speaking to me. "You sound hangry."

"No, I'm frustrated." He places his hands on his hips, looks down and back up at me. "I'm also not wearing pants. Excuse me."

He disappears down the hall. The door to his room softly clicks closed.

A few minutes later, he returns wearing jeans and a long-sleeved dark gray t-shirt.

"Let's go get some food." He slips on a green fleece jacket the same color as my ensemble.

We look like an old couple who has been together for so long they've started wearing matching outfits. Given his annoyance with me, I keep this observation to myself. My filter must be functioning better at lower altitude.

CHAPTER TWENTY-TWO

JAY

For some reason, seeing Snowbird with a phone really burned my biscuits.

I'm not sure her having access to weather reports would've made a lick of difference in her actions. The other AT hikers told her about the storm. She admitted she knew it was coming but still went off on her own and didn't heed the warnings.

I shouldn't be mad. All's well that ends well, right? We're both safe and uninjured. She still has all ten toes and fingers.

As far as her losing her common sense, I'm not sure how much she had to begin with.

We're both quiet as I drive down the dark, winding road leading out of the park and into the neighboring hills. I pass the right turn to Green Valley and keep going straight for about half a mile.

Daisy's Nut House sits at the back of a gravel lot. Thankfully only a half-dozen cars are parked in front, meaning we won't have to wait for a table and there should be pie left, maybe even more than one selection.

"I love this place." Snowbird grins at the sign and then back at me. "My grandfather and I used to sneak off to have breakfast in a silver diner on the west side of Manhattan when I was a teenager. Just the two of us."

"This place ain't fancy. Just good, honest food," I warn, wanting to temper her expectations.

"And pie. What's not to love?"

There's a bounce in her step as we walk from my SUV to the entrance.

"You want the counter or a booth?" I ask.

"Booth, please."

We're shown to our table by a young waitress who also takes our drink order.

Snowbird peruses the menu, making frequent comments about how delicious something sounds, suggesting we get several appetizers to start, along with burgers, fries, milkshakes, and at least two slices of pie for dessert.

"Do you like yours a la mode?" She finally tilts her menu down to look at me.

"How many other people are joining us for dinner? You want to order one of everything on the menu." I laugh and set mine down.

"No, I don't. I definitely do not want the soup. Or the chili. I've had enough of both to last me a lifetime." She sighs. "You're right, though. My eyes are definitely bigger than my stomach. I'm going to get a double bacon cheeseburger, fries, and a chocolate shake, malted if they have those here. And pie. And probably a slice to go so I can also have pie for breakfast tomorrow because pie is my absolute favorite."

"Sounds like a plan." I nod, glancing around for our waitress.

Daisy herself sees me looking and walks over to our table instead.

"Ranger Daniels, good to see you." She flashes me her warm smile. "Who's your friend?"

I've been calling her Snowbird for the past two days, but using a trail name out in civilization is weird. How much of an explanation should I give? The pause between her question and my answer lengthens as I debate what to say. I feel two sets of eyes watching me.

"I'm Olive." Snowbird waves at Daisy, but her eyes flash to mine. "Nice to meet you."

"You too," Daisy says. "What can I get you?"

We place our orders and she leaves.

Olive sounds like a trail name. It's pretty, but it's going to take me a while to think of her as anything other than Snowbird.

"Olive, huh? Just come to you?" I tease her.

"Nope. It's my name. Want to see my ID?" She pats her pockets. "Darn it. I left my wallet in my backpack."

I arch an eyebrow. "Convenient."

She laughs at my dry tone. "I'll pay you back. Trust me, I'm good for it."

"How can I trust you when I only met you three minutes ago, Olive? If that is your real name." I keep my tone light.

"Just because my name isn't pinned or sewn onto my clothing doesn't mean it's not mine," she teases back.

"Olive," I repeat the word. "It suits you."

"Why? Because I'm dressed in green?"

I laugh because she's right about the color of her outfit. "I had no idea when I bought it for you. The options were limited."

"I'm not ungrateful. It was sweet of you."

"Don't tell anyone. I have a reputation as a grumpy misanthrope to uphold." I frown to prove my point.

Her mouth pops open. "Who calls you that?"

"My sister, mostly. At least to my face."

"Siblings don't count. My older sister calls me a flake. I mean, she's not wrong. Or at least she was right about younger me. Doesn't matter how old we get, our family sees us the way we were as kids. Cryogenically suspended in time."

We don't know each other. Not after two days.

Hell, I only learned her real name a few minutes ago.

It doesn't matter, though.

This connection I feel with her is real.

* * *

Two extra pieces of pie tucked inside a paper bag sit on my kitchen counter, a slice of coconut cream and a slice of pecan.

Snowbird—I mean Olive—keeps staring at them.

"If you want to have your second piece tonight, you should just eat it instead of gazing longingly at it from across the room." I poke her ankle with my foot.

We're sprawled on opposite ends of my sofa. I have my feet on the dinged and scratched coffee table I inherited when I took over this cabin. Same goes for the couch. It predates me by at least a decade. The only thing in here belonging to me are my mattress and the family photos. Everything else will stay after I leave, whenever that day comes. I don't plan to live in ranger quarters for the rest of my life.

Someday I'd like to have a partner and a family if we're lucky. We'll spend our evenings together, hanging out at home. Not unlike tonight.

I'm not having these thoughts about Olive.

Of course not.

Nor did I think of her naked in my bathroom and have to take matters into hand, so to speak, while I took my own shower.

From the far end of the couch, she yawns, mouth wide, her head tipping back.

"We should go to bed." I nudge her foot with mine again.

"I thought you'd never ask." Standing, she stretches. "Do you have extra sheets and blankets?"

"Why?"

"So I can make up the couch?"

I give her a blank stare. "I'm not going to make you sleep out here."

"I can't make you give up your bed."

"Didn't we already have this discussion earlier?" I stand up, too.

"I'm not comfortable sharing a bed with a guy who has a girl-friend," she explains, her words tumbling together with how quickly she speaks.

"Who has a girlfriend?" I'm not denying. I'm confused.

"Don't lie. I saw the picture in your bedroom." She sits back down. "I'm fine sleeping here."

"What photo?"

"The two of you are hugging, looking adorable and in love. She's pretty."

I dip my head before rolling it back on my neck to stare at the ceiling. "You're talking about my sister."

Uncomfortable but not ashamed, I decide we're having this conversation now. "Follow me."

Without waiting for her, I head down the hall to my bedroom. The frames on my dresser haven't been moved, so I assume Olive didn't look at all of them.

She pauses in the doorway.

"Is this the photo you're talking about?" I point at the small silver frame.

With a nod, she confirms it is.

"In case you're wondering, neither of us was adopted." My voice bristles with old defensiveness.

Her brows scrunch together. "You don't look anything alike. Is this your dad? You have the same hair color.

"It is. Most people say I resemble him. I was six in this picture. My dad took us all to an auto show. He lived for cars." I slide it to the right and pick up a smaller gold frame tucked behind the silver one. "And this is my mom holding me."

She takes the frame from me and lifts it closer to her face to study the image. "This is you? You're such a chubby baby."

It isn't the comment I'm expecting. "Yes, I just said it was me. And my mother."

"She's beautiful." She shifts her gaze to my face. "You have her smile. Your sister does too. There's definitely a resemblance. Sorry I accused you of dating your sister."

"You're missing the elephant in the room." I point at the picture of me as a baby. "My mom is Japanese."

"I see." She tilts her head. "Was she born here or in Japan?"

"In Japan. My dad worked over there in the late eighties and met my mom."

"How sweet." Her mouth curls into a small smile. "Oh, that's why you've been there, and why you said your mom doesn't have family close by. Makes sense."

"That's it?"

After a quick glance at the photos, she focuses on me again. "What am I missing?"

"You don't think this is a big deal?"

"Why should it be? I know a lot of people from different ethnicities and backgrounds. My best friend Campbell is half Persian, half Dutch from Kansas. Her boyfriend is Irish, German and Taiwanese. You never asked about my background either—I'm an American mutt, in case you were wondering."

Now I feel stupid for acting like I have this big secret. I sit down on the end of my bed. "My entire life I've dealt with being *hāfu*."

"You've lost me. I'm sorry, but I don't know what *hāfu* means." She sits next to me.

"It means someone with one Japanese parent and one non-Japanese parent. Often, it's used in a derogatory way. I don't fit in with either the Japanese or the American sides of my family." I stare at the family photographs. "I'm both, but I'm also neither, which makes me nothing."

"I disagree." She touches my knee. "I can tell this is a big deal to you. I don't understand, but I'd like to."

Exhaling, I brace myself. "Everyone says I look exactly like my dad. You saw the photo. I've always been his mirror image, except my eyes are more similar to my mother's and I never got his thick chest hair. Otherwise, it's obvious we're related."

"I can definitely see the resemblance."

"It means I look white."

"But you are white, no more, no less than you are Japanese. It shouldn't matter." Her voice is gentle.

"Ah, there's the issue. Half doesn't count when you look like my sister. She has our mom's dark hair and Japanese features. People used to assume my mother was my babysitter."

Olive blows out a long breath. "Ouch."

"Yeah. Then there's me. I pass."

"You pass?"

"As a white guy. Even you called me white back at the cabin, like I'm king of the world because I have a dick and light skin."

She cringes. "I assumed. I'm sorry."

"You don't have to apologize. Most people do." I shrug off her apology. "The funny thing is I'm not Japanese enough for my mother's family. They see my dad when they look at me, and they were never fans of his because he wasn't Japanese. That, and he took my mom with him back to America."

For a few moments, we sit in silence. "Because of our biases, we assume others who look like us must be like us. Doesn't mean you need to wear a name tag declaring your ethnic background. This isn't the 1940s."

"No, this is America now. Growing up, both my sister and mother bore the brunt of bigotry. I didn't. She suffered through racist jokes where she was the punchline and sexist comments about being a geisha, had assumptions made about her personality, and was the object of attention from guys with a fetish for Asian women. Same for my mom. Not me. The worse I get is someone asking me where I'm from or where I was born, like they sense I'm different, but can't put their finger on it. So yeah, I have some issues." Exhaling, I knot my hands between my knees and dip my chin to my chest.

She doesn't say anything, just slips her fingers into the space between mine.

We sit together holding hands for a while.

CHAPTER TWENTY-THREE

JAY

*W*e fell asleep on top of my bed last night, fully clothed and holding hands, passing out after a long day of hiking and an evening topped off with me dragging my emotional baggage out into the open. I think my body shut down, not from exhaustion so much as self-preservation.

Sharing about my family and my failings isn't something I do on the regular. Or ever. Normally, I avoid all discussion of my life. Easy to do most of the time. Yet, for some reason, I dumped out the entire mess to Olive last night.

The therapist I had to see in high school would be proud of me for opening up. After too many fights, my mom negotiated with the principal: therapy instead of expulsion. Dr. Nielsen taught me coping skills. They worked too well. Instead of random explosions of violence, I switched to locking everything down. Avoiding people became easier than risking confrontation or facing rejection.

And then Olive showed up.

Beautiful, nutty, strong, stubborn, sexy Olive.

* * *

There's a staff meeting this morning to discuss storm damage, so I leave Olive asleep on my bed after covering her with a blanket. She doesn't stir at all. I can't imagine how exhausted she must be after months on the trail.

After leaving her a note explaining how to operate my coffee machine and when I'll be back, I head over to the main ranger station.

For some reason, Cletus Winston is pouring a cup of coffee from his thermos in the employee lounge. Bearded like his other brothers, but stockier, he reminds me of Jethro.

"Morning, Ranger Daniels. Can I interest you in a hearty morning beverage? I brewed it myself knowing how weak and disappointing the coffee is here." His hazel eyes challenging me to disagree with his assessment.

The strong scent of molasses barely masks the tang of warm apple cider vinegar in the steam hovering above his coffee.

"No, thanks. I'm good." I hold my hands up to ward off the toxic cloud.

"Sure about that? This will fortify you for whatever awaits. Good for your digestion, too." He waves the mug from side to side between us. "How is your digestion these days?"

I'm not going to share personal information with him or anyone else, so I stand quietly waiting for him to move on to the next topic or someone to interrupt us.

"What's the awful stench? Are we having a skunk problem again?" Guy asks before cutting herself off. "Oh, hi, Cletus."

Our guest grumbles about skunks and bear relocation. "The problem is with procreation and an overpopulation of progeny."

Griffin enters the room. "This is why we need a skunk adoption program. I keep telling you they're going to be the new ferret in pet trends. Once their mercaptan production is eliminated with the removal of their scent glands, they're good to go. Why should weasels get all the glamor and glory?"

Guy closes her eyes briefly before she seeks me out with a pleading expression. With a single look passing between us, an entire conversation takes place. "Griffin, I like your creative, out-of-the-box thinking, but we have protocols in place that we need to follow."

"The US Department of Agriculture issues permits to breeders. I've done my research with the Domestic Skunks of America Owners Association." He begins to plead his case for a skunk adoption day next spring.

"Hold on," I interrupt him. "We are not getting into the business of illegal skunk trade. It's our duty to protect wildlife, not sell it. If you need to complain to someone, bend the game warden's ear or call your senator."

At his sides, Griffin's hands ball into fists and then open again. "Nothing will ever change if we wait for politicians to lead us. The revolution must start at home."

Guy's eyes open wider, and Cletus pauses with his mug halfway to his mouth.

"Just kidding." Griffin bursts out laughing. "It's a quote. In a movie. You should see all y'all's faces right now."

Doing what she does best and ignoring him, Guy asks Cletus, "What brings you to the ranger station this fine morning?"

"Dr. Runous and I have an appointment to discuss wild boar. I have a new sausage recipe I'm testing. According to TCA 70-4-115 of the Tennessee state code, I can legally possess wild boar if it isn't a federally protected species and as long as I use the meat for personal consumption. My understanding is if someone hits a boar and doesn't want the carcass, I can claim it. Much easier than going into the mountains and hunting one."

"I don't think we have a phone tree for roadkill," I tell him.

"Well, we should." Griffin adds his two cents even though no one asked him. "Some folks like to honor the traditional foods. Venison, boar, and even squirrel can be good eating."

First, he wants to domesticate skunks and now he's talking about mountain delicacies.

Cletus nods, slurping his brew. "Shame when all the old recipes are lost because no one wrote any down unless the ladies of the Methodist

Church have some copies in their cookbook archives. Someone should check in their basement."

If this conversation is any indication of the rest of my day, I should turn around and go back to bed, skip the meeting entirely.

I wonder if Olive is awake yet.

I could bring her a real cup of coffee. The campground store recently got an espresso machine and their egg sandwiches are made with thick-cut bacon. It's the best thing on their menu.

As I'm debating my exit strategy, Dr. Runous arrives with Ed, the head ranger.

* * *

"Jay, you have a minute?" Ed stops me as I walk out of the small conference room at the end of the group meeting.

There's enough weather-related damage at the higher elevations that the AT will stay closed for at least three more days. That said we don't have enough personnel to guard all the trailheads to prevent people from stealth hiking at their own risk. The best we can do is post signs and warnings.

Other than some extra work, I'm happy about the closure. Means spending a few more days with Olive. Not mad about it at all.

"Sure, of course," I respond to Ed's question.

"Let's talk in my office." With a friendly smile, he gestures for me to follow him down the hall to the back of the station.

He shuts the door behind me while I stand in the middle of the room, unsure if I should sit, hoping this will be a quick enough conversation that standing will be fine.

"Have a seat." Ed gestures at the old rust colored upholstered chair opposite his desk. Running my hand over the frayed edge of the hideous seat cushion, I wonder if the chair showed up the same time Ed did. I swear all the furniture in this place was purchased in the nineties and has never been updated.

After complying, I cross my ankle on my knee. "Everything okay?"

Being a worrier by nature means my brain is already coming up with scenarios where I could be in trouble. The AT sweep is top of the list. Had I not disobeyed Guy's warning, I never would've gotten stuck in a cabin for two days. Rangers should be the search party, not lost in the woods.

"If this is about the storm rescue—"

"I wanted to talk to you about my retirement."

"—I can explain," I continue. "Wait, what?"

"Hold on, what are you talking about?" He leans back in his office chair.

"Getting stuck in the old moonshiner's place with the solo female hiker?" I pick at the hem of my pants.

He tips forward, resting his forearms on the desk. "And? No one died up on the mountain, right?"

I dip my chin.

With a shrug, he dismisses my concerns. "Then I'd say you did your job successfully, which brings me back to why I wanted to speak with you. I'll be retiring early next year. Time for a change around here."

"Congratulations." I flash him a genuine smile. "You going to buy an RV and travel the country?"

"Maybe. Marcia has another couple of years of teaching to get her retirement. Kids are spread out all over the country, and she misses the grandkids." He straightens the files and lines up his pens. "Making myself sound old."

"Nah, you're still in your prime," I lie.

Ed's been a father figure to me since I started here five years ago. Fresh out of grad school and eager to prove myself, I was kind of a kiss-ass the first couple of years I worked for him. Somehow he got me, and understood my need for solitary assignments and lots of space.

"I want you to take over as chief ranger," he declares in a tone that warns me not to argue with his decision. "You've proved yourself and will make a great leader. Of course, there's the added bonus that you'll increase our diversity at the management level."

No, no, no. I don't want to manage people. I'm happy being a peer, not a boss, and me ticking off the Asian box doesn't make the work-place more diverse if everyone assumes I'm another white guy.

Ignoring his declaration, I protest. "What about Gaia? She's been here as long as I have, maybe even a year or two longer, and she has her Masters in environmental management and conservation. No one here is more qualified than she is."

Plus, she likes people. Well, everyone except Griffin, but she knows how to manage him, which proves she can handle difficult employees.

Ed brushes his index finger over his white mustache. "You're saying you don't want the job?"

Do I? "I'm happy being a wildlife ecologist and resident avian specialist."

"There's more to life than birds, Daniels."

A tangle of dark hair. Soft skin and delicate fingers. My mind conjures up images of Olive asleep on my bed.

"I know." My voice is hoarse, so I clear my throat. "I'm happy doing what I do. I've applied for a grant for a new research project starting next year if I get the funding. I feel I can best serve the park in a scientific capacity."

Ed studies me, his finger still petting his facial hair. "Most people want to advance in their careers. The money is better."

"I already have my dream job, and it doesn't involve pushing papers and sitting in an office. No offense." I cringe at the uninten-tional insult. "I spent summers working as a seasonal ranger out in Yellowstone and Grand Teton, hoping someday later in my career a position would open up in the Smokies. These mountains are my home. With promotion comes more responsibilities and expectations."

More exposure to people and society, which I try to avoid.

"What if I tell you it's temporary? As a federal position, it will be posted nationally. No guarantee any local applicants will get it."

I'm not sure if he's trying to reassure or deter me.

"An even better reason to appoint Gaia. We both know she's better at the soft skills. Other than Griffin, she enjoys the company of people."

Ed knots his fingers together behind his head. I'm being studied with a familiar look, observed like one of the creatures we're charged with protecting. A rare and unusual species.

"You're kind of an odd duck, Daniels."

He's not the first to say this about me. "To an ornithologist, being called a duck isn't an insult."

"Figured. Okay, I'll take your comments under advisement. Don't tell anyone about this conversation, especially not Gaia. If I change my mind, no need for her to feel like second best."

"What conversation?" Standing, I wait for him to respond.

He plays along. "Exactly."

Dismissed, I casually exit and run right into Guy.

"Everything okay?" she asks, peering over my shoulder.

I shuffle both of us down the hall. "Totally fine. Ed's happy as long as everyone makes it out alive. Less paperwork."

"Good. What happened with your hiker? Did she head into town until the AT reopens?"

"No, she's still here." I avert my eyes. "Any word on when we'll officially open the trails? We encountered a lot of debris and blocks on our way down Anthony's Creek."

"Thru-hikers can head back out in a couple of days unless we get more weather. The Appalachian Trail Club is advising everyone to stay put on their message boards. If it were me, I'd be eager to finish before more snow arrives."

A couple of days.

My time with Olive officially has an expiration date.

"Aren't you off today?" Guy reminds me.

"I am. Probably gonna head back to my cabin and get some laundry done. Catch up on sleep."

"Speaking of laundry," she says with a sly look. "I went to do mine last night and found some hiker gear in the dryer. You think one of the campers snuck over to our quarters? Weird, huh, given the door was locked and only rangers have keys. Wonder if I should bring it up to Ed. What do you think?"

Her warm brown eyes sparkle with knowing there's no security issue.

I completely forgot about her laundry. "It's none of your business, but Olive stayed at my place last night. I did a load of her laundry because it was covered in mud."

Guy's mouth pops open. "Repeat the first part. Olive?"

"The hiker I was stranded with. No big deal. By the time we hiked back, the campground was full."

"And you invited her to stay with you?" She presses the cool back of her hand to my forehead.

I jerk my head away. "What are you doing?"

"Checking to see if you're delirious with fever after your arduous hike."

"I'm fine," I grumble. "Quit making a mountain out of a molehill."

"When was the last time you had a woman in your place who wasn't me?" She stares me down.

"I have no idea." I keep my tone flat and disinterested so she'll hopefully take the hint that this isn't a conversation I want to have right now. Or ever.

I've dated over the last five years. Not often and not seriously, but I haven't lived the life of a monk. Not completely. I don't appreciate what she's implying.

"Is Olive her trail name?"

"No, she goes by Snowbird."

Something shifts behind Guy's eyes. "Olive? Dark hair? Blue eyes? Heart-shaped face? Curvy?"

"How do you know what she looks like?" I glance behind me to make sure Olive isn't standing there. Confused, I ask, "Did you see us in the park last night? Or at Daisy's?"

"Oh my god. She's still here?" Guy's voice goes up an octave.

Not sure why she's so excited, I explain, "I think she's still asleep back in my cabin. You can meet her later—*if* you stop acting like a weirdo about me hanging out with a woman."

I'm seriously concerned Guy might scare Olive away with her intensity about my romantic life.

She gives me another strange look, her hand squeezing my arm. "You don't know, do you?

"Huh? Know what?"

"Oh, Jay." With her hand tucked around my elbow, she drags me to her desk and plops me down in her office chair. Leaning over me, she opens a brower window and types something.

"If you're sitting me down for the birds and the bees talk ..." I stop talking as she hits enter.

Olive's face fills the row of images at the top of the page. The name Olive Perry repeats over and over again on the screen.

"What the hell?"

"Your hiker is Olive Perry," she explains.

"I can read," I grumble.

"Have you heard of the Runaway Fiancée?" Guy clicks on the first link.

"No. You know I don't watch reality TV."

"This isn't a show." She leans away so I can read the screen.

Olive Perry, 29, granddaughter of former President Theodore Perry, earned the nickname the Runaway Fiancée after she called off her third engagement. Now she's done it again. A live video that captivated everyone's attention shows a romantic mountain top proposal from her boyfriend Sutton "Tye" Wallingford III. No wedding date announced yet. Scroll down for pics of the gorgeous ring and the happy couple. We all hope the sixth time is the charm for Olive.

It's possible my Olive has a doppelgänger. I tell myself this until I get to the first image. Staring back at me is Snowbird, wearing her blue backpack and grinning at the camera while a blond man kisses her cheek.

"Maybe my hiker is a different Olive?" My voice sounds weird to my ears.

"You okay, Jay?" Guy places her hand on my shoulder.

"I'm ..." I have to clear my throat "Fine."

"Not to get personal, but you didn't sleep with her, did you?"

I want to ask her to define sleep, but I don't. "No."

"Okay, good. Sorry I assumed anything happened."

I flinch at the pity in her tone.

"Yeah, no worries. I'd probably think the same thing if I found men's underwear in your laundry. We should probably set up a rotation so we don't have conflicts with the machines. Missing socks are already a problem around here." I don't know what I'm saying. Words spill out of my mouth in a rush. "I should go."

I stand up quickly, sending the chair spinning on its wheels.

"You sure you're okay?" Guy's eyes hold sympathy and her forehead is lined with worry.

"Of course." I look away. "I'll see you tomorrow."

Shoving open the front door of the station, I walk outside and then pause. I have no idea where I'm going.

Should I wake Olive and confront her?

Avoid my cabin and hope she decides to leave on her own and I never have to see her again?

Pretend nothing has changed? Pretend I didn't open myself up to her, the first time I've done so in ages?

Storm back to my place and confront her while I'm feeling … what? Anger? Hurt? Disappointment? Sadness? All of the above?

I need to calm down, restore the protective layers I peeled away last night.

Instead of turning right to return to my cabin, I make a left.

CHAPTER TWENTY-FOUR

OLIVE

*A*fter finding Jay's sweet note, I set the coffee machine to brew while I take my second shower in the last fourteen hours. I'm going to soak up every joyful moment of hot water and fluffy towels I can before I get back on the trail.

Ever since I began my SoBo hike, I've been focused on finishing the AT, enjoying the moments but not the miles.

Now I'm sad when I think about leaving and saying goodbye to Jay.

Which is ridiculous.

We've known each other for three days.

I can't be falling for him.

A quiet voice in the center of my chest whispers, "Oh, but what if you are?"

No, no, no.

I try to ignore the way my heartbeat quickens with the idea of falling in love with Jay.

You could stay and find out if he feels the same, my heart whispers.

My breath stalls in my throat. This isn't rational. I can't stay here. What would I do? Work in the campground store? I'm not qualified to be a ranger. I'd suck as a diner waitress.

What am I doing? I stop this crazy train of thought.

I have a goal, and I'm within ten days of completing it.

Once I have the all-clear on the trail, I'll walk out of here, leaving the way I arrived.

I may have started this trek because of a guy, but I'm not going to bail because of a guy.

There's no indication Jay wants me to stay.

We're not together.

That kiss, though …

He kissed me back, slowly taking control of what I started.

And he did open up to me last night, revealing parts of himself I don't think he shares with most people. Which makes me feel like an even bigger asshole for my own assumptions. I hate how he feels like he doesn't belong.

I hate how well I can relate.

Feeling guilty for all the hot water I've used during my existential crisis, I turn off the shower and dry off.

Dressed in my new favorite sweats, I pour coffee and ponder what I should do with my morning until Jay returns.

Reorganizing my pack and jettisoning anything I won't need for the next week and a half sounds like a productive way to spend my downtime. I will not spend the morning fantasizing about the ranger. Definitely not about the fit of his olive cargo pants or the strange fluttering low in my belly whenever I see his hat.

* * *

For some reason, my pack is lighter than normal. I unload the gear from it and stare in confusion at the small piles. Among my reduced food stash, the Cartier box stands out. Ugh. I hate it. Soon I'll be able to give the ring back and be done with my old life.

"Where are all my clothes?" Perplexed, I sweep my gaze around the room. "I had them when I arrived last night," I mumble.

Takes me at least five minutes to realize I gave them to Jay to wash and I don't remember ever getting them back.

My shoes still sit outside the front door, a small breadcrumb Jay dropped for me to figure out his background. How many others did I miss?

Sounds of vehicles, conversations, and birdsong fill the air of the campground. I don't see anyone near the cabins to ask where I can find the laundry room, so I wander around.

I smell fabric softener and follow the scent to the end of a low building. The door is held open by a large, river rock wedged next to the jamb. Inside, my meager pile of clothes are folded on top of the dryer. I check to make sure everything is there, including my under- wear. Grateful for the laundry fairy, I scoop everything into my arms then walk out the door.

And right into a woman in a ranger uniform.

"Sorry," I huff out.

"Miss, this laundry is reserved for staff. You'll need to use the one in the main campground area." She's stern but not unfriendly as she chastises me.

"I'm all set." I clutch my clothes against my chest.

Her attention shifts from the pile in my arms to my face.

"You're Olive Perry," she states, eyes wide with surprise. It isn't a question; she recognizes me.

I want to say no, she has me confused with someone else, explain my name is Snowbird. However, she's a ranger. Which means she's a colleague of Jay. Sweet Jay who doesn't know who I really am.

Unable to find my voice to lie, I simply nod in agreement.

"You're the hiker Ranger Daniels rescued." Her attention shifts to my clothes. "He told me he did your laundry. He's a good guy. One of the best."

"Rescued might be exaggerating a bit. I would've been fine if I had to camp at altitude." I straighten my spine and roll my shoulders back. "While we might disagree about what happened on the mountain, I agree he's a good man."

I don't know this woman's relationship to Jay, but I know territory- marking when I see it. She thinks she knows me and doesn't want me anywhere near him.

"By the way, congratulations on your engagement." She says this casually like we're old friends who haven't seen each other in ages, just two women chatting about our lives.

And then I know.

My real life has caught up with me in Tennessee.

"Where did you hear I'm engaged?" I keep my tone even, nonchalant.

"The announcement was everywhere a few months ago. Died down after you refused to make a public appearance and your family didn't comment to the press." She gives me a pointed look.

This is good news. If everyone has moved on from Tye's stunt, it will be easier to move on with my life without the added scrutiny of the masses.

"Thanks for the update. I've been hiking the AT solo for the past five months, so I'm completely out of the loop when it comes to gossip." My grin would be the envy of the Cheshire Cat.

Her lids close almost all the way as she stares at me. When she begins laughing, I'm caught off guard.

"I like you. I can see why you were able to crack through Jay's grumpy veneer."

I have no interest in her approval or disapproval of me, yet relief still floats through my body. If she's close to him, I don't want her as an adversary.

This woman makes me nervous with her directness. "By the way, who are you?"

"Gaia." She doesn't offer her hand.

Named for the Mother Earth goddess. No wonder she's fierce.

"You obviously know who I am."

She gives a quick bob of her chin. "Only the gossip I've read online."

"I think I like you, too." I laugh, the fight-or-flight tension leaving my body.

She goes back to her serious expression. "Don't hurt him."

"I don't plan to."

Her eyes meet mine again with a meaningful stare. "Good."

"It was nice meeting you," I saw, awkwardly because this hasn't been nice. Not at all. "I should get back to my packing."

Shaken after my encounter with Gaia, I realize I need to come clean with Jay. If his colleague knows the truth, does he?

Panicked at what's going through his mind and what stories he's believing, I run back to his cabin.

When I open the door, I find Jay standing over my things.

"We should talk," he says, his eyes cold and his jaw locked.

He knows. Or thinks he does.

CHAPTER TWENTY-FIVE

JAY

*N*eeding to clear my head and quiet my emotions, I take a walk after Guy shows me the articles about Olive.

I scroll through the memories of our conversations, looking for the clues I missed. She never used any first or last names when talking about her family. Then again, neither did I.

Her grandfather is retired. True. He lives on acreage in California with cows—more like a large ranch, but still true. He supports the national parks—also true, but not through donating money. He created thirty-four new monuments and protected over half a billion acres, more than even Roosevelt.

Theodore Perry did more for land conservation than anyone since Wilson created the national park system. He's a hero among Park Service employees.

Olive never mentioned any of it to me. Rationally, I know I shouldn't feel betrayed. We barely know each other, having only spent half a week in each other's company. For all intents and purposes, we're strangers. Casual acquaintances at best.

How does someone casually disclose their family connections?

I never told her about how my mom's father, the CEO of a

Japanese car maker, disowned her when she fell in love with my father. How she gave up her trust fund to move to America and build a life with him. Seems we both kept some family secrets to ourselves.

Once I'm calm again, I walk back to my cabin.

Olive isn't there, and my first thought is she's already left the park without saying goodbye.

I notice her pack and the small pile of her belongings on the floor. Reassured she wouldn't leave those behind, I study the contents.

A red jewelry box from Cartier draws my attention. I've never seen it before. Then I remember how protective Olive has been about her bag.

Why would she still have the ring if she's not engaged?

I'm only standing there for a minute or two before she comes flying through the door like she's being chased by a bear.

"We should talk." I can barely get the words out.

"I know," she says, breathless. Beautiful.

"You're Olive Perry. Your grandfather with the cows on some acreage is a former president."

"Both true." Her eyes are wary, nervous. "Jay, whatever you think you know, I can explain."

Having trouble meeting her stare, I drop my gaze to the floor. "How about the ring?"

Tossing her clean laundry on the floor, she picks up the box and places it into my hand. "Open it," she commands. "I have nothing to hide."

Inside, nestled on white fabric is the largest diamond I've ever seen in person.

"Is this real?" My eyes snap to her face.

She nods. "Of course."

"And you've had it with you the whole time?" My stomach sours at the idea of her truly being engaged to another man.

"Since Massachusetts, yes."

"This has to be worth a fortune."

"Depends on the fortune, I guess."

"More than I make in a year?" I cringe at the question. We both know it is. NPS employees don't do these jobs for the money.

With a sad smile, she bobs her head yes.

I study the facets of the sparkling rock, thinking about how nature is simultaneously incredible and cruel.

"The size of the ring means nothing to me. It never has." Emotion clogs her voice. "Love shouldn't be correlated with carat size. True love can't be bought."

"Why do you still have his ring?" I close the box and hand it back to her. "I thought he dumped you."

She exhales. "He did, after he proposed and I said no. He left before I could give it back. I've been stuck with it."

"Why not mail it back to him?"

"Would you trust the post office to not lose it?" She cocks her head.

"Probably not. Why didn't you tell me back at the cabin?"

"The first night? Because you were a stranger and my entire life I've been raised to keep secrets. I didn't lie to you. My relationship with Tye was over months before we met."

"According to the media, it isn't."

She flinches. When she stares up at me, her expression is defeated.

"Really? You're going to believe them over me? They don't have the whole story. Everything they know is based off of a few pictures on Tye's social media feed and an unfortunate live video."

"So you're not engaged anymore?" My voice sounds foreign to my ears, disconnected and weary.

She flings her arms out in exasperation. "Tye and I were never engaged. Aren't you listening? I never accepted. I'll make him issue a statement, a retraction."

This should make me feel better, but it doesn't.

"And the other ones?" I ask.

Her lips pull into a pout. "What are you referring to?"

"The other times you did say yes. How many were there? Four?" My tone is cruel and full of hurt.

She grimaces. "Five."

I lock my jaw, grinding my teeth together to the point a muscle ticks in my cheek. "I see."

"You don't," she argues, but there's no fight left in her voice.

"No, I think I do—clearly for the first time."

With a sigh, her shoulders slump. "I guess it doesn't matter if I tell you I was young and under a lot of pressure to settle down, to make a good match. I never went through with a single wedding. Didn't even come close."

"Did you love them all?" I hate that I care.

"At the time, I thought I did. Now, I'm not sure I've ever been in love with anyone. Until recently." Her eyes are full of unspoken words.

My frown deepens. "What changed your mind?"

"You."

"Don't." I cross to the other side of the room. "This is crazy."

We haven't known each other long enough to have genuine feelings. There's no such thing as insta-love.

Her eyes water and her smile barely curves. "It's true. Even if we never see each other again, I'm different because of you."

"You're confusing bonding over trauma with other emotions." I dismiss her confession because I'm not willing to admit the same is true for me.

"Okay, you're right." She sighs again, resigned. "I'm not emotionally aware enough to know myself and what I feel. Thank you for explaining it to me so clearly."

Did she ... did she just accuse me of mansplaining?

"You know I didn't mean it like that."

"No, you're right. We don't know each other at all." She kneels on the floor and quickly stuffs her belongings inside her pack.

I scrub my hands over my face. "Olive, I'm sorry if I gave you the wrong idea."

"Don't." She holds up her hand to stop me. "You didn't do anything. I have a problem with falling in love. Can't seem to help myself."

Standing, she straps her pack on before glancing back at me over her shoulder. "Bye, Jay."

Rationally, the right thing to do is let her go. We come from two different worlds and have nothing in common. She's a serial monogamist with commitment issues. I'm a loner with trust issues.

We could never work.

This is for the best.

Yet I know when I look back at this moment, I'll regret watching her walk out my door.

CHAPTER TWENTY-SIX

OLIVE

*I*f you scream your lungs out in frustration and no one is around to hear you, does it matter?

I'm not mad about Jay's hesitation to believe me. When it comes to love, I've proven myself to be fickle. My heart is undependable.

The only person to blame is me, the old Olive, who always said yes even when she meant no.

There are too many people around for me to release the primal scream I want to unleash. Instead, I stomp across the campground.

It isn't nearly as satisfying.

My mission is to find some hiker trash and set up camp with them. Or better yet, convince someone to hit the trail today. Sun's been out for hours. Snow's melting. We can traverse any blocks or slides we encounter.

Because we are AT thru-hikers. Hear us roar.

I'm smart enough to know I shouldn't head out on my own. The last thing I want is a nice ranger being forced to bring me back here.

My bag begins ringing when I'm halfway down the main road. Weird. I don't remember turning it on today. Or turning it off after sending the selfie to Campbell.

The sound of my old ringtone is unfamiliar to my ears after months of not hearing it.

Deciding if I ignore it, it will go away, I keep walking.

And the phone continues ringing.

"Fine," I shout to the sky, the only witness to my frustration.

My mother is calling me.

Perfect timing.

"Hi, Mom." I do my best to keep the exasperation out of my voice.

"Olive, do you ever think about anyone but yourself?" She doesn't give me the same courtesy. Annoyance bleeds into her words.

Excellent. Who else can I disappoint today?

"We've tried to tolerate your whims and fancies, your need to always be different, but this is unacceptable. For weeks, no one has known where you were or how to contact you. You may be able to run away from your romantic obligations, but—"

I cut her off. "Is there a point to your call? Because I'm very aware of all of my failings and really don't need the reminder today. I've been updating Campbell every time I've had service."

"I'm well aware. That's how we tracked you to Tennessee."

Our conversation from months ago comes back to mind. The subtle methods my family uses to maintain knowledge about my life without direct contact.

She sighs. "I know the two of you were close when you were little. This will be difficult for you to hear, but it should come from me before you pick up a newspaper or see it on television."

I'm about to tell her I haven't done either since June when the meaning of her words hit me.

"What's happened to Grandfather? I spoke to him not long ago." I try to remember when I last called him. The hotel in Damascus. A week? Ten days? The conversation was short and he sounded tired, but he laughed when I rambled about my adventures.

"As you know, he never fully recovered from the stroke last year and has been slowly declining ever since." I hate how disconnected she sounds.

"Did ..." I gulp air. "Did he die?"

"No, but hospice doesn't think he has much time left."

"I need to see him. I need to say goodbye." I start running but then stop when I realize I can't run all the way to California.

"Exactly why I've been calling. You have a ticket waiting for you in Knoxville. A car is on the way to pick you up." There's rustling and muffled conversation in the background. "Sorry. Where was I? Right. The car should arrive at the Cades Cove ranger station at eleven-thirty. Can you be there or do we need to make other arrangements?"

"How do you know where I am?" I spin around.

"We tracked your phone. At least we didn't have to send out a search party."

Checking the time on my screen, I see I have ten minutes before my ride will arrive. "I'll be there."

"Good. We'll see you in California. Be safe."

She ends the call.

"Love you, too." Tears fill my eyes.

Adjusting my pack, I quickly follow the signs to the station. The walk only takes me five minutes, so I linger across the road outside the store, hoping to avoid running into Jay.

A black Tahoe with tinted windows winds its way down the drive, slowing as it approaches me. I hold up my arm so the driver knows I'm here.

"Olive!" Jay's voice calls from the entrance to the station.

Our eyes meet briefly and I give him a small, sad wave.

He doesn't walk toward me, but his eyes search mine.

The SUV passes me, blocking my view for a few seconds. The driver gestures to let me know he's going to turn around.

My eyes seek Jay again.

He's still standing by the door, watching me.

I don't know whether to apologize again or tell him I love him. Neither would make a difference.

Checking for traffic, he jogs over to me.

"Olive? Are you okay? You just left, and I should've followed you. I'm sorry I didn't." He stuffs his hands in his front pockets.

The Tahoe pulls up behind him, and he glances over his shoulder as a man in a classic security guard dark suit hops out and opens the rear passenger door.

"What's going on?" His eyes search mine.

"I have to go." Hot tears burn my eyes. Without asking permission, I invade his personal space one last time to hug him. I don't even care if he hugs me back.

When his arms wrap around my shoulders and he tucks me close to his chest, the dam threatens to break. I cannot cry in front of him.

Wiggling out of his embrace, I stare at his boots for a second.

He gently lifts my chin with his finger. Confusion, sadness, and another emotion swirl in his beautiful green eyes.

"Ready, Miss Perry? We need to get on the road or you'll miss your flight." The security guard stands awkwardly a few feet away. "I can take your bag."

Jay's attention swings between the man and me. "You're leaving? You're not going to complete the AT? How can you quit now when you're so close?"

"Goodbye, Ranger Daniels. Thanks again for all of your help." I extend my hand.

Reluctantly, he shakes it. "Always happy to be of service."

He stares at me like I've lost my mind.

Maybe I have.

All I know is my heart is breaking and I'm leaving part of it behind with him.

* * *

Left, right, left. Repeat.

One step leads to another as I walk to the open passenger door.

I refuse to look at Jay again.

"Watch your head," Mr. Security instructs me.

His warning only adds to the feeling of being arrested and detained against my will.

I wish I had time to explain everything to Jay. How my grandfather is dying and I'm filled with guilt over not being in better touch with him. How no one can know because then the media will start the death watch and our private grief will become national mourning.

I'd try to get him to see how an omission isn't always a lie. How who I'm related to doesn't change the time we spent together. How I'm not the same person I used to be and I'm not sure I ever want to go back to being her.

Instead, I close my eyes and rest my head against the seat, unwilling to watch the park disappear behind me as the Tahoe drives away.

I must fall asleep because the security guard is standing by my open door, his hand gentle on my shoulder.

Blinking away the fog of my nap, I remember who he is and why I'm in the backseat. "Are we here?"

"We're in Knoxville, ma'am." His warm brown eyes are friendly. "You'll be catching a flight from here to Los Angeles then you'll have a short layover before your flight to San Luis Obispo. Your parents will meet you there."

"Are they flying commercial, too?" I ask, still obviously confused.

"No, ma'am. They are scheduled to take off from Teterboro around the same time as you."

"So in theory, they could swing by and pick me up?"

"I don't know anything about their arrangements, ma—"

I interrupt him. "Please stop calling me ma'am. I'm younger than you are."

"Sorry, m— Miss Perry."

"Better, but you can call me Olive. It's nice to meet you." I hold out my hand.

"Kade. Like Cades Cove with a K instead of a C." He wraps his dark fingers around mine. "Nice to meet you as well."

"Kade," I repeat. "Thank you for helping out today."

"It's my honor. I served in the Marines when your grandfather was president. He is a great man." He straightens and gives me the smallest of salutes.

A gesture of respect from a stranger shouldn't make me cry, but the tears spill down my cheeks. "Thank you for your service."

The driver steps into view behind Kade. "I have your bag. An agent is meeting us and will escort you to your gate."

Wiping my cheeks, I exhale a shaky breath. "I must be an absolute mess."

Kade gives me a sympathetic smile. "You look fine, Miss Perry. There's a box of tissues on the floor, if you need one. Or take the entire thing."

"I wish I had sunglasses." I hold my thumb to the corner of my eye, hoping the tears will abate.

"You can have mine, ma—, Miss Perry." He reaches into his chest pocket and hands me a pair of Ray-Ban aviators.

"I can't take your glasses." I wave him off.

"You can if I offer."

"Give me your card. I promise to send them back to you."

He hands me the slip of paper and the sunglasses.

"Thank you," I tell him softly.

Hiding behind the dark lenses feels safer, less exposed. I step out of the SUV and plant my feet on the ground. My battered backpack rests against the wheel, looking shabby and sad like the rest of my appearance. With worn shoes, a stained puffy jacket, and grubby socks, I don't fit in with the rest of the people at the airport.

I should've made them stop so I could buy new clothes, something appropriate for the granddaughter of a president. Making sure my hair is tucked under my black beanie, I run a hand over my braid.

A friendly but stern-looking woman in a blue skirt suit approaches us. With a smile, she introduces herself. "I'm Letitia Ramirez and I'll be your VIP agent today. Do you have all of your luggage?"

She's good at her job, her professional demeanor never faltering when I hoist my pack onto my shoulder. "Yep, this is everything."

I thank Kade and the driver again before saying goodbye.

I always knew I'd return to my real life when I completed the AT. Just figured it would be on my own terms.

We pause for the automatic doors to open. The whoosh of stale airport air slams into my face. I haven't been inside a building like this in months. Feels like a lifetime.

One foot in front of the other, I remind myself.

CHAPTER TWENTY-SEVEN

JAY

November

$\mathcal{F}$ive days after I watched Olive climb into the back of an SUV and disappear out of the park, Theodore Perry died. The flags in the park have been lowered to half-staff.

I have no way to contact her to send my condolences.

A week later, the funeral is being televised on every network and news station. I don't have a TV but there's one in the staff lounge. Normally, I wouldn't watch a state funeral. These are not normal times.

If someone, specifically Guy, asked, I'd deny that I'm sitting on the couch waiting for the camera to pan to the Perry family so I might get a glimpse of Olive.

It finally shows them sitting in the front pews of the National Cathedral in Washington. There she is.

I'm not sure I would've recognized her if we passed each other on the street. Dressed in an elegant, tailored black dress and heels, she's the epitome of a city girl. The mess of hair has been tamed into shiny waves. Her natural beauty is hidden behind makeup. Restrained. Tempered. As if someone turned down the volume and desaturated the color of the woman I fell in love with.

Hold on—love? Where did love come from? I shake my head at the randomness of my thoughts. I'm not in love with Olive. The woman on screen is a stranger to me.

"Olive Perry, seated next to her sister, Grace, recently called off her engagement to Sutton Wallingford the third. This will make the sixth time she's failed to walk down the aisle," a male commentator states like it's anyone's business.

"The Runaway Fiancée strikes again." His female colleague giggles. "Maybe the seventh time will be the charm."

"Can you imagine being number seven? You'd have to be crazy or stupid," he responds, chuckling at the idea.

"Or living under a rock," she sneers. "She's no Elizabeth Taylor."

Finding his co-anchor hysterical, he laughs heartily. "No, definitely not. Plus, she'd have to actually get married."

Is this her reality? Strangers picking apart her life for their own amusement? I've never had much empathy for celebrities complaining about details of their lives being splashed across tabloids. They knew what they were getting into. Olive, however, didn't make the same decision. All she did was be born. We don't choose our parents.

I clench the remote so tightly I swear it's going to be pulverized into dust. Flipping the channels, I switch to another broadcast.

The camera scans the crowd and the female host rattles off several names I don't recognize. "I see the Wallingford family is also in attendance. This could make for an awkward moment in the receiving line."

A well-preserved older couple sits next to a human Ken doll with artfully messy hair. His suit probably costs more than my monthly pay. I don't have to guess who he is. Or why Olive would date him.

He fits perfectly in her world. He also looks exactly like the giant tool I imagined. A self-satisfied smirk lingers on his face and I get the impression he knows exactly where all the cameras are in the vast space.

My mood soured, I change the channel once again. Thankfully the hearse arrives outside the cathedral, indicating the beginning of the service and the media vultures finally quiet their commentary.

"My father is probably there." Drew Runous sits down on the

couch next to me.

Dr. Runous and I aren't exactly friends, but we enjoy each other's company. I've always had the feeling he's a kindred spirit, someone who prefers his own company, maybe a bit of a misfit in the world he came from.

We sit in silence while the choir sings.

"I didn't know your father was in politics." In fact, I don't know much about most of my colleagues' families. Except the Winstons, and that's only because they're local.

He frowns at the television. "Money and connections don't make you a better person."

"Society says they do," I mumble.

He turns his attention to me and I feel the weight of his scrutiny. "The measure of a person's worth is synchronicity between their words and actions.No one should be judged on the color of their skin, or the money they do or don't have, nor should we bear the weight of our family's deeds and words.

"Most people, with the exception of his political opponents, agree Theodore Perry was a good man. I'm sure his children and grandchildren love him. What you probably don't know is his father was a state representative in California in the early forties who supported the internment camps. Do his children bear the guilt? For how many generations? Who shall be responsible for the sins of the father?"

In typical Dr. Runous fashion, a simple conversation doesn't skim the surface of small talk. He's dropped a bomb of information and doesn't realize it.

I sit in silence, processing his words. Not only is Olive the granddaughter of a president, her family supported racist policies and incarceration of innocent Japanese Americans. My people.

I feel sick, bile rising in the back of my throat at the idea of concentration camps on American soil.

"You might not remember because you're young, but it was Theodore Perry who opened up the investigation into the camps during his presidency. He's responsible for the reparations act and issued a national apology to the detainees and their heirs."

"I vaguely remember studying that in school. I think it took up about five lines in our history book." At the time I didn't relate because my mother came from Japan in the nineties. We didn't know anyone directly impacted. It all felt like a long time ago and far away. "I do remember after the chapter on Pearl Harbor a group of kids pulled on their eyelids, stretching them sideways while they spoke gibberish to imitate Japanese, and the awful Asian jokes that followed. I wanted to disappear. My mother is Japanese."

"I didn't know," he says, his voice kind.

"I've always struggled with how to bring it up in conversation." I chuckle, but it's a brittle sound.

He studies me. "It can be difficult to be authentic when you feel like an outsider among the people who are supposed to be your community."

"Any advice?"

"Be true to yourself."

"Easier said than done." I give him a weak smile.

"Better than the alternative of leading a false life to appease people whose opinions shouldn't matter."

I'm still mulling over his words well after the funeral ends.

* * *

The next day, I find a postcard from Washington, D.C. in my mailbox.

No signature, but I know it's from Olive.

Washington, D.C.
Day 13
Miles walked: Less than one

What do you call a sad bird?
A bluebird.

CHAPTER TWENTY-EIGHT

JAY

April

Kyoto, Japan

*T*he cherry blossoms are blooming in Kyoto.

Pink petals transform the trees into cotton candy.

My grandmother wraps her hand around my elbow as I escort her down the path in the park. With her gray hair, she might look frail, but she's not using me as a support. She's tiny, but she's strong and healthy as a hummingbird. I think she could outlive us all.

Ahead of me, Jenni and my mom have their heads together, giggling about something.

We've been in Japan a week, and despite all my protests and reluctance about coming, it's been a nice visit.

Even my aunties have been warm to me. No one has called me *hāfu.*

There was one unfortunate incident with mayonnaise on pizza. I'm trying to block it from my mind.

Obaasan's English is not very good, but it's better than my Japanese. Yet, we've communicated with each other well enough through our limited vocabulary and charades..

She squeezes my arm and points to the koi pond. I lead her closer to it. We stare into the dark water, watching bright orange and white koi swim close to the surface.

Speaking in rapid Japanese, she gestures to the park around us. She then points directly to me and repeats a sweeping pattern on the ground.

"I'm sorry, I don't understand," I tell her. "Mom? Can you translate?"

My mother listens and begins to laugh.

"What is she saying?" I peer at my grandmother's smiling face.

"She's asking if this is like the park where you work. She wants to know if you are in charge of the fish or keeping the pathways clear."

Shaking my head, I laugh.

Pantomiming tall mountains, birds flying, and a growling bear complete with sharp claws, I try to explain how wild the Smokies are.

By the time I finish, all three of them are laughing. At me.

"She was teasing." Mom has to wipe tears from her cheeks.

Obaasan says something in Japanese and makes a typing action with her fingers before stretching up to pat my cheek.

"Now what?" I grin at her.

Jenni stops giggling long enough to explain, "She says she knows how to use the internet, sweet boy."

Obaasan covers her mouth as she laughs, her wrinkled eyes pinching together with amusement.

"How did you know what she said?" I ask Jenni.

"Because my Japanese is much better than yours. You should practice more," my sister chastises me, but I agree with her.

"Mom, can you give me lessons?"

"No," she says with a smile. "But I will help you practice. I should've spoken more Japanese with you when you were growing up. It's my fault you aren't bilingual."

"No, it isn't," I reassure her. "I take responsibility for not being more curious."

Obaasan tucks her hand around my elbow again, indicating she's ready to continue our walk. Speaking so softly I can barely hear her, she wiggles her finger for me to dip my head closer to hear her. I comply and listen intently.

"To be better, you must do better," she says in her choppy English.

Her words could apply to learning Japanese or to living life.

Choosing to believe it's the latter, I think about the changes I've made in my life over the last six months. I'm trying to be less of a cantankerous hermit hiding under my bridge. Socializing more. Visiting Knoxville and Nashville to hang out with Jenni and Mom.

Ed retired, and Guy has taken over as our temporary chief ranger until the national search is complete. I think she'll get the permanent job. She knows the park inside and out. There's no way there's anyone more qualified than her.

We hired a new seasonal ranger to take over for her. Daphne fits in well with the rest of our motley crew.

I received my grant to continue my research on the Black-throated Blue Warbler. When I spotted the return of the first flock in the park this spring, I thought of Olive.

I think of her often.

She still sends postcards. The second arrived for Thanksgiving. An illustration of a bald turkey with "I'm so plucked" above it. The other side simply said she was grateful for me. Another showed up in December: "I hope your Christmas is pheasant."

January's card: "Ibis you so much."

February's read: "I have no egrets."

March featured a woodpecker. She wrote, "I think you're im-peck-able."

The problem with postcards is they don't have return addresses on them.

Pointlessly, I tried to find Olive's contact information online. No phone number. No mailing address. After wading through the swamp of articles speculating about her life, I gave up.

She's not on social media, or at least in a way that would allow a stranger to find her.

If not for the postcards, I couldn't be sure if we'd actually met or if I imagined it.

I have to trust our paths will cross again.

CHAPTER TWENTY-NINE

OLIVE

April
Springer Mountain, Georgia
Mile 1

I don't send a postcard letting Jay know about my return.
I want to surprise him.

There's a small part of me that worries he'll disappear if he knows I'm coming back. The rational part of me knows he has a job to do and taking off work to avoid me would be out of character for him.

Still. Doubt and her evil stepsisters, Fear and Insecurity, have taken up residence in my head. I'm hoping it's more of a short-term rental than a lease-to-buy option.

Sending postcards instead of calling the ranger station meant I could reach out without risking rejection. A coward's way of reminding him I still exist out here in the world.

Back in February, I began checking long-term weather forecasts for Springer Mountain, Georgia. A March start would have put me back in the Green Valley area a little earlier in April, but it also would have risked more snow and delays due to bad weather.

Mother Nature and I are barely back on speaking terms after her stunt last October. Yes, I'm happy her surprise storm led me to Jay. No, I'm still not over getting kicked off the trail with less than a hundred miles to go.

A year ago, walking a hundred miles wasn't in the realm of possibility. Now I'm eagerly looking forward to getting back on the trail.

When I was in California with my family last fall, waiting for my grandfather to pass, I started researching the Pacific Crest Trail. A little over 2,600 miles, it's longer than the AT but allegedly easier. Someday I'd like to find out for myself.

Like most things in my life, the sweet moments are tucked between bitter. Meeting Jay, losing my grandfather, finding myself ... the events will forever be entwined.

* * *

Unlike the start of my original NoBo hike last June, when I arrive at the trailhead to Springer Mountain I'm prepared. My pack is unburdened of extra weight from stuff I don't need. I have a new pair of trail-runners on my feet and a spiffy new pole. With under a hundred miles until I officially complete the AT, I'm eager to get started and have to resist overdoing it on the first day.

While my mind is ready, my body definitely needs time to remember how to do this hiking business. The distance to my destination is much shorter than before and I'm grateful.

At the official start of the AT, I sign my name in the register. Because Tye and I began our hike at a random point, I never got to do this. A few hikers are celebrating by passing around a bottle of cheap champagne and I join them in a toast.

These are my people, the crazy dreamers who decide they want to live their life off the beaten path. At least for a little while.

A few smartphones are used to take group selfies, capturing the last moments of before.

I'm dragged into the frame by two women who yell "Girl power!" as the photo is taken.

"Do you mind if we tag you on social?" the shorter blonde asks me, thumbs hovering over the screen. "What's your Instagram handle?"

"I don't have one," I tell her.

They both gasp like I've announced I don't believe in electricity or deodorant. The second one is pointless on the trail, as they'll find out soon enough.

"But why?" they ask at the same time. "Are you banned?"

Laughing, I shake my head. "Long story. I decided life is more interesting when I'm not on my phone. Isn't that the whole point of hiking the AT? Living is what happens when we put down the screens."

I sound like I should end my statement with a bow and a softly whispered, "Namaste."

I stand by my words.

The women contemplate me with new awareness. The blonde powers down her phone and slides it into the side pocket of her enormous pack. I want to tell her to ditch half of what she has packed, but I don't. It isn't my place.

Everyone does their own hike.

There's trail magic everywhere on the first stretch of the AT, giving the days a festive vibe. So far, we've had free pancakes in the morning, hot dogs and cold sodas for lunch, and cake one afternoon. Everyone is in a good mood, not yet worn down by the miles and challenges.

When the subject of trail names comes up, I tell the story of how I earned mine and the irony of being blocked from finishing by the freak snow last October. I explain I'm only hiking as far as Tennessee this trip.

At the fork in the trail splitting the AT from the shorter spur leading to Cades Cove, I'm greeted with an impromptu party. A bottle of champagne is popped to celebrate me officially completing the trail. There's no sign for me to climb for my picture like there was at Katahdin, so I opt for hugging the nearest tree with a white blaze.

I did it.

2,190 miles by foot.

Five months on the trail.

Five months off.

Five months of not hiking and my body has forgotten how to cope with the challenges of life on the AT. I'm grateful my journey is over. A few more miles and a half-day of hiking then I'll truly be finished.

With a promise to keep in touch and a hug for each of them, I wish my new family good luck. They're off on a great adventure, one they'll never forget and that will change them forever.

My solo hike takes me past the unmarked trail leading to the moonshiner's cabin. I can't resist a visit for the nostalgia and to confirm I didn't dream the place into existence.

In contrast to the snow-covered ground from October, the spring conditions make the narrow path easy to follow. I spot the stone chimney first, followed by the steeply pitched roof extending over the narrow porch.

Wildflowers bloom in the mossy earth around the little building.

A "NO TRESPASSING" sign sits propped in one of the grungy windows, and a thicker padlock secures the door.

Rubbing through the grime with my sleeve, I peer inside. Everything looks exactly how we left it. Still no moonshine.

I pull out my phone and snap a photo.

Once I'm on the trail leading me down to the valley, nerves take residence in my belly, beating their tiny wings at the knowledge I'm less than ten miles from seeing him again.

No risk, no reward, I tell myself.

* * *

Unlike the riot of color in the Smokies in October, April is all about green. A lot of the trees aren't back in leaf yet, but the ground is saturated with spring grass and wildflowers. Wisps of blue clouds cling to the tops of the mountains like trails of woodsmoke. I feel like I'm hiking through a fairy tale. Any moment now a fawn and squirrels will join me as I march into the valley.

Crickets chirp and birds tweet all around. Always scanning for flashes of blue feathers, I have trouble keeping my eyes on the trail, stumbling a few times because I'm not looking at my feet.

Finally, there he is, looking handsome and dapper in his blue and black feathers. My Black-throated Blue Warbler.

"Hello, handsome." I wave at him. He doesn't notice me but lets out his familiar call before flying away.

Today is a very good day.

I'm home.

The thought makes me laugh. Me? At home in these mountains? A place I've spent months walking through but have never lived in. My inner New Yorker scoffs at the idea. The skeptic in me blames the thought on exhaustion. The liar in me declares the feeling has nothing to do with my unresolved feelings for Jay.

Ignoring all of them, my soul says yes, this is where we belong.

Two miles from the ranger station, I slow my pace as doubt and insecurity settle into my chest. I should've let him know I was finishing my hike. What if he doesn't want to see me? I should've reserved clean clothes so I don't show up smelling like roadkill from a week of living on the trail. What if he's moved on? He could have a girlfriend. Or a wife. Some people fall in love and get married right away.

Stopping myself from spiraling into a champion-level round of the what-if game, I decide I'm going to head directly to the ranger station.

But first, I'm going to enjoy the joy of an indoor bathroom.

Detouring to the one-story building housing the campground restrooms, I'm practically giddy. Hello running water, my old friend.

Inside, I dump my bag by the door and then take care of the usual protocol. Spare a quick glance in the mirror, something I don't normally do while I'm on the trail. Which I'm not anymore, so I guess it's okay.

The toilet flushes in another stall.

"Yikes," I whisper, observing myself flinching at the sight of my reflection. I have a smear of dirt on my forehead, a scrape on my chin, and what were once braids have turned into matching birds nests on my shoulders. "You can't show up looking like a hot mess."

A woman in a ranger uniform steps up to the sink next to me.

"Olive?" her reflection asks mine.

My hands still wet with soap, I reply with a smile, "Hi, Gaia."

"What are you doing here?" she asks, not sounding happy to see me. In fact, she frowns, the exact opposite of the smile I gave her. "Does Jay know?"

"I'm going to surprise him."

And now my very brilliant idea seems like the most foolish thing I've ever done.

"He's not here." She presses the button on the dryer, the noise so loud I can barely hear her.

"Sorry?" I ask when she finishes drying her hands, hoping for clarification.

"I said he's not here." Not exactly helpful.

"Can you elaborate? Is he in the backcountry? Or out of the park?"

"He's out of the country. In Japan."

My stomach sinks at her words.

Without prompting, she continues, "He took two weeks of vacation."

I repeat the information back to her.

"That's what I said. He's in Japan for two weeks." She frowns. "Maybe you should have given him a heads-up you were coming back."

"I wanted to surprise him," I mumble, wiping my hands on my pants.

She shrugs. "Bad timing, I guess."

This isn't the happy ending I've been imagining. Defeated and exhausted, I hoist my bag onto one shoulder. "Thanks for letting me know. Guess I'll ..."

I let the words drift off. I don't have a contingency plan.

In my fantasy, I was going to show up here and he'd welcome me with open arms. He'd kiss me again, birds would sing, and we'd start our happily ever after.

With my free hand, I cover my face. "I'm such an idiot."

"Sorry, you were mumbling—can you repeat your last sentence?"

Removing my palm from my mouth, I mumble, "I'm an idiot."

A grin breaks out on her face. "I thought that was what you said."

Remembering how defensive she was about Jay, I'm guessing she's taking delight in this moment.

"Come on," she says, stepping around me. "Let's find you a campsite."

"Why?" Confused, I follow her.

She stops walking to answer me. "I figure you'll want to hang around until Jay comes back. Or do you have somewhere else to be?"

Standing with my mouth open, I slowly process her words. "But you said he's gone for two weeks."

"You're not willing to hang and wait that long for him? Doesn't sound like too much of a commitment to make for the man you love."

"I didn't say I love him," I protest.

Leveling me with a strong look, she asks, "Then what are you doing back here, Olive? Passing through on your hike?"

Damn, she's intimidating.

"I finished the AT."

"Congratulations." She gives me a high five before returning her face to its resting serious expression. "Now what?"

"I don't know. I'm here to figure it out."

"Well, you have a few days to do just that."

When she starts walking again, I jog to keep up with her. True to her word, she leads me to the camp office, where I register for a site.

Before Gaia leaves, she tells me, "If you need anything or get bored, swing by the ranger station. You're welcome to hang out."

Still uncertain about her motivations, I thank her. It's possible she hates me. It's also possible she's helping me. Either and both could be true.

Sniffing my t-shirt, I decide laundry will be the first order of business after a shower. The public camp showers aren't nearly as nice as Jay's, and I wear my water shoes to avoid catching cooties.

* * *

In the campground, I use the wifi to pull up my flight search app. I type in Knoxville to Tokyo.

What am I doing?

I close the app.

Proving a point? Making a grand gesture?

I reopen the app.

Chasing Jay to Japan is crazy. Interrupting his family vacation is presumptuous at best, deranged on the opposite end of the scale.

I close the app and delete it from my phone.

Gaia is right—if I'm not willing to wait for him, what am I even doing here?

Spending two weeks hanging out in the campground is much more rational than twenty hours of flights. Plus, how would I even find him? I doubt Gaia or anyone else would give me his phone number.

If this is one-sided, I can slink away into the woods.

Plan of action decided, I celebrate with an ice cream sandwich at the small store.

There are bikes to rent for use in the area. I debate peddling into Green Valley to check out the town. I could always hitch a ride there and back.

"Tomorrow," I tell myself. There's no rush. Unlike clocking miles on the trail in order to hit my daily goal, now that I'm here and officially done with the AT, I am free to do whatever I please. Or nothing at all.

I think I'll choose the latter option.

Near the store is a little free library. According to the brass plaque on the door, it's a gift of the Friends of the Green Valley Library in honor of a Bethany Winston. Inside are at least a dozen assorted books. I'm not surprised to find two copies of Bill Bryson's *A Walk in the Woods* tucked among the fiction, along with some non-fiction, children's books, and a few comics. Bryson's account of hiking the Appalachian Trail is one of the most famous. I decide to skip it.

On the bottom shelf are five books of poetry, ranging from Whitman to E. E. Cummings. Not what I expected to find in a campground. I end up selecting a romance about a highwayman with a pretty yellow cover. Uncertain about my own happily ever after, reading about one might give me hope.

CHAPTER THIRTY

JAY

*M*y sister insists on driving me back to Cades Cove from Knoxville. We arrived yesterday and immediately crashed. Jet lag means I have no idea what time or day it is. I can't wait to get home and sleep.

Jenni drops me at the station after making me promise to visit soon when I have a Saturday off.

Inside, I find Guy and Daphne hanging out at the counter.

When she spots me, Guy's eyes widen into saucers. "Welcome back!"

Her enthusiasm worries me. Guy is never exuberant. Dry, sarcastic, exasperated? Yes.

"Wow. Thanks. I missed you too." Cautiously, I drop my bag by the door. "What's going on?"

"Oh, nothing interesting." She presses her lips into an exaggerated frown. "Right, Daphne?"

My eyes cut to Daphne, who appears as confused as I am.

"Uh," is all she manages before she sneezes. "Sorry. Allergies."

Guy's head is tipped in the direction of the back office. "Besides spring allergies, we've had some rare bird sightings while you've been away."

"Oh, really?" She has my attention. "What species? The Red-throated Loon? Great Blue Heron? Snow Goose?"

"Ooh, Griffin was talking about a snowbird recently," Daphne interjects.

Guy beams at me. "Oh, right. There was a sighting in the campground."

"What kind of snowbird?" I watch Guy's eyes dart down the hall again. The tempo of my heartbeat increases.

Guy's dimples pop out as she presses her lips together tightly. She looks like an unrepentant chipmunk with a mouth full of stolen nuts. With a nod, she answers, "The same one who came through this area last fall."

She barely finishes speaking before I'm speeding down the hall-way. At the threshold to the office, I pause to collect myself.

The awful overhead fluorescent light is off and the room is dark, lit only from the fading afternoon sunlight coming in through the window. I pause, waiting for my eyes to adjust to the dimness.

The woman I can't get off my mind, the one who occupies far too many of my thoughts while awake and my dreams at night, is curled up in the corner of the old sofa, reading a book. Completely at ease, maybe even a little bored, like she's waiting for a doctor's appointment or hanging out at home on a lazy weekend afternoon. She looks like she belongs in this space. A half-empty cup of tea rests on the floor within reaching distance. Obviously, she's been here a while.

Unobserved, I indulge in the joy of reacquainting myself with my favorite parts of her. She worries the corner of her fuller bottom lip with her teeth. Long lashes hide her eyes and her long neck is bent as she dips her head to read. Elegant fingers turn the page.

My eyes follow the winding S curve of her body from shoulders to the narrower tuck of her waist before widening over her hips and thighs. She's curvier, healthier than she was in the fall. I want to retrace those lines with my hands first, followed by my mouth.

"You're here." Her voice is husky, like she hasn't used it in a long time. It reminds me of her waking up in the morning, still tipsy from sleep.

Damn, I've missed her voice.

While I was devouring every detail of her body, I missed the moment she noticed my presence.

"I am. So are you. Imagine that," I say, amused because I can't believe she's really here. I've imagined seeing her again. Over and over again I've thought about this moment, the impossibility of being in the same place together again.

Her dark brows pull together, confusion filling her blue eyes. "You're supposed to be out of town."

"I flew home yesterday." I shove my hands in the pockets of my uniform pants.

She untangles her feet and stands.

Moving across the room in three quick strides, I stop when I'm a few feet away from her. I'm close enough to inhale her clean scent but not to touch her. Inside, I'm battling the urge to pick her up, throw her over my shoulder, and walk out of here, not stopping until we're back at my place.

I don't know what brought her back or why she's hanging out in the office like it's the local library.

"I'm sorry I left so abruptly." Her eyes hold traces of her grief.

"I'm sorry about your grandfather. I wanted to send a card or call or something to let you know I was thinking of you, but I didn't have any way to reach you." I hope my sincerity shows. "I know what it's like to lose someone you're close with. I'm so sorry."

"Thank you." She blinks away tears. Her attention flicks between a spot over my shoulder, her feet, and the window—anywhere but my face. Is she nervous?

"What are you doing here?" I ask, voice rough. I wonder if she can hear the restraint I'm battling.

She finally meets my eyes, and the same pull from before anchors itself in the center of my chest, sending a current straight to my heart. "I came back for you."

Without overthinking, without hesitation, I wind my hands through her braid, gently tugging until her head dips back, angling her chin closer to my lips.

"Olive," I whisper, her name holy, sacred. My lips brush against the corner of her mouth. Not a true kiss, but a promise. "Tell me to stop and I will."

Leaning away slightly, my hand still in her hair, I search her eyes for reluctance or rejection. If I've misread the situation, if I have somehow misunderstood her motivations for being here, I'll walk away, let her go. I've done it once and survived.

She blinks up at me, her pupils dilated in the dim light and darkening her blue eyes.

"Why would I do that?" Her voice is barely more than a breath, not loud enough to be a whisper.

"Because this won't be just a kiss. Not this time." I pause, letting my meaning sink in. "If we do this, I'm all in. You need to know before we start anything. This isn't going to be a one-time thing. At least not for me."

Her breath catches and her eyes grow wide. Slowly her lips part and a warm sigh of an exhalation escapes.

"Just so we're clear ..." I drag a knuckle down her cheek and along her jaw, "I want you. I want this."

In response, she shivers beneath my touch. A warm flush of color spreads across her cheeks. With a nod, she steps closer, pressing her body against mine from chest to thigh.

Her curves, her softness melts against where I'm hard, the planes of muscle in my chest, my abdomen, my cock. My instinct tells me to grind against her, to seek friction to relieve the ache, but I maintain control. Angling my hips away, I'm stopped with her hand low on my waist.

With both hands, she pulls me flush against her, locking her arms around my back.

"I came back for you," she repeats, eyes blazing with desire. The look is familiar, and I realize now it was always there, simmering beneath the uncertainty, visible if I'd only been brave enough to believe.

My lips find hers, not a gentle caress, with intention.

A soft sigh breaks the silence, a moan of relief.

She's kissing me back, her mouth opening for me. I slide my tongue inside, seeking hers, wanting to taste and devour her.

Her hands move from my back, up over my arms to tangle in my hair, first at the nape of my neck and then near my temples. I lose myself in her, surrounded by her scent and her warmth.

Voices drift into the office through the open door. If anyone were to walk down the hall now, we'd be busted. The last thing I want is to stop kissing Olive. Second to last, is being interrupted by one of my fellow rangers.

And then I remember the office door has a lock.

CHAPTER THIRTY-ONE

OLIVE

*J*ay has a feral look in his eyes when he closes the office door and turns the lock.

"Here? Now?" My voice squeaks. "Where?"

His eyes dart from the ancient sofa over to the desk and then to the wood-paneled wall, lingering on the shelf with the taxidermy skunk who stares down at us.

"No," he says, firmly. Resolved. His eyes return to their normal state of being pretty, but not untamable. "Not here. Not for our first time together. Nothing wrong with hard and fast, but I want to savor this moment. What I want to do requires privacy, which we won't have here."

Part of me is disappointed, but I'm also relieved.

I wasn't expecting him to reappear today. I need to gather my thoughts around the fact that he's here.

And he wants me.

I took a short hike this morning to hand out coffee to the AT hikers like I do most days. It's not a lot, but I know how much hot coffee is appreciated. A few miles up and back is easy for me, but that doesn't mean I don't sweat. With no one to mind, I also haven't washed my hair in … I try to remember by counting on my fingers. It's been three days.

I could use a shower and fresh clothes, though the clothes are optional because I'm planning to be naked. With Jay.

However, I'm not going to get naked in the back office of the ranger station.

"Do you have plans tonight?" he asks, sounding more rational and a little uncertain.

"Some of the hiker trash are having a campfire with s'mores, but I can skip it." I shake my head. "Unless you want to go?"

He's asking me out on a date. At least I think he is, and I'm babbling.

My lips still tingling from the feel of his kiss, I press my finger against them to quiet my words. "No, I don't have plans."

"Good. This is me, asking you out. To dinner." He's serious but also irresistibly nervous. "To avoid any confusion or misunderstanding, this is a date. Don't try to split the check or pay. We're doing this the proper way."

I beam at him, my happiness like rays of sunshine. "How proper are we talking here? Should we have a chaperone? I bet Gaia would be delighted to join us."

"You're adorable and hysterical, but I've never been more serious about a first date than I am right now. The last thing I want is to share you," he grumbles. "I think we'll be fine without supervision. I managed to remain a gentleman when we were trapped in the cabin. Should be able to act like a decent human in public."

If real people swooned, this would be me swooning over his words.

"Just so I'm clear this time: this is a date?" I ask, teasing him a little.

"Yes, a real date—the kind where you should bring an overnight bag." His eyes twinkle with mischief and intention. He confirms the meaning of his words with a solid kiss, taking up where we left off before he locked the door.

Backing me up to the wall and then pressing me against it, he devours my mouth with his, a thirsty man taking his first sips of water, a dying man praying for his soul.

Wishing I had a third hand or maybe a fourth, I want to touch him everywhere. I can't decide if I should twist my fingers in his hair or grab his biceps to steady myself, or perhaps neither when his strong back is within easy reach. Oh, and his abs. And his pecs. Those are more difficult to access because he's flush against me, my boobs squished against his chest.

Unlike me, he doesn't appear to be paralyzed by indecision. He skims his hand down my waist and over my hip, lifting my thigh to his side. This changes the angle of where we connect below the belt.

A deep, husky, loud moan escapes me when he hits the right spot. We're fully clothed and he still makes my knees buckle.

"Shh," he whispers along my neck, sending a cascade of goose-bumps over my skin.

Raised voices and laughter reach us through the door.

My eyes bug out. "Do you think they heard me?"

"No, of course not," he says while nodding.

"Totally did." I'd cover my face with my hands, but they're currently buried deep in his back pockets where they're busy grabbing his ass.

"And this is why we need to get out of here." He leans away but is trapped because of my hands. "Um, Olive?"

"Right. Sorry." I release him.

"You never answered me about the overnight bag. Did I overstep? I don't want to presume." He sweeps his hands through his hair and ducks his chin like he's shy or embarrassed.

"I only have my pack, so there's not a lot to bring besides my toothbrush."

He steps back, shock in his eyes. "Wait, you hiked here?"

"Of course. How else would I get here?"

"By plane? In a car? Hold on, if you walked here, does that mean what I think it means?" His expression switches from confusion to elation. I prefer his wide, happy grin.

I nod, my own mouth curling into a wide, tooth-showing smile.

He scoops me into his arms, lifting me clear off my feet before spinning me around. "You did it!"

"If you mean complete all two thousand one hundred and ninety miles of the historic Appalachian Trail, then yes, yes I did."

He's squeezing me tight and still turning us in circles. "Congratulations!"

He sets me down but keeps his arms wrapped around my shoulders, hugging me tight against his chest.

If we stand like this for more than a few seconds, we'll end up making out again. I'm not opposed, but we really need to get out of this office.

"When did you finish?" he asks.

"Five days ago." My voice is muffled by his chest.

"You've been here for almost a week?" Incredulous, he holds me at arm's length, his beautiful face a mix of emotions, both joy and sadness. "I wasn't here to celebrate with you."

"We still can. There's no time limit."

Walking into the campground did feel anticlimactic. If anything, I looked like a quitter who gave up less than a hundred miles into the hike. I wanted a laminated placard for my pack with the route and dates of my miles. I wanted a trophy and ribbons. No balloons, though, because they're bad for birds and turtles.

"I'm sorry I wasn't here and missed it." He hugs me again. "I'll figure out a way to make it up to you. Maybe we can recreate your arrival, give you the proper welcome."

"Historical reenactment of an event that took place a week ago?"

"Works for me." His warm green eyes meet mine. "This is a big deal. We need to do it right."

He could be talking about more than the AT.

My being here is a huge deal, and I do want to do this right.

His lips find mine again and we seal the promise with a kiss.

"Okay, tonight. I have ideas." He slides his fingers between mine. "Where's your tent?" At my worried expression, he laughs. "I'm walking you there so you can gather your things, nothing more. As you know, I have a perfectly good bed at my place. Unless you prefer sleeping on the ground?"

Laughing, I shake my head.

He unlocks the door and swings it open. The conversation among his coworkers immediately stops, like birdsong quiets when a predator approaches.

"I'm leaving," Jay announces, even though everyone is busy looking busy at their desks.

Gaia spins in her chair and stares at me. "Be easy on Daniels."

Next to me, Jay groans and squeezes my hand. "Guy, I don't need you acting like a mama bear. I've got this."

Something passes between them.

Ranger Baum raises her hand like she's in class and waiting for the teacher to call on her. "Can I ask what's going on? New girl here is confused."

"Daphne, this is Olive. Jay's —" Guy pauses, glancing between Jay and me. "—Jay's friend."

I give her a small wave.

"Oh, you're the hiker who's been hanging around," Daphne says. "Griffin said you were waiting for some bird to fly back to the park."

Ranger Lee pops his head, around the corner. "Daphne, you're going to have to be quicker if you're going to last longer than a season around here. What kind of bird did I say?"

Guy groans and closes her eyes.

Lines appear in Daphne's forehead as she thinks. "It wasn't a crow. Owl? No."

Griffin lets out a frustrated sigh. "Not even close. I'm disappointed, Daphne. I said it was a blue jay."

No one laughs.

"Get it?" he asks the group. "His name is Jay and he's been a mopey bastard for months?"

Sweet Daphne at least tries to fake a laugh.

Griffin doubles down on his terrible joke. "It's funny."

"Not if you have to explain it," Guy chides.

The two of them bicker about the subjectivity of humor.

Next to me, Jay rolls his eyes.

Dipping my head closer to his shoulder, I whisper for only him to hear, "I think it's sweet you missed me."

He squeezes my hand. "More than you know."

CHAPTER THIRTY-TWO

JAY

Gaia tips her head in Olive's direction. She thinks she's being subtle. "There's a jam session in town tonight. People around here generally say it's a fun way to spend an evening. You know, if you're looking for something to do. Would make a fun date if you wanted to go out."

I pierce her gaze with imaginary lasers from my eyes. "Thanks for the social calendar update."

"Jam session?" Olive asks. "Like a group of people canning preserves?"

Gaia's eyes widen. "Why would I suggest Jay take you on a date to hang out with the Methodist church ladies?"

"Guy," I growl low in my throat, avoiding glancing at Olive. I don't want her to think I've been gossiping about us to my coworkers. Griffin's joke was bad enough.

Shifting my attention back to Olive, I explain. "Bunch of local musicians get together and play at the community center every Friday night. Nothing formal, but the music is good and they have some pretty decent barbecue."

"What kind of music?" Olive asks.

"Probably nothing you'd like. Old-time country and bluegrass from

Appalachia, songs you've never heard, handed down generation to generation around here."

"Are there fiddles? Banjos? Mandolins?" Olive's eyes grow wide and her knee bounces with excitement. She lowers her voice. "Please tell me someone plays a washboard."

Guy's eyes seek mine and she shrugs. "Probably?"

Olive grips my arm, tight enough I'd hate to thumb-wrestle her. She has a strange amount of strength in her fingers. "We have to go. What time does it start? Can we go now?"

Still thinking about the possible bruise on my forearm, I remove her hand. "It's mostly locals playing music together. Nothing fancy. Best not to think of it as a concert or anything. Don't be expecting Nashville or New York."

Olive narrows her eyes at me. "Why are you trying to convince me not to go? Is it because I'll stick out as a city slicker?"

I glance at her wild hair and the scrape on her cheek. I doubt anyone would mistake her for a socialite now.

"How about we take a raincheck for next week?" I hope she understands my meaning.

"Deal." She beams at me and I feel like I'm the only man who's ever fallen in love.

"Ready to get out of here?" I whisper loudly to her. "Before my colleagues invite themselves along on our date."

Laughing, she nods and waves at the weirdos I have to deal with on a daily basis.

"Remember, only you can prevent forest fires," Griffin says as parting advice.

Outside, I lean down to give Olive a quick kiss.

When we part, she asks, "What's next? Jam session?"

"Another time. I have something more private in mind." I give her another soft peck. "Stay here. I need to make a phone call."

I step inside again, ignoring the commentary from the peanut gallery, and move into the office for privacy.

Energy courses through my body, and not the jittery kind from coffee or the buzz from alcohol. This is new. My pulse quickens and my heart beats in double-time. This is crazy. She's here. She's back. She's been waiting for me.

A quick call and my plans are settled.

"Everything okay?" Olive asks when I return.

I've missed her. All of her. Her lack of filter and her stubborn determination. How she makes me laugh and pushes my buttons. The way she is easy to talk with about stuff I never share with anyone. How she's both fearless and a little absurd. Those are only the first things to come to mind. She's here now, in front of me, and I don't want to waste a moment of time with her by making mental lists in my head.

I slip my fingers between hers, lifting our hands to my mouth to place a kiss to her wrist. Her touch grounds me. "More than okay."

"So where are you taking me on this date? Do I need to get fancy?" Olive gestures to her leggings and puffy jacket.

"Do you have other clothes?" I hadn't thought about her lack of clothes appropriate for a nice dinner out.

"Maybe."

My brows draw together. "You don't know?"

"Guess it depends on where we're going." She bobbles her head. "I might have an adorable GSM sweatshirt a guy bought for me. Not sure if it's date appropriate."

I finally catch on to her trickery. "I'm not telling you where I'm taking you. Think of it as a surprise."

"This makes me a hypocrite, but I hate surprises. Or at least being the surprisee."

"Given there are three options for a nice dinner in Green Valley, you have a thirty-three percent chance of already knowing."

"I haven't really left the campground to explore the area. Rode one of the rental bikes down to Green Valley. Looks like charming little town, but if we're not going to the diner or the Piggly Wiggly, I haven't a clue."

I realize she's genuinely nervous about being unprepared. Last time, we went to Daisy's and no one cared if she was in sweats.

With empathy for how she's feeling, I confess, "I made a reservation at the Lodge."

"For dinner?" she asks softly.

"To start." I confirm.

"What time?" She toes her shoe into the dirt.

I clear my throat, unexpectedly nervous. "Does now work for you?"

"Yes." Her smile fades. "No."

"Okay." I wait for her to explain.

"I'd love to, um, freshen up before we go." She doesn't quite meet my eyes.

"How about you can shower there? I also booked a room. For you. For … us." I stumble over the words and the meaning lurking behind them.

Her eyes brighten. "When can we check in?"

"How about now?" I kiss her again, because she's adorable and she's here and I can.

CHAPTER THIRTY-THREE

OLIVE

*J*ay packs up my little campsite in record time. I've never seen a tent collapsed and stuffed into its bag so fast. If there's a camping Olympics, he should enter.

I'm not-so-secretly hoping he drags me back to his cabin, locks the door, and ravishes me. I don't think I've ever been ravished, and I'd like to find out what I'm missing. Jay seems like he'd be a natural.

We swing by his place so he can drop off his suitcase. He surprises me when he comes out of his bedroom with a small backpack.

"What's that for?" I ask.

"I wasn't joking about this being an overnight date." He rolls his lips together and drags his teeth over the bottom one.

"Oh," I whisper. "We're not coming back here after dinner?"

"No." He sways back on his heels. "I told you—I'm taking this date seriously. Go big or go home."

"I don't want to go home."

"Good." He takes my hand. "Ready?"

Sliding my fingers between his, I'm reminded of the night we fell asleep on his bed. All we did was hold hands. And it remains one of my favorite moments with him.

* * *

The Lodge is exactly how the name makes it sound. Constructed of old timber, it's a wood-lovers paradise.

Beams, wide plank floors, tons of stone and iron, and more wood decorate the lobby.

I feel like we've stepped back in time.

Jay checks us in and gets the key while I warm up by the enormous stone fireplace.

"It's a little different from our cabin." I gaze around the large space. Delicious scents from the restaurant make my stomach grumble, but it's the man strolling toward me who makes my mouth water.

I take a moment to observe him: his faded jeans and a black thermal, his hair in messy waves, his green eyes intently focused on me like I'm the only person in the world.

He takes my breath away.

I was too stunned when he walked into the office to really study him to see if he's changed during the time we've been apart.

Then the kissing started and I couldn't have cared less.

I realize something has changed about him.

"You trimmed your beard." I touch his face.

"You just noticed?" He leans down to kiss me. "I don't normally let it get as wild as it was when we met."

I drag my nails through the shorter whiskers. "I like it like this. It's softer."

He gives me a sheepish smile. "Beard oil."

"Hmm," I hum. "I wonder if it will prevent beard burn."

His eyes flash to mine. Without a word, he pulls me to the staircase and up to our room.

* * *

Our room is dominated by a large king-sized bed. It's huge and screams sex—in a tasteful, mountain lodge kind of way. There's a stone fireplace on the opposite wall and next to it a door, which I assume leads to the glory of the modern bathroom.

"Want to go first?" he asks, setting our bags on the chair next to the window.

"I'll only be a few minutes. Thank you." I give him a quick kiss and hug him.

He hugs me back, his head resting on mine, telling me, "You're welcome, and take your time."

I do. Steam billows around the small but beautiful bathroom when I'm done with my shower.

Feeling bold, I get dressed in my bra and underwear and nothing else. We can eat dinner later.

When I open the door, Jay is sprawled on the bed … sound asleep.

I remind myself he flew back from Japan yesterday. Jet lag is no joke.

Glancing at the alarm clock on the nightstand, I notice it's only four-thirty. Plenty of time for dinner—and other activities—later. Better to let him rest.

Deciding to join in on the napping, I crawl under the duvet and snuggle into his side.

The bed is soft and comfortable and Jay is warm, so warm.

My lids grow heavy as I settle in.

* * *

I wake up, alone in the bed. The fireplace has been lit and gas flames dance behind the glass screen, casting shadows around the darkened room. The sound of running water carries from behind the bathroom door.

I have zero regrets about the nap.

Stretching, I enjoy the feel of being in bed. The fluffy white comforter covers me from chin to toe. Please forward my mail, I live in this bed now.

The bathroom door opens, releasing misty clouds of steam. Jay walks out, dressed in pants but no shirt.

For some reason, I jump out of bed.

In my head, I start listing every kind of bird I can think of.

Robin.

Raven.

Red-tailed Hawk.

Redheaded Woodpecker.

Swallow.

Not helping, Olive.

Jay is standing RIGHT THERE. Shirtless. The fly and button of his jeans are undone, revealing the black band of his boxers.

I'm so busy staring at his shoulders and pecs and enjoying the peekaboo his abs are playing with me, I don't notice when he catches me. I only know he does.

And he's blushing.

Or maybe he's flushed from the warm glow of the fire or his shower. Sure, because what man who looks like Ranger Daniels is capable of blushing?

I'm in only a black sports bra and underwear. In my opinion, I'm wearing the equivalent of a conservative bikini. However, Jay's eyes and the way he keeps blinking tell another story.

We're standing on opposite sides of the enormous four-poster bed. A mile of white sheets separates us. I'm nervous like a virgin on her wedding night. Only this isn't our wedding night and I haven't been a virgin in a long time.

His chest heaves with breath like he's run a mile instead of walked a dozen feet from the bathroom.

Feeling bold, I peel the bra over my head and drop it to the floor.

In response, he stalks over to my side of the world's largest bed. The desperate look is back in his eyes, as if he's barely able to restrain himself around me. I find the idea of him losing control because of me beyond sexy.

Without a word, he lifts me by my waist and tosses me on my back in the middle of the mattress. The fluffy duvet pads my landing. I open my mouth to speak, but Jay drops his jeans to the floor.

And then he's above me, mouth covering mine, tongue sweeping into my mouth. He's gone from awkward to wolfish in seconds.

He takes control, shifting my body to settle his hips between my spread thighs. I've caught glimpses of him through his uniform pants, but I'm wholly unprepared for the feeling of him with only two thin layers of fabric separating us.

Breaking from kissing my mouth, he drags his bearded jaw along my jaw. The sensation of whiskers brushing against sensitive skin has me arching my back as I imagine his face between my thighs.

His tongue sweeps a line down my neck. He pauses to nip the skin at the curve above my collarbones. While his mouth is busy, his hand is on my breast, kneading and rolling my nipple between his fingers. The sensation sends a direct current to the gentle throbbing between my thighs.

He dips his head to draw the other breast into his mouth, sucking and dragging his teeth over the tender nipple. My back arches and my hips buck, seeking rhythm or friction or something to ease the building ache deep in my belly.

Without even touching me below the waist, he's pushed me to the edge. Feeling selfish, I reach for him, drawing his face closer to mine. He obliges, roughly kissing my lips. His hips grind into mine and I know I'm not the only one desperate for more.

Each kiss becomes slower and lighter. When there's a gap between them, I open my eyes to find him staring down at me.

"What?" I whisper, worried he's having second thoughts.

"Nothing. I said I wanted to savor this moment with you, so I am."

I don't know whether to fall in love with him on the spot or scream with frustration.

Too late. I'm already in love with him.

I skate my hands over his shoulders and biceps, down his torso until I reach the band of fabric at his waist. Palming him through his boxers, I say a silent thank you to the first deity who comes to mind: Eros, the god of lust. I slip my hand under his waistband to feel him against my skin.

Jay sucks a breath between his teeth. Dropping his head until his forehead presses against mine, he breathes deeply for a few beats as I stroke him.

"Olive ... damn. Your hand feels amazing."

Inwardly, I preen.

"But you need to stop or I'm going to come from a hand job, which is not at all how I imagined this evening going." With an embarrassed laugh, he rolls to the side and unclasps my fingers. Encouraging me with his hand on my hip, he whispers, "Come here."

I climb on top of him, legs astride his thighs, his erection trapped between us. Leaning forward, I capture his mouth with mine, gently biting on his bottom lip.

Slowly, torturously he rolls his hips, driving himself against me. It doesn't relieve the ache. Instead, he multiplies it by tenfold.

My head thrown back, I find a rhythm above him, grinding down when he thrusts.

His hands knead my breasts, eliciting a throaty moan from me. Lifting his head, he sucks a nipple into his mouth and drags his teeth along the taut bud.

Everything becomes too much. My skin heats, a warm flush blazing across my chest and up my neck as tiny beads of sweat gather between my breasts. My movements become erratic as I both delay and seek pleasure.

All this and he hasn't removed my underwear.

Sweet lord.

I exhale and let my chin drop to my chest.

This man, this beautiful, complicated man.

It's entirely possible I might not survive the night.

Death by pleasure might be the best way to go.

Peering down at him, I see his long lashes cast shadows on his high cheekbones. There's a small scar near his left eye. Could be from the chickenpox. His Cupid's bow lips are parted and his tongue rests heavy in his mouth. The cords in his neck strain and his fingers dig into my hips, guiding me over him.

How can I suspend this moment forever? This bliss that only exists in these fleeting seconds between before and after?

I sweep my fingers through a lock of hair on his forehead. In response, he opens his eyes, the green deeper and darker with lust and pleasure.

His movements pause as he drinks me in, his hands lifting to cup my face. Simultaneously, arching his neck and dragging my head down, he finds my mouth and kisses me, deep into my soul. His intentions are as clear as the love in his eyes.

I have to bite my tongue to keep from saying the words aloud.

CHAPTER THIRTY-FOUR

JAY

*O*live is above me, kissing my neck, her hips rolling in slow, agonizing circles.

Tangling my fingers in her hair, I pull back, less gently than I did when I kissed her in the office. "If we're going to continue, we need to stop. I've waited months for this moment, fantasized about variations whenever I masturbated."

Her eyes flash open. "You thought about me?"

"For months. I have a very good imagination."

"Oh god, you can't say things like that to me." Her hips still and her eyelids flutter closed. "What did you imagine?"

"I could tell you, or I can show you." I cup her breast and squeeze.

She releases a soft moan. "Show."

I place my hands on her hips, leveraging her weight to slide her off of me and then flipping her to her back. "We'll need to lose these."

I nip the black fabric at her hip before removing it.

Her thighs part, exposing her center to me. Climbing off the bed, I kneel near the side.

"You don't have to." She stills my head near the apex of her thighs. "It's okay."

I sit back on my heels. "Didn't you just ask me to show you what I've been fantasizing about?"

Her eyes are closed, but she nods.

"Look at me, Olive."

She barely opens her lids.

"If you say you don't like something or want to stop, I will. Always." I pause to kiss the soft skin of her thigh. "Now if you're saying you don't want me to go down on you because you think I'm doing it out of obligation, you're wrong. Got it?"

She nods again.

"Good." I nuzzle her sex with my nose, inhaling her arousal before dragging my tongue through her wetness.

In response, her hips buck off the bed. I flatten my tongue and lap at her clit until she's a writhing, begging mess. Slipping one finger and then a second inside her, I curl the tips against her inner wall, seeking the spot to send her over the edge.

"I'm close, so close," she murmurs.

I continue my steady rhythm, reaching my other hand to her breast, losing myself in the way her body responds to my touch. When I feel her begin to fall apart, I open my eyes and still my tongue. With a groan, I watch as her orgasm rolls through her body. She's magnificent.

My cock throbs in response, hard with desperation. I need to be inside her as soon as possible.

"That was …" She exhales. "Everything."

"I aim to please." Smiling, I kiss her hip, sending small tremors across her abdomen. Slowly, dragging my mouth along her skin, I make my way up to her shoulder.

With my lips against her ear, I whisper, "I'll be right back."

"No, don't go." She wraps her arms around my neck.

Chuckling, I unwind her arms so I can go get a condom.

"Please tell me you brought more than one." She cracks open an eye to find me.

"I have a fresh box," I admit.

"Good. We should plan to use all of them."

I'm up for the challenge if she is.

After she left in October, I spent weeks thinking we'd never get here. I convinced myself she wasn't the one for me. I had a long list of all the reasons why we could never work out.

If I die from delayed gratification, I have no one to blame but myself.

I make quick work of sliding the condom on, giving myself a quick tug. Part of me wants to give her another orgasm with my mouth, delaying the inevitable quickness of my own climax. It's been a long time since I've had sex, and I know I won't last. Not with the way I already throb for her.

"Jay?" Her voice is a siren call.

I climb over her and kiss her deeply, the tip of my cock nudging her entrance through the slick of what we just created.

"Please," she pleads, her hand sliding between our hips to grip me.

I groan at her touch as I slide into her warmth. My forehead falls to hers as I pause, breathing deeply through my nose.

"Are you okay?" she whispers.

"Give me a second," I mumble with my mouth against her temple.

She giggles, lightening the moment. I feel her body's shaking in my cock.

"Not helping."

"Don't aim for perfection. We have all night to get this right." Her hands slide down my back to my ass, encouraging me to move.

Confident I won't come in two strokes, I thrust deeper into her. The sensation overwhelms me. She feels incredible. My skin slides against hers, our bodies connected deeply.

Emotion rises and crests over me.

"I love you, Olive."

Shit.

Once again, I still my hips, mortification helping to delay my orgasm.

With my eyes closed, I confess, "I can't believe I said that to you for the first time during sex."

"Do you mean it?" she asks, her ankles against my thighs.

"Without a doubt." I peek down to find her staring at me with wide, emotion-filled eyes.

"I love you right back." She rolls her hips, reminding me that we're still joined as intimately as two people can be.

"God, I love you," I repeat.

She cups my cheek. "Show me."

My pleasure hits the point of no return. My movements become erratic before I thrust deeply, emptying myself inside of her.

Collapsing, I roll us to the side, limbs tangled together. I pull her head to my chest and stroke her hair. "I love you."

She rests her hand over my heart. "I'll never get tired of hearing those words from you."

"Good, because I plan to tell you every day."

* * *

"What about dinner?" she murmurs a while later, not lifting her head from the pillows.

I grin as I slip out of bed. "One of the reasons I suggested coming here—room service."

"You are a genius, Dr. Daniels." She rolls over and the sheet slips.

"Best idea I've ever had." I crawl up the bed until I can kiss her shoulder. "Wait, did you call me Dr. Daniels?"

"It's your name, right? You have a Ph.D. in conservation biology from Ohio State."

I pin her with my hips. "You looked me up?"

"I may have done some online research, yes." Wiggling beneath me, she kisses along my jaw.

On instinct, my hips roll, my cock thickening.

"Your dissertation was on a particular bird." She gazes up at me, fighting a smile. "Do you recall what it was?"

She obviously knows the answer. Resting my weight on one forearm, I sweep a strand of wild hair from her forehead with my other hand. "I believe I studied a species of warblers."

"Hmm, interesting. There are so many."

"There are. Almost forty different species in the Great Smokies alone." I kiss a line across her collarbones.

Her thighs spread farther apart, welcoming me closer. "I don't suppose you'd be considered a leading expert on the Black-throated Blue Warbler, would you?"

A grin slips across my face. "Perhaps."

"Ranger Daniels, would you say you lied to me by omission?" Her laughter fills the space.

"Maybe. In my defense, I was in too much shock that you picked *my* bird as the one you wanted to spot. I also knew you were too late in the season to see one."

"I have a confession." Her brows pull together. "Remember how we met?"

"I don't think I'll ever forget your first words to me." I chuckle against her skin.

"I lied. I was off the trail because I thought I saw a warbler. When you showed up, I thought I'd be in trouble."

I lift my head to stare at her before cracking up. "Seriously?"

She nods. "It obviously worked. Not only did I escape arrest, I charmed the pants right off of you."

"I love you, Olive." I hold her gaze. "I wanted to tell you again since I messed up the first time."

"It was perfect." She kisses me and with her lips hovering a breath away from mine, whispers, "I love you, Jay."

My heart expands at the words on her lips.

I want her beside me as I take this journey through life. She's both the path I'd follow anywhere and my destination.

I might not fit neatly into any box, but I'll never doubt I belong with Olive.

CHAPTER THIRTY-FIVE

OLIVE

May

*J*ay navigates the official white National Park Services SUV through the crowded parking lot to the back of the community center housed in a charming, old school building.

Everything about Green Valley screams quaint, small town America with the adorable main street full of little businesses and a nice library. Feels like walking back in time to a simpler way of living. Not saying things are easier around here, but after months in the woods and mountains, the frantic pressure of city living holds less and less appeal to me.

I've stuck around because I don't want to go back to my old life and even more than that, I want to see if I can make a new life here with Jay. He doesn't seem eager for me to leave either. In fact, my departure has never been discussed. Maybe that's how people who aren't born here end up living here: they visit and just stay. Sounds good to me.

"Popular place to be on a Friday night." I gaze out the window at all the cars.

"Really the only place to be unless you like bars or strip clubs." He parks the large vehicle with ease.

"How come you didn't tell me about those options?" I keep my voice neutral to gauge his reaction.

It's a good thing we're parked, because Jay's head jerks so hard to the right to stare at me he might have crashed.

"Um, I didn't think either of those would be your thing. If ... if you'd like to go somewhere else, there might be a book club meeting at the library. Or we could grab some pie at Daisy's again."

"What's the name of the strip club?" I ask, hoping to catch him off guard.

"The Pink Pony," he answers without hesitation. "Why?"

"I've never been to one, so I'm curious."

His ears pink at the edges and he swipes a hand through his light brown hair. "I doubt a backroad strip club would hold much interest for a big-city girl like you."

"Have you been to this Pink Pony?" I twist and lean in my seat to get a better view of his expression.

"Once. One of the summer interns thought it was appropriate to have his birthday-slash-going-away party there a few years ago." His hand drops from his head.

"Good time had by all?" I grin.

"Some, yes. The majority, no." He grimaces. "Work functions should require everyone to be wearing pants."

"Sounds awkward."

He groans. "You have no idea."

"Why did anyone go? Couldn't you have said no?" Now I'm genuinely curious.

"My boss asked me to go to make sure no one got in too much trouble."

I lean against my window. "Chaperone at a strip club?"

"Could anything be worse?" He closes his eyes before opening one and sneaking a glance at me.

My laughter fills the small space, and his soon follows.

"Shall we go inside?" he asks after a few moments.

Muffled sounds of music, banjo and fiddle, drift across the lot when I open my door.

Up until now, I've played it cool, showing only minor interest in the jam session, hiding how thrilled I am to hear real Appalachian music.

He jogs around the hood to close my door.

"Excited?" He squeezes my hand.

"Almost as excited as I was when the warblers returned. Did you know there would be so many? They're the pigeons of the Smokies." I wink at him.

"Pigeons? Really?" he grumbles, his voice gruff.

"Kidding. I kid." I give him a quick peck on the cheek. "They are magnificent and tiny and everything I'd dreamed of."

We take a few more steps, the music growing louder as we approach the entrance. I stop and he keeps walking.

"I have a secret to confess," I whisper.

Stopping and turning back, he asks, "Does it have anything to do with birds, bodily functions, or getting arrested?"

I think about it for a second. "No."

"Okay, tell me."

"Remember how I said I played the violin as a kid but gave it up?"

"I do." He sounds wary and I can't blame him. My filter is better but half the time I don't know what's going to come out of my mouth until I hear it.

"Part of the reason I quit is because everyone insisted I play classical music. My parents, my tutor, and the music teacher at school."

"Sounds typical." He nods. "What was the issue?"

"You may not have noticed, but I have a small rebellious streak."

This makes him laugh. "Microscopic really."

"I wanted to play folk music." I'm serious.

He tilts his head to the side. "You're a fiddle player?"

"Well, the closest I ever got was *Appalachian Spring* by Copland. Other than sneaking some sheet music into my room, fiddle-playing was deemed unworthy of my time. Beneath me."

His jaw drops open. "It's classic Americana."

"I know," I agree.

"Your family sounds like a bunch of horrible snobs." He grimaces. "Sorry. I shouldn't say that."

"No, you're right. They are." I frown. "I love them, but they have a very narrow definition of what is culturally acceptable."

"We'll find you a violin and you can play all the fiddle music you want. My mother can get one for you. She'll be thrilled. Recently, she's been studying the oral history of Appalachian musicians, doing interviews with people up in the hills."

"She has?" My heart skips a beat. Not because he's being sweet, which he is. "I've dreamed of getting back into music in some way. I'm not delusional enough to think I'll ever be good enough to be a professional. Does she need funding? Research and grant writing I can do."

He pulls me into a hug. "I don't know, but if it lights you up like this, then we'll make it happen."

I hug him back, tightly. "What are the odds of my dream coming true?"

He whispers against my hair, "About as good as the two of us finding each other in the middle of nowhere."

Inside the door, there's congestion around a table where a glass bowl is set out for donations. Jay drops in a few bills as we slip past. Everywhere I turn, people of all ages chat amongst small groups. Teenage girls gather in circles, giggling and whispering. Their male counterparts do the same, only without the giggling and with more staring while trying to not get caught doing so. Smaller kids, wild with excitement, weave crooked paths through the crowd.

In the background, I can hear the music. Jay explains how some nights, each of the old school rooms will have a different group playing. I want to visit every one and stay forever. If no one opposes, I'll set up my tent and not take up too much space.

Across the main room, I spot a group of particularly handsome men.

"Wow. They're like a pack of bearded Hemsworths."

"Those would be the Winstons," Jay explains as if he's pointing out a flock of house sparrows, AKA nothing exciting at all.

"How many of them are there?" I don't hide my amazement.

"Do you need a hankie for your drool?" Jay teases.

"I love only you, Ranger Daniels." I softly kiss his cheek. "Think of this as birding, only we're observing humans in their natural habitat instead of wildlife. People watching is one of my favorite sports."

He gives me a sidelong look before answering my previous question. "I only see two of the six brothers. The tall blond man with the guitar case is Dr. Runous, the federal game warden for the Smokies. He married into the family. The ginger next to him is Beau, one of the twins. The stockier one holding the banjo with the suspicious glint in his eye is Cletus. He's with Jennifer, who runs Donner Bakery."

"The source of the cookies?" He distracts me from the Appalachian Hemsworths with talk of baked goods. I doubt he does this by accident. He knows my weakness.

"One and the same."

"Ooh, she's a genius. I feel like I'm in the presence of baking greatness."

"Do you want to meet her?"

I nod, perhaps overly enthusiastically. "I promise I won't fangirl too hard."

"Okay. I'll introduce you." He gives me a reluctant smile. "Do you think you can handle being around the Winstons?"

"I'm merely curious about the gathering of beards—or is it a mob of beards? I'm not sure about the collective noun."

Jay ponders my question for a moment. "There isn't one."

"We should change that. Wait, are the brothers part of a religious sect? Like a casual Mennonite offshoot?"

"I have a beard and I'm not in any religious order." He laughs, at me and not with me, but I'm okay with it. "Some in Green Valley think their dad is the devil himself, so no, they're not part of a conservative religious sect."

"That's interesting. This place is growing on me."

Unlike the big city filled with strangers, I like the idea of living somewhere with real community. I don't tell Jay I'm already thinking about moving here permanently. I don't want to scare him off, even if I have already made up my mind.

I love it here. More importantly, I love him. He already feels like home.

Life isn't about the destination. We all end up at the same place.

Love is what gives our journey meaning. How we travel this winding trail of life and who walks beside us makes all the difference.

I want Jay beside me for every step and each new adventure.

EPILOGUE

JAY

November

Knoxville, Tennessee

*W*e arrive at my mom's house, a Craftsman bungalow on a quiet, tree lined street. A wreath of fake autumn-colored leaves hangs on the front door, the porch light glowing in the fading light of the late afternoon. Smoke from the fireplace scents the cool air.

"It's so charming." Olive gazes around with a small smile curling her lips.

Nervous, I rub my hand over the back of my neck. "I know it isn't as fancy as you're probably used to, but it's—"

"Home," she finishes for me. "This is your family home and it's perfect. I love it."

The door swings open and my mother steps out, beaming at us both. "Welcome!"

"This is for you." Olive points to the hostess gift I'm holding by the handle.

"Oh, you shouldn't have. It's wonderful to see you again, Olive."

Mom pulls her into a hug. She's petite but stronger than she looks. The two of them whisper to each other and Olive pulls away, laughing.

"What are you two sharing secrets about?" I ask, my voice more grumbly than I intended. I'm left holding the world's largest gift basket.

"Come in, come in." Mom takes it from me. "I've already pulled out all of our photo albums from when he was little. Wait until you see him in the Power Ranger costume when he was four. Absolutely adorable."

"Mom."

The single word uttered with raw pleading stops her mid-step.

She narrows her eyes at me. "Don't ruin my fun, Jay. I've been waiting for this moment forever."

As we follow her into the house, Olive catches my attention and whispers, "You've never brought a girl home before?"

With an innocent expression, I lift my shoulders. "For the holidays? No. You're the first."

"All the girls used to flirt with Jay, but he never paid attention." Mom pats my arm.

Wanting to change the subject, I ask, "Where's Jenni? Running late like always?"

"She's stuck in traffic but will be here soon. Can I get you anything, Olive? Tea? Water? Wine? I have iced tea. It isn't sweet. Don't tell any of the neighbors I'm offering unsweetened tea in the South. They'll stage an intervention."

While I'm reserved, she's warm, welcoming. As an extrovert, she actually loves people.

Mom leads us through her house to the warm, modern kitchen where she's placed a round table next to a picture window overlooking the backyard. The scent of ginger and garlic carries through the air from a pot simmering on the stove.

"Sit, make yourselves comfortable. I'll just find a place for Olive's generous gift." She places the basket full of food and wine on the counter.

"I know Jay said I didn't need to bring anything, but I couldn't show up emptyhanded." Olive slides her glance to me and flashes a smug smile.

"It's wonderful. I plan to eat everything myself and not share. Especially the apple butter." Mom knows she's poking the bear with that comment.

"I bought three jars at the harvest festival at one of the local churches," Olive says innocently.

"And Jay let you part with one?" Mom winks at me.

"Reluctantly," I mumble. "She knows how much I love apple butter."

Olive slides her fingers between mine and squeezes. "I do because you ate an entire jar yourself."

"Should've bought more." I kiss the top of her head. "And we shouldn't be giving away any of our limited supply. No offense, Mom."

"We'll have it on toast for breakfast tomorrow." She pats my cheek. "Or waffles."

Olive snorts and my face breaks into a grin as I laugh.

Mom glances between us.

"Sorry. Inside joke," I explain. "Had to be there."

With a knowing smile, she waves off my apology. "I know what it's like to be young and in love. Now, who wants to help me make dinner? I figure we'll have something light tonight before the big feast tomorrow."

"Prepare yourself," I warn Olive. "Thanksgiving is my mom's favorite American holiday. She goes a little crazy."

"I can't wait." Olive rubs her abdomen.

"Are you making ramen?" I lift the cover of the pot and inhale.

"Of course. It's your favorite."

"My mother's broth is the best you'll ever taste," I tell Olive. "It's the cure for everything."

"I should get the recipe. I'm not much of a cook"—Olive's eyes meet mine—"but I'm learning."

"I'll send some home with you. You can put it in your freezer."

Mom smiles sweetly, but it doesn't escape my notice that she's dodged the recipe question.

Under Mom's supervision, we wash, chop, slice, and peel the ramen ingredients. She asks Olive a string of questions, never over-stepping or prying. Mom isn't the kind to get starstruck. Some of her music students have gone on to be successful musicians in Nashville or LA.

It's been a year since Olive's grandfather passed and she's faded out of the spotlight again. No more gossip about engagements. No more social media scandals.

Maybe it's just me, but she seems to be content living in the Smok-ies, away from the big city. I'd like to think I play a major part in her happiness.

Olive is renting a small house in Green Valley, and most mornings I make the commute to the park from there. Depending on the weekend, we spend time at my cabin or hiking nearby. Sometimes we drive to Knoxville to see my mom. Or go over to Nashville if we have more time.

I found a tattoo artist there who studied in Japan and uses tradi-tional Japanese techniques. He did a piece on my shoulder featuring a red koi in blue water with a sprig of pink cherry blossoms. The blos-soms are in honor of my grandmother, and the fish is to remember my father.

For Halloween, we went to Jenni's annual costume party. Olive insisted on dressing like a bear even after I told her it wouldn't be appropriate for me to wear my uniform off-duty. When I refused to go as either Goldilocks or a honey pot, she reluctantly agreed I didn't have to wear a costume.

"Olive," Mom says. "Did you bring your fiddle?"

"It's in the car with our other bags," Olive answers. "I didn't forget. I've been practicing."

Mom nods her head in approval. "Still playing at the jam sessions?"

Olive nods, happiness radiating off of her. "I've never had so much fun. Last week, I drove up past Gatlinburg to meet an old-timer at his cabin. He played for me and I can't get the tune out of my head. I'll have to play the field recording for you. Incredible."

I frown and cross my arms. I don't like it when she heads into the hills to meet with God knows who to record a song as part of their quest to document traditional Appalachian music before it disappears.

"I can't wait," Mom says, enthusiastic. "We should plan another trip to Chapel Hill to spend some time at the Southern Folklife Center."

The two of them spent four days in the music archives over the summer while I dealt with rogue tourists taking selfies too close to black bears. That's how I ended up in the national press—or at least my picture did. Thankfully, I was only identified as an NPS ranger.

A loud chime from the doorbell announces Jenni's arrival.

"I'll get it," I offer, already moving down the hall.

Arms full of grocery bags and totes, Jenni is using her elbow to press the button.

"Here, take something. My arms are going to fall off." She hands me three heavy reusable bags.

"Why? Did you fly here?" I ask, preceding her back to the kitchen.

She groans loudly behind me and Olive moans.

"How do you handle the bad bird jokes?" My sister gives Olive a hug.

"He has other charms and talents that make up for them." Olive lifts her eyebrows in surprise at her own words as a flush of pink covers her cheeks.

"I'm not even going to touch that one." Jenni coughs out a laugh.

"Good," Mom says.

Olive refuses to look at me.

"Dinner's ready," I announce even though I have no idea if it is.

Mom dishes up the large bowls of ramen, topping each with pork belly and a boiled egg.

"*Itadakimasu*," Mom says when we're all seated at the table.

"*Itadakimasu*," the three of us repeat.

While we eat, Jenni and me slurping our noodles like it's a competition, Mom and Olive chat more about music.

"*Obaasan* was asking when you're going to bring your *kanojo* to meet her." Jenni stares at me.

"What's a ka-no-jo?" Olive asks.

"Sweetheart," my mom explains.

"Well?" Jenni asks.

Olive's eyes meet mine. "I'd love to go to Japan."

"Then let's go," I tell her. "My grandmother will love you."

"We could go over Christmas if everyone can get the time off work. Although, I don't want to take you away from your family for another holiday, Olive. April is my favorite time to visit, for the cherry blossoms." Mom beams, happy at the idea. "My mother will be so pleased to see Jay two years in a row."

"Great, I always knew he'd end up being the favorite," Jenni complains. "*Dōitashimashite, otōto.*"

"What did she say?" Olive asks my mom.

"You're welcome, little brother," I answer before she can.

"Ah, you've been studying." Mom claps softly. "Good for you."

"A little bit when I have the time." I flash her a proud grin.

Jenni mumbles something more about patriarchal societies and beloved sons.

"Don't feel neglected, sweet daughter. I bought your favorite black sesame ice cream for dessert." Mom pats Jenni's arm.

Olive leans close to my ear, and I dip my head to hear her.

"I love your family. I'd happily spend every holiday with them."

I kiss her temple and whisper that I love her.

I'm different than I was last year, but not because I changed for Olive. If anything, I'm more myself than I have ever been.

Love is the most powerful force of change. I never imagined falling in love would bring me full circle to who I'm meant to be. There is no struggle to embrace the different sides of me. I am myself at last.

* * *

After we finish gorging ourselves on the Thanksgiving feast, Jenni and Olive sprawl out on the sectional in my mom's living room. A fire warms the room, increasing the post-meal sleepiness. Mom went to lie down in her room while I finish up the dishes.

My hands are covered in soapy water as I scrub the roasting pan when she comes back in the kitchen.

"Coming to save me?" I joke.

She glances at the non-existent pile of dirty dishes. "Darn it, I'm too late."

"I wouldn't have let you help. Tradition says this is my job. You cook and feed me, I clean." I bump her shoulder with my elbow.

"I trained you well." She beams up at me. "It's nice to have you and Olive here."

"We're happy to be here. She loves spending time with you and Jenni." I glance over my shoulder in the direction of the living room and lower my voice. "The two of them are thick as thieves."

"They're asleep. We'll have to wake them up for pie."

"Olive will be mad if she sleeps through dessert and no one wakes her." I give my mom a serious expression. "She really loves pie."

"Not more than she loves you. The two of you radiate love." Mom curls her hand around my elbow and leans her head on my bicep.

"She's my person. I don't think I ever imagined loving someone this much. How did I get so lucky?" I beam down at her.

"Do you think you're going to propose?" Mom asks with a mischievous spark in her eyes.

I chuckle. "Olive doesn't have the best history with engagements."

Over the last year, I've thought about marrying her, what our lives together will be, and, if we're lucky enough, raising kids together. She moved to Green Valley to be with me and give us a chance. Says it's the best decision she's ever made.

Yet ... I've hesitated. How do I propose to a woman who has already had six proposals and make it original?

I share these worries with my mom while she dries and puts away the clean dishes.

"There is a reason none of those worked out." Mom hands me a towel so I can dry my hands.

"What?"

"Those other men weren't you. Her heart knew to keep waiting. Now the wait is over. I have something for you." She dips her hand into the pocket of her pants. "It isn't big or fancy, but it symbolizes true love. I want you to have it to give to Olive when the time is right."

In her hand is the ring my dad gave her, the one which she wore for many years after his death. A simple setting with two small round diamonds flanking a slightly larger diamond in the middle. All three are wrapped in gold edging and rest almost flush with the band. Understated but beautiful, kind of like Olive. I try to refuse, because I know how much this ring means to her. It's one of the few pieces of fine jewelry she has and one of the even fewer things from my father.

"Mom, you should keep that. It's your ring from Dad." I curl her fingers into her palm.

"That's what makes it perfect. I still have my gold band." She holds up her hand to show me the thin circle on her ring finger.

While distracting me, she slips her engagement ring into my shirt pocket. "Don't argue with your mother. This will make me very happy. Are you going to deny me happiness?"

"Never," I whisper, pulling her into a hug. "Thank you."

* * *

April
Kyoto, Japan

My family walks through the botanical garden, pink blossoms filling the trees and drifting down like snowflakes.

Obaasan strolls with one hand around my elbow and the other hand holding Olive's. They don't share many words in common but speak the same language of smiles and laughter.

Jenni snaps Polaroids and shows them to our grandmother.

"Somewhere at home, I have a box of old Polaroids of your dad as a boy. I'll have to find them next time we're all together," Mom tells us and then translates for her mother.

Obaasan says something in Japanese and my mother laughs. My understanding is better, but I miss a lot when the two of them speak together.

"She said she expects us to visit at least once a year. Especially you, Jay, and you're to always bring Olive with you."

"I'd be delighted to be invited back. Dōmo arigatō, Sobo."

Grandmother's face lights up and she squeezes Olive's arm while speaking excitedly.

Olive gives me a helpless look. "What did I say?"

Jenni's eyes widen while Mom interjects. "You called her grandmother as if you are family. She is excited about the news that you are getting married."

Olive's eyes flash to mine, worry visible. "How do I explain that I misspoke?"

My heart thumps strong and loud in my chest. "What if you didn't?"

Grandmother glances between us and then steps forward to take my mother's arm. Jenni's mouth pops open before she clamps it shut and spins on her heel to join them.

"What's going on?" Olive asks.

I've carried the ring with me almost every day since November, always prepared should the right moment present itself. Tucked in a pocket, my father's ring has been a talisman these past five months.

Kneeling doesn't feel right, so instead, I take both of her hands in mine. "Olive, I love you."

She smiles, a confused look in her eyes. "And I love you."

"I wasn't planning to do this today, and I'm not sure I know the right words to say." I wonder if she can hear my heart pounding.

Her eyes widen and she slips her right hand from mine to cup my cheek, already tears pool in her eyes. "Jay, I love you. More than anything. More than I ever imagined. Loving you is the easiest thing in the world for me. My whole heart belongs to you. I can't fathom a life without you by my side." She pauses, tears trailing down her cheeks.

"Hold on, this is my proposal to you, not the other way around." I gently take her hand and kiss her palm as I stare into her eyes.

A small gasp escapes her mouth.

My mind goes blank. All the romantic, heartfelt words I've been chanting to myself for months are gone.

"Olive, I love you." I sigh. "I said that already."

Tilting back a little so she can meet my eyes, she says, "And I love you, Jay."

"You are my forever. You're my person. For the past five months, I've carried this in my pocket, waiting for the right moment." I release her hand to locate the ring in my jacket's inside pocket. "This is the ring my father gave to my mother as a promise to love her forever. We're not given endless days together, and our forever can be shorter than we'd like. I don't want to wait another day or keep waiting for some imaginary perfect moment. I want to spend my life beside you, making you happy, no matter what the future might hold. Will you marry me, Olive?"

Her fingers shake as she covers her mouth, extending her left hand toward me.

"Is that a yes?" I hesitate to slide the ring on her finger.

Swiping her cheeks with her right hand, she nods.

Once the ring is in place, I lift her fingers to my mouth and kiss the band.

Crying and giggling, she stands on her toes to kiss me. "Yes, yes, a million times the answer is yes."

I kiss her back and the rest of the world disappears.

Once we break apart, she gazes up at me. "Can we do one thing?"

"What's that?" I smile down at her.

"Can we skip the engagement and get married as soon as we get home?"

"Don't you want a wedding with all your family and friends?" I'm a little confused.

"None of that matters. You, me, and a justice of the peace would be fine. I don't want to wait." She entwines her fingers with mine and I feel the cool metal of the ring.

"Afraid you're going to jinx us?" I ask, finally catching on.

"No, you're stuck with me until death do us part."

I lean down to kiss her and remember something important. "Why wait until we get home? Jenni is proudly ordained in the Church of Universalist Life. She can marry us right now."

"Did I hear my name?" Jenni calls over from the bench where my three family members are observing this private moment between Olive and me. They're not even pretending they're not watching every moment. All they need is popcorn.

"How much of that do we need to repeat for you?" I ask them, strolling over with Olive.

"There were moments when you whispered and we had to fill in the gaps, but we got the gist." Jenni stands and hugs Olive. "Congratulations and welcome to the family."

Obaasan and Mom are next, hugging us and laughing and crying.

"Now, I'm happy to perform the ceremony, but legally you'll have to fill out the license and paperwork when we're back in the great state of Tennessee."

"Not a problem," Olive says.

Mom explains all of this to *Obaasan*, who responds with a big smile and points to the row of blooming cherry trees as she says something.

"She said we should have the ceremony over there and that this is a very good time for a wedding because the blossoms symbolize a new beginning," Mom says.

"Then let's do this." Olive squeezes my hand.

"We're getting married." I kiss the corner of her mouth.

"Right now," she whispers against my lips. "I've never been more certain about anything."

"Save the kissing for the 'I do'," Jenni teases.

The four of us make our way over to a particularly large tree, its branches creating a canopy above our heads like a natural chapel.

"This is perfect," Olive whispers.

I nod, suddenly overcome with the truth of this moment. Tears prick at my eyes as I hold both of her hands and face her.

Jenni pulls up the traditional wedding ceremony on her phone. "Ready?" she asks.

Not taking my eyes off of Olive, I say yes.

Standing under the cherry blossoms, I'm reminded how precarious and brief life is. How precious and beautiful love is. How lucky I am to spend the rest of my life loving and being loved by these women, my family.

ACKNOWLEDGMENTS

To Penny Reid, thank you for creating Smartypants Romance and allowing me to play in your world. I am grateful for your faith in my writing, your encouragement, and your friendship.

To my readers, thanks for following me to Tennessee and a new series.

To the Reiders, thank you for taking a chance on this book. I hope you enjoyed *Happy Trail.*

My fellow Smartypants Romance authors, thank you being a sisterhood of awesome. Not only are you all talented authors, you are kind, inclusive, funny, kick-ass women. So proud to be on this journey with you.

To my editor, Caitlin Nelson, thank you for your patience, faith, and editorial wisdom. To Janice Owen, thank you for proofreading. Any remaining errors are entirely my fault.

Fiona Fischer, thank you for everything you do. Someday, we'll have dinner in Rome again. Brooke Nowiski, thank you for all you do for the Smartypants Romance authors.

Thank you to my PA, Jennifer Beach, for keeping me afloat this year. Lots of gratitude for Christina Santos, Heather Brown, Kiersten Hill, Elizabeth Clinton, Lauren Lascola-Lesczynski, who beta read the early version of this and whose insightful comments made it better. To my street team and review crew, thanks for being incredible. To the members of my Facebook reader group, Daisyland, thank you for chatting about books and life with me.

To all the bloggers and bookstagrammers, thank you for sharing your passion for stories. I'm grateful for supporting me and my books.

To Abi and Oscar, thank you for sharing your story with me.

I love hearing from readers. Come find me on social media and say hi, or email me at daisyauthor@gmail.com.

ABOUT THE AUTHOR

Daisy Prescott is a USA Today bestselling author of small town romantic comedies. Series include Modern Love Stories, Wingmen, Love with Altitude, as well as the Bewitched and Wicked Society series of magical novellas. Tinfoil Heart is a romantic comedy stand-alone set in Roswell, New Mexico.

Daisy currently lives in a real life Stars Hollow in the Boston suburbs with her husband, their rescue dog Mulder, and an indeterminate number of imaginary house goats. When not writing, she can be found in the garden, traveling to satiate her wanderlust, lost in a good book, or on social media, usually talking about books, bearded men, and sloths.

* * *

Find Daisy Online
Website: http://www.daisyprescott.com/
Facebook: https://www.facebook.com/daisyprescottauthorpage
Goodreads: https://www.goodreads.com/author/show/
7060289.Daisy_Prescott
Twitter: twitter.com/Daisy_Prescott
Instagram: instagram.com/daisyprescott
Mailing List: https://www.daisyprescott.com/mailing-list/

Find Smartypants Romance online:

Website: www.smartypantsromance.com

Facebook: www.facebook.com/smartypantsromance/

Goodreads: www.goodreads.com/smartypantsromance

Twitter: @smartypantsrom

Instagram: @smartypantsromance

ALSO BY DAISY PRESCOTT

Happy Trail

Tinfoil Heart

Love With Altitude Series

Next to You

Crazy Over You

Wild For You

Up To You

Modern Love Stories Series

We Were Here

Geoducks are for Lovers

Wanderlust

Wingmen Series

Ready to Fall

Confessions of a Reformed Tom Cat

Anything But Love

Better Love

Small Town Scandal

The Last Wingman

Very Merry Wingmen

Made in the
USA
Middletown, DE